WOLF UNLEASHED

WOLVES OF WILLOW BEND

HEATHER LONG

WOLF UNLEASHED

Change swept through the packs of North America, leaving in its wake seven packs where once only five stood. Old enemies still lurk, past hatreds fester, and the shadow of invaders linger. The challenge of diplomacy, evaluating the old laws, and instituting the new ones falls squarely on the shoulders of the pack Seconds. It's a whole new world, and what took so long to construct...remains vulnerable.

Luc Danes is Second, and best friend, to Brett Dalton, the Alpha of Hudson River. He has his hands full training healer and Alpha's mate Colby in how to defend herself as well as hone her wolf senses. It's not a bad life for a bachelor wolf, not really—except lately, all the eligible females have turned him down. No dates. No playing. Nothing. He's *untouchable.* Turns out no one wants to lay a finger on what rumors have labeled the Alpha's property as the third to the Alpha's pairing, leaving Luc one shocked and frustrated wolf ...

Just the position he wants to be in when paired with the stunning Charlie who doesn't know him at all, so why can't he even earn a second look?

Charlotte "Charlie" Miller works in the city, an urban wolf, she rarely sheds her skin for fur. As an executive handling day-to-day meetings for her Alpha in New York and around the world, she knows how to handle even the most difficult of individuals. But changes in pack structures across the country require a different kind of handling, and Brett calls in his chief negotiator to back up his Second, and to give him a crash course in diplomacy.

Unfortunately, Charlie has dealt with wolves and humans just like Luc before, and it doesn't matter how sexy he is, she refuses to be impressed.

Rogue Wolf

Salvatore & Margo

Bayou Wolf

Lincoln & Serafina

Untamed Wolf

Dylan & Chrystal

Wolf with Benefits

Matt & Shiloh

River Wolf
Brett & Colby

Single Wicked Wolf
Giovanni & Murphy

Desert Wolf
Cassius & Sovvan

Snow Wolf
Diesel & Ranae

Wolf on Board
Jake & Mimi

Holly Jolly Wolf
Collin & Rory

Shadow Wolf
Mitch & Amelia

His Moonstruck Wolf
Hugo & Lesley-Anne

Thunder Wolf
John & Hadley

Ghost Wolf
Julian & Dallas

Outlaw Wolves
Rayne & Luciana

Wolf Unleashed
Luc & Charley

Sign up for Heather's Newsletter.

FOREWORD

Hello my darlings!

I am thrilled to return to the world of the Wolves of Willow Bend. This series has always been told in a series of arcs. We began with the Rise of the Alpha (*Wolf Bite, Caged Wolf,* and *Wolf Claim*) then to Dawn of Three Rivers, the Wolves of Change and finally the last arc, Guardians of the Wolves.

Wolf Unleashed kicks off a new era for the North American packs—now comprised of seven packs instead of just five. The addition of new packs requires setting new treaties and working out trade and more. This job will fall to the pack Seconds. First up, we're heading back to Hudson River and fan favorite Luc!

First introduced in *River Wolf,* Luc Danes is smart, witty, and brutally loyal to his best friend and Alpha, Brett and Brett's mate, Colby. He's also the perfect romantic comedy hero.

You do not have to read the earlier books in this series, but I think you will get a lot more out of the overall series.

Thank you so much for reading!
Heather

For every single fan of the Wolves of Willow Bend!
You are my pack!

HUDSON RIVER WOLVES

Brett Dalton—Alpha of Hudson River, mate to Colby, cousin to Dallas Dalton and Chrystal Royce.

Colby Jensen Dalton—Latent wolf, healer, and mate to Brett Dalton.

Luc Danes—Second to the Hudson River Alpha, and Brett's best friend.

Charlotte "Charlie" Miller—Special counsel to Hudson River's Corporate Office, and official representative of the Alpha and CEO.

Charles Dalton—Father of Brett and mate to Margie, chef. Son of previous Alpha.

Margie Dalton—Mother of Brett and mate to Charles, nurse. Daughter of Hatcher, previous healer

Babette Danes—Mate of Gil. Mother to Luc, Samantha, Simone and Taylor. Something of a gossip.

Gil Danes—Mate of Babette. Father to Luc, Samantha, Simone, and Taylor.

Samantha Danes—Daughter of Babette, sister to Luc, Simone and Taylor. Wary with a chip on her shoulder.

Adele Miller—Senior Pack Hunter, Mother of Bishop, Duke, Noah, Sullivan, and Charlie.

Bishop Miller—Pack Hunter, Twin of Duke, brother to Noah, Sullivan and Charlie.

Duke Miller—Pack Hunter, Twin of Bishop, brother to Noah, Sullivan, and Charlie.

Noah Miller—Pack Hunter, Twin of Sullivan, brother to Duke, Bishop, and Charlie.

Sullivan Miller—Pack Hunter, Twin of Noah, brother to Duke, Bishop, and Charlie.

Pierce Donovan—Senior Hunter for Hudson River, counselor to Brett.

Harris Ryder—Teenage human dominant.

Rita Standish—Maternal, diner owner.

Debbie Locke—Executive assistant to Charlie Miller, Human

Trent Lawson—Fifteen-year-old wolf with Healer Potential, apprentice to Gillian of Willow Bend.

Owen Chase—Hunter, Willow Bend, counselor to Mason and mate to Gillian.

Gillian Chase—Healer, formerly apprenticed to Emma, trainer for Trent and Colby; and mate to Owen

CHAPTER 1

*H*e didn't slam out of the restaurant, he didn't growl at the lady he'd just had dinner with, nor did he act in any way save walking her to her car and opening her door for her. Amanda gave him an apologetic look as she touched the door near his hand without actually touching him. "I'm very sorry, Luc. I just...I hope you understand."

Not even a little, but he gave her a smile and brushed his hand against her shoulder. Wolf to wolf, they were fine. "Thanks for a lovely dinner, Amanda. I appreciate that you could meet me." Even if dinner had been a stilted, almost embarrassing affair where she'd avoided his gaze, and his flirtation.

Relief had her sagging, and Luc wanted to kick himself for being an asshole. He was pack Second, if nothing else, his regard mattered to the wolves in the pack, and it must have taken her a lot of courage to admit she wasn't interested, much less why.

"You good to get home on your own?" As he studied her, he grew more aware of the faint upset in her scent. She'd been masking it, and that made him want to hit himself harder. No female should ever feel pressured to *put up* with him. "I can call someone," he offered to make it clear it wasn't him trying to work his way around her very clear dismissal of his attention.

"Lord no, I'm fine," she said with an exasperated huff. "This is all my fault, I wound myself up, and I appreciate how graciously you accepted everything...and I really did enjoy dinner. You're just as fun and funny as Simone said you would be."

Luc made a mental note to strangle his middle sister and gave Amanda another smile as she slipped into the car, then he closed the door and backed off with a wave to head over to his own truck. He'd invited Amanda to meet him for dinner at a steakhouse about forty minutes away. Just a nice evening out where he hoped to learn a little more about her and maybe charm his way into her bed.

She was a gorgeous, leggy brunette, with fantastic boobs, a killer smile, and wit for days. The fact she'd waited until they were in the middle of their steaks to confess, "Luc, all of this is really quite wonderful, but I feel like I should be up front. There will under no circumstances be sex for you at the end of this evening."

The fact she'd been blunt about it was fine, in fact, Luc had never been one for beating around the bush. If a female found him attractive, and he reciprocated, there was absolutely nothing wrong with either party propositioning the other. He wasn't fussy, nor did he stand on ceremony. If a woman wanted him, hell, he was down for that.

While Amanda wasn't the first—she was actually the sixth in as many weeks—female to turn him down, she was the first to do so in between discussing his travels as a Lone Wolf and her time in college before they even got to anything remotely risqué. Some of his surprise must have shown, because she tried to walk the words back, but there really was no softening the blow.

No sex was neon sign flashing clear.

At least they'd actually gotten to have dinner. The others hadn't even made it that far, one to drinks but that was about it. It was like he was cursed. Banging his head back against the seat, he started the engine, and checked his phone for any missed messages. Maybe someone had lost a kid down a well, and he could go be heroic and studly or something.

Not that he wanted anyone falling down a well, and cubs were a lot tougher than they looked. Maybe one could misplace themselves, and he could go track them down. But alas, not a damn thing had happened other than one of the Hunters wanted to let him know the camp grounds on the other side of the national park area were closing early this year. Low funding meant fewer hours for the rangers, and the decision had been made unilaterally to free up this whole area, since the pack could look after it and enjoy the extra time without having to worry about campers or hikers.

Translation, the Hunters and probably more than a few of the younger wolves wanted to have a big party next weekend. Fuck, the last thing he wanted to do was ride herd on a bunch of wolves drinking, carousing, and likely stinking up the woods with all the sex they got to have while he sat out like the designated driver at a kegger.

Just...no.

He sent back a *I'll think about it.* Then left it at that.

Not the kindest thing he'd ever said, but it wasn't especially mean. Still, Patrick sent back a *You okay man?*

Fine. He answered. *Bad date. Probably fine for party.*

There was a beat with three little dots appearing on the message, like Patrick was typing something, then finally...

I don't get why you date. Just getting temp of pack?

He stared at the message. Looking for some hidden meaning.

What?

Another long pause and Luc checked the time on the dash. It was going to be a far earlier night than he planned.

His phone buzzed, and he glanced at the message, then stared. He read it three times, then he hit the call button and put the phone to his ear.

Patrick answered on the first ring, "Yeah?"

"What the fuck do you mean 'I'm off limits'?"

There was a hollow laugh, like he wasn't sure he should even be making the sound, and Luc could almost hear the unease through the phone.

A growl rumbled in his chest at the lack of a forthcoming answer. "Patrick."

"Man, don't make me say it…" Then, he said, "Okay, fine. Gimme a sec to go outside."

The background noise said he was out at the roadhouse, a lot of the Hunters liked to head there in the evenings. They could catch up, trade info, have a drink, and play billiards before going their separate ways to homes, or conversely heading out for a run.

Abrupt quiet echoed over the line along with the crunch of gravel. "Okay, I'll tell you…but man, promise not to kill the messenger."

"My patience for that long since expired, Patrick. Just explain already." Off limits. Who the hell marked him off-limits?

Five minutes later, he'd disconnected the call and backed out of the parking space before putting the vehicle in gear and heading out for home with his hands locked in position on the steering wheel. He stewed on the information for the next forty-five minutes, bypassing his place and continuing up toward Brett's house and the Alpha compound. He'd stayed either at Brett's or the healer's house for several months, and only recently moved into his own place, though he still spent more time at Brett's than he did his place.

The pack's "on loan from Willow Bend" healer Gillian and her mate Owen occupied the healer's house, which had formerly belonged to Hatcher, Brett's grandfather. Hudson River had been without a full time healer since Hatcher died, the victim of a mad wolf, one of many. Brett and Gillian had also been almost victims, in fact, Brett had worn his scars for a long time after the incident when the mad wolf burned him.

It wasn't until after Luc, who had literally been hit by a car, and ended up in a hospital in the boondocks of Maine, persuaded Colby to bring him back to Hudson River that Brett began to wake up from his self-imposed exile. Now, Brett and Colby were happily mated and very secure. Colby was getting a handle on her wolf and learning self-defense, while also training her very powerful and natural healing ability. Since she'd finished her journeyman sabbatical in Three Rivers a few weeks earlier, she was almost ready to take up the mantle of full time healer in Hudson River.

It was all going *well*. The Russians were gone. The packs were settling down after far too much upheaval. The Enforcers made up their own pack, and even Three Rivers, upstarts that they were, had settled nicely. It was a good time to be alive, and Luc was a bachelor with plenty of time on his hands, even if he spent most of it acting as Brett's Second and dealing with issues to free up his Alpha.

Or it had been.

He pulled right up to the garage and parked off to the side. Lights were on at the healer's house, but so were they at Brett's. It was mid-week, and still early, and while Brett rose before dawn most days, he rarely went to bed before midnight. Letting himself in, Luc followed his nose right to the kitchen where Brett was pouring coffee.

"I can't get laid," he announced, probably louder than he intended, but he couldn't help it. It was so fucking ridiculous. "And it's all your fault."

Brett paused in mid-reach for a third mug, and studied him as if he'd grown a second head. His best friend pursed his lips before sliding the carafe back into the coffee maker and opening a cupboard where a bottle of whiskey hid. Unscrewing the cap, he filled a tumbler with a couple of fingers and slid it over toward Luc.

"Okay," Brett said slowly. "I'll bite. How is it my fault?"

Grateful for the whiskey, Luc tossed the whole glass back and let it burn its way through his system before saying. "Because some damn fool has decided that dating me would be tantamount to stepping on your property, and no one will cross the line with you."

A frown gathered between Brett's brows, and he squinted at Luc. "Come again?"

"Yeah, sounded fucking ridiculous to me, too, but apparently—I'm off-limits, the *secret* third of the Alpha pairing, and no one will step on your toes." He shook his head. Patrick had repeated it to him twice, and Patrick wasn't a wolf prone to practical jokes. He was too sober by half. The fact he'd been practically squirming verbally over sharing what was probably the juiciest gossip in Hudson River—Luc was going to kill his mother—lent the whole idea that wolves believed that crap more weight.

Brett hadn't said a word, but had instead, unscrewed the bottle of whiskey and poured another two fingers into Luc's now empty glass.

"For weeks, I've been asking out a few of the ladies, you know—dinner date or drinks, and most of them find excuses or just turn me down. Can't get them to look at me twice.

Got Sabra to have drinks with me, but she pretty much finished her drink, patted me on the head, and told me to tell you hi before she took off." Luc shook his head, at the time it hadn't seemed anything more than a genuine comment—but *now*... "Not an hour ago, Amanda and I are out to dinner for steak...Amanda, the gorgeous brunette who works over in Reeves End..."

"Crazy crystal shop," Brett said with a nod. "Colby loves her stuff."

"Exactly. I've wanted her to go out with me for months, and we're sitting there, having a good time—or at least I thought we were—and in the middle of our steak, she just says, to be clear at the end of the evening, there will be absolutely no sex for you, Luc Danes." He tossed back the whiskey, then pinched the bridge of his nose. The burn was helping with the knots in his shoulders, but he'd need to drink the whole bottle, and maybe most of a second for it to do any good. "Fucking ridiculous, I mean sex would have been great, but that wasn't why I took her out to dinner."

"Clearly, that's why it's my fault you can't get laid." The dry delivery pulled Luc up short, and he glared at his best friend. Brett picked up his mug and took a sip of coffee. "But why don't we get to the part where it's my fault..."

"I told you—the word through the pack is I'm off-limits, no one will touch *your* property." Even saying the words made him want to spit.

Another slow blink. "Because you're the secret *third* to my *mating* with Colby?"

"Right?" It was fucking stupid.

Then Brett did the very last thing he thought he would do.

He laughed.

"Man," Luc exhaled, hands braced on the countertop. "Not funny."

"Depends on your point of view," Brett said, amusement filling his eyes. "From over here in the expensive seats, it's pretty hilarious."

Luc groaned. "I hate you."

"Eh, I'm used to it. Besides, you're you—you going to let a rumor kill your reputation?" As if his reputation hadn't been hard-won, and built over years of skillful dating technique. He liked women. He liked them all, and he liked them in every size and shape. If he ever settled down, he wanted a demure and sweet wolf—like Gillian, maybe. A docile, little submissive. Until then, he planned to have as much fun as possible.

"Doesn't really seem to be up to me," Luc muttered. "No one wants to piss you off or make you jealous."

The derisive snort carried just enough hilarity to rake over Luc's nerves. "You are very much *not* my type, brother."

"Apparently they think Colby is." There was an inherent risk in even bringing that suggestion up. During Colby's early days in Hudson River, before she and Brett settled their mating bond, Brett's possessiveness included not liking Colby's interest in healing Luc—at least not after her first shift and absolute refusal to listen to Brett.

But that was another story.

Brett eyed him before he took another long swallow of his coffee. "You might want to explain that comment, just a little more." No threat, but the promise of potential violence was very real. He and Brett had known each other far too long to stand on ceremony. Especially not since Luc had returned to the pack full time, and taken the place as Second at Brett's request.

Groaning, Luc scrubbed a hand over his face and reached for the bottle of whiskey to refill his tumbler. "Someone has it in their head that I'm with Colby and you. Or at least, enough with Colby that I'm part of your pairing."

The absolute silence would probably shut up other, smarter wolves. Or at least wolves with enough savvy to protect their own skins. Three way bonds weren't unheard of, but they were also not common either.

"I'm guessing the fact I've been training Colby doesn't help." While Luc was more than happy to cover her skills training and keep it private for her defense, it meant they did meet secretly, and they did keep it quiet, and they absolutely spent a lot of time together.

"Maybe, but you and I know where everything stands, and so does she." Brett eyed him. "Do you need me to make some public announcement and save your sex life?"

"Ass," Luc said with a roll of his eyes before he tossed the whiskey back.

"Sometimes," Brett told him cheerfully. "But you know, not being busy chasing tail can be good for the soul. Give you time to figure out what you really want out of life."

"I spent several years running alone to do that, I'm good." Setting the tumbler down, he blew out a breath. Brett had gotten out a second coffee mug, but he'd seen no sign of Colby. And as much as he loved the little wolf, she rarely stayed out of their conversations. Not that he or Brett had ever asked her to leave them alone to talk. In fact, they'd had more than a few conversations since returning from Three Rivers.

Colby's little healing trick of an entire pack and their bonds was a closely guarded secret. Luc was only the fifth to know, and Brett wanted him aware, particularly when they had to linger in Three Rivers for so long. Colby's gift was exactly that, a blessing and a gift, but a wolf who could repair pack bonds and heal them, could also tear them apart.

That made Colby a very dangerous wolf in some circles.

As her primary instructor and defender when Brett

wasn't there, Luc definitely fell into the need to know category.

"Speaking of Colby…where is she?"

"Out for the evening with my mother, your mother, and your sisters—and probably Gillian, and I think the Barrister twins. They just turned twenty-one, so they were invited to ladies' night."

Luc grimaced, and Brett's grin seemed to grow at his discomfort.

"Probably doesn't help your case much, does it?" The smirk coupled with the laughter lacing his words just rubbed Luc's fur the wrong way.

"You don't have to sound so damn cheerful about it," he grumbled, then motioned to the second mug. "If she isn't home, who's that for?"

Brett's home smelled undeniably of him and Colby, but so many wolves came and went that the common areas—including the kitchen—held any number of wolf scents. Just standing there, he could pick out his and Brett's parents, Gillian, and her mate Owen, Trent, the teenage healer who trained with Gillian and Colby, and Pierce Donovan, their senior Hunter, and a couple of other wolves he recognized as familiar but couldn't put a name on them.

And that was just right there in the kitchen.

"Come on back," Brett said, as he refilled his mug then added fresh coffee to the second one. "Probably a good thing you dropped by tonight anyway."

He led the way, leaving Luc to follow him. Luc took a couple of steps, and then on second thought, retrieved the whiskey and his empty glass before following. If the rest of his evening went as well as the beginning of it, he definitely needed more liquor.

They reached Brett's office when the fresh scent hit him. Sweet, with a tang, like smoked ribs, slow cooked to perfection and leaving the mouth watering for more. There was a distinct hint of woodiness beneath the sweet, but the brown sugar and honey were just damned inviting. While the nuances of her—definitely feminine—scent also held an element of pack, he didn't know this wolf. Brett had been holding out on him.

"Charlie," Brett was saying as he carried the mugs in. "Sorry for the delay, got waylaid in the kitchen."

"I heard." The rasp of her husky voice scraped over him, and Luc's blood traveled south with sudden raging force and need. Clamping down on the reaction, he pushed open the dark oak door, and sought out the source of that provocative scent and sexy as hell voice. "Sounds like your man has problems."

The droll humor let the air out of him, and Brett turned after setting the coffee in front of her to motion to Luc. "While you shouldn't believe everything you hear," Brett teased. "Luc's definitely my guy."

Ass. Hole.

If looks could actually cause damage, he'd have pounded Brett flat. As it was, his Alpha—and asshole best friend—smirked at him. "Luc Danes, meet Charlie Miller. Charlie's our senior attorney and chief executive, and she's been handling most of our asset negotiations for the last twenty-two months, in addition to running day to day at Hudson River International for the last few years."

"Ms. Miller," he said, crossing the room to extend his hand to her. The wolf behind Brett's desk had killer green eyes, nearly the color of pure emeralds, and her red hair added to the effect, the length of it falling in straight lines to the shoulders of her royal blue jacket. Her business attire probably fit right in at the office, but they tended to be more casual at home. "Where have you been all my life?"

"Working, Mr. Danes," she said, shaking his hand once,

then dropping the grip so fast, he was almost left with his hand hanging in the air. "A concept I hear is relatively new to you."

Ouch.

"Luc, Charlie is my Second in the business, she's a brilliant negotiator and exactly what we need for some of our upcoming projects." Brett continued to be far too amused for Luc's taste.

Well, as for the rest of it, yay for her. The less Luc had to do with the business offices side of things in the city, the better. Too many people in too close a quarters, and having to work with people who lied like they breathed wouldn't leave him in a particularly pleasant mood, as evidenced by Ms. Miller's cool, expressionless demeanor.

"Charlie, Luc's the reason you're here…"

Wait.

What?

Surprise flickered in those emerald eyes, and Brett's grin just grew. Yeah, if he wasn't Alpha, Luc might have already punched him. What was he talking about? "Come again, boss?"

Brett motioned to the chairs. "Have a seat, both of you." It wasn't a request, and Luc avoided any appearance of disregard for the command, even if he wanted to roll his eyes. Giving Brett shit in private was acceptable, but he didn't know Ms. Miller, so for the time being, Luc would behave like a Second and keep everything as professional as possible.

But he did pour himself another drink. Once Ms. Miller circled the desk and took the seat next to him, she crossed one leg over the other and cradled the coffee mug in her hand. Like her jacket, the skirt was royal blue, and gave him a great view of her spectacular calves and the pair of blue heels she wore.

If not for the hint of fur in her scent, he might not pick

her out for a wolf at all. There was no sense of dominance play, no aggressive stares, and no attempt to determine her place opposite his. Then again, Brett just said she held a position equivalent to his, but ranking in the pack didn't work that way—no matter what position she'd been appointed to or held.

Seated, Brett tapped a couple of keys on his laptop, then turned the larger monitor. The map on the screen detailed pack territories, current lines, and who held what—up to and including Willow Bend's ownership of Tennessee, Three Rivers' rather significantly smaller holdings in Nebraska, Sutter Butte's cleaner lines cutting into California and north to Nevada from Arizona and New Mexico, and finally the largest of the territories with Delta Crescent sweeping most of the Gulf States to Florida and up to South Carolina with some incursions into North Carolina.

The Yukon Territory existed above the lower forty-eight, primarily in Alaska and parts of Canada. There were some disputes over Washington State, but currently it was considered open territory because Diesel didn't bother with it.

"So what you see here is the standing of our territories post the meeting of the Alphas a few years ago in Willow Bend. With Three Rivers having achieved full status, we've locked the territory to what they hold currently, but there's room for them to grow..." He marked out a zone of plus a hundred miles or more along the boundaries of Willow Bend's territory, the closest to Three Rivers. "Barring crossing these lines to their north and east, and..." He added another set of demarcation to Sutter Butte. "These to their south and west. It's plenty of room, several thousand square miles for growth they likely won't need for a hundred years or so, but it's better to be prepared."

Luc kept his focus on the conversation, but really—land mass? Who cared? Three Rivers had less than two hundred wolves, and they'd nearly self-destructed once. If they made it another fifty years, they could worry about it then. Not that Rayne and Luciana were horrible people, despite their history, he found himself liking them and almost rooting for their success. The fact they'd won over the Reagans didn't hurt.

But...that wasn't the point of this discussion, or was it?

He stole a peek at Ms. Miller, but her calm, unreadable face remained turned in Brett's direction, and her gaze on the map.

"The seventh pack—the Enforcers—don't have a specific territory, however, Julian has suggested and several of us agree, they need one. Even if it's a smaller one where they can raise families when that begins to happen for them."

Which was an alien concept for all of them, Luc included. He'd run into his fair share of Enforcers while running as Lone Wolf. The idea of their forming a pack of their own seemed anathema, and yet at the same time, felt like the most natural thing ever. The irony of that contrast wasn't lost on him.

"For now, southern Washington state, all of Oregon, a section of Northern California, and quite possibly pieces of Montana and Wyoming are to be included in their tacit territory," Brett continued. "Unlike our territories, though, Lone Wolves will still be able to move freely in Enforcer controlled territory, Enforcers will continue to supervise Lone Wolves, and proceed with their other duties up to and including protecting the packs from external incursions, and maintaining a semblance of order."

Not yawning took effort, particularly when Ms. Miller nodded her head as if she expected the information and her focus was so absolute. "So that's what we *know*, at the moment?" Clarifying what Brett had already said, fine. Not that Luc needed to make him repeat himself.

"Precisely," Brett told her, but his smile didn't quite reach his eyes as he leaned back in the chair. "Now for the hard part."

Now, Luc focused. Brett's demeanor had gone from playful and indulgent, to sober and absolutely serious.

"Treaties are what keep our territorial boundaries where they are, treaties negotiated some hundred to hundred and fifty years ago. The last major changes were installed after Sutter Butte won their independence. The only significant changes since then have been some withdrawing inside the marked areas and more recently, Serafina ceded Tennessee to Willow Bend. They're more or less holding it jointly at the moment, and some of her wolves requested permission to stay because of businesses and ties, and Mason's been cooperative—it's a big ol' lovefest."

Despite the description, a hint of sarcasm marred the last few syllables.

"But you don't think it's going to last," Ms. Miller stated, probably unnecessarily, yet this time, Luc couldn't fault her for it, because Brett wasn't the easiest wolf to read when he wanted to keep his thoughts to himself.

"For the next twenty or thirty years? I'm sure it will be fine. As long as Mason and Serafina have such close ties—her mate is a triplet to his second, and they were friends long before Mason was Alpha. They have every reason to maintain good relations."

"But they won't always be the Alphas," Luc summed it up. The reality for all of them. Eventually they grew old, and sometimes, the old were supplanted by the new, whether through direct challenge or through the need to cede their power to someone stronger. It was what Brett's grandfather had done, while rumor had it that the Hounds held the power Serafina's father, then the Alpha, until the day he died, and only then did the Alpha challenge happen.

"Exactly," Brett said with a nod. "We're in a rare place at the moment, our packs are closer than they've ever been historically. We're territorial by nature, and our natures are kept in check by our laws, and our laws are negotiated along with our treaties."

"Spell it out for me, Brett..." Luc was getting a headache. "What are you asking me to do?"

"I'm not asking," Brett reminded him, and fine, Luc deserved the reprimand, but he still needed the rest of the answer. "I'm tasking you with this. As Alphas, we agreed to the formation of the Enforcer pack, in large part because we were also acknowledging and granting Three Rivers full status, and that would put us at an even pack number, the Enforcers puts us at seven."

"Avoids deadlocks on anything major that needs to be decided," Ms. Miller said with a firm nod. "Smart."

"Thank you," Brett said, then gave Luc a small smirk like why couldn't he be a suck up, too? Luc sucked up. He didn't flip Brett off. His Alpha seemed aware of the fact, because he almost chuckled. "That said, we need to revisit our treaties with all of the packs, and establish new ones. We're talking territorial lines, trade, rules for passage, and those are just the top items I can think of—there will be more. Everyone needs something."

Wait...

"You want me to negotiate with the packs on laws and territorial boundaries? Shouldn't that be you?"

"I want you there representing me and our interests," Brett told him laconically. "Charlie's going to handle the negotiations. Good cop," he motioned to Luc. "Bad cop," he said with a nod to Charlie.

That was almost insulting, but Brett's eyes flashed so Luc kept it to himself.

"You two are going to have to work together, and that means getting along…"

"We'll be fine," Ms. Miller assured Brett. "I've accomplished more with far less."

That insult landed. Cocking his head, Luc let his gaze skate over *Charlie* from head to toe. "Just tell me we don't have to travel to all these packs…" he said turning his attention back to Brett. The Dolce and Gabbana wolf seated at his side would require far more protection than even Colby, and she was supposed to be bad cop?

Had mating finally addled Brett's brain?

Or was this revenge? It had to be revenge.

Luc wasn't sure for what yet, but he couldn't put it past Brett.

"You'll travel as needed. Some meetings will need to take place in neutral territory; others will require you to go to them. We may even consider bringing one or two here. They will have to have meetings of their own. I am, however," Brett said as he stood and rapped his knuckles on the desk, "leaving you both to figure it out. Charlie has a list of the attorneys for the various packs, and you have the names of all the seconds…"

That he did.

"Handle it." Then he glanced at his watch. "I need to go pick up my mate, you two can let yourselves out, right?"

He didn't wait for their answer before striding out and leaving Luc with the coolly impersonal Charlie, before he could open his mouth though, she stood and carried her mug toward the door. "I believe we're best suited to our own tasks, so once I've made arrangements, I'll contact you and brief you on what you need to know."

That sounded all well and good, but that wasn't how this worked. Rising, he faced her before she could open the door and escape. The wolf in him peeked out as he studied her, and she went still.

"I don't think so," he said, folding his arms.

"I'm the negotiator," she told him, as if that answered everything. "Brett is trusting me to get this done."

"I'm his Second," he reminded her, and for a split second, her wolf peeked out at him then retreated.

Her chin lifted, and he'd give her this, she held his gaze a beat longer than he thought she'd be able to. Exhaling, she squared her shoulders and nodded, her gaze directed somewhere just past him. "Yes, you are."

"So, let me buy you a drink?"

The flash of irritation across her face poked another hole in his already bruised ego.

"Just a drink, sunshine. Don't get your fur in a knot. We need to make plans...and that includes being on the same side for all of this." Maybe he wasn't a negotiator, but he understood what the lines of alliance should look like and right now, they were definitely *not* on the same side.

"Understood," she told him, her gaze flicking to his. "And I'd prefer if you called me by my name...just so we're clear."

"You got it, Charlie," he reached past her and opened the door. "I'm Luc. Shall we?"

She took the invitation, but her sigh drifted back to taunt him. "Yes, but I have to work in the morning, so can we make it coffee?"

"Whatever you want," he said with a forced grin.

Great, he couldn't get laid, and now he had to work with *Charlie*. His night just kept getting better and better.

CHAPTER 2

*C*harlie followed Luc Danes from their Alpha's home to the diner over on Route 5. It was pack owned and pack run. Considering his position, they would find a table without delay. She would rather have scheduled this for an afternoon meeting on Monday, or even a conference call. She and Luc did not need a sit down face to face to make plans, not yet anyway. Not when she had so much research to do and presentations to prepare.

Yet, here she was, pulling into the lot behind him and parking her hybrid next to his oversized truck. He was at her door before she even had the engine turned off, and opening it for her. Irritation scraped beneath her skin. Presumptive. Arrogant. Overbearing.

Drop dead gorgeous.

These were all descriptions that applied to him, and none of them could influence the work they needed to do. So, she kept her claws from flexing, a restraint long-honed in the business arena where she dealt with arrogant, self-aggrandizing pricks on a regular basis.

Her wolf batted at her.

19

Okay, perhaps that last was harsh. Pasting on a professional smile, she said, "Thank you." She allowed him to close the driver's side door as she opened the rear passenger and removed a messenger bag and her purse. The scent of steak, the faint trace of a woman's perfume, and a general scent of woods and green made her nose itch. It had to be the perfume. Even those formulated for wolves tended to aggravate her sense of smell.

Thankfully, he didn't offer to take her bag. So she locked her car and then drew up short following him when he stopped and eyed the car then her.

"Problem?"

His frown seemed more curious than furious, so she waited him out. "Most folks around here don't lock their cars." The implication being why would they? Wolves understood territorial boundaries and possession. Her scent would be on the car, no other wolf would touch it without her permission—in theory of course. Also, the humans who lived in and around the pack, those aware of them, were also rarely foolish enough to challenge the wolves on these subjects.

However, her answer was far simpler. "I don't really live around here, do I?" She gave him a beat, and then nodded to the diner. "Shall we?" It was almost nine, and she still had to drive back to Manhattan for a conference call with Japan in a few hours.

"Oh, let's." The dry sarcasm wasn't lost on her; she just refused to rise to the bait. She had four older brothers, every single one capable of irritating the feathers off an angel with their comments, tone, and attitude. She loved them, but she had a quadruple dose of inoculation for male egocentric behavior.

The door pushed into the diner, and a cheerful bell announced their arrival. There were easily a dozen customers scattered amongst the tables—a college student with coffee steaming the cup next to her as she poured over a textbook, and had a digital pad open next to her where she was writing things in with an electronic pencil. A pair of gray-haired older wolves with wrinkled faces and gnarled knuckles had coffee and pie, while playing chess. A human dressed in a delivery uniform sat tiredly at the counter, filling out paperwork in and around eating a burger.

Luc passed those tables, garnering nods, smiles, and greetings. He paused to give the human at the counter a shoulder squeeze and asked about his wife and new baby. Well that explained the lack of sleep. The student glanced up and gave Luc a quick smile, that never crossed the line into flirty.

"Mr. Danes."

"Laurie," he greeted her. "How's the math going?"

"It still sucks," she said cheerfully enough. "But I've got it on the run."

He laughed, and then continued on. Four teens hunkered down in their seats, making themselves look smaller, while trying—and failing—to avoid being noticed. Luc paused at their table, and his gaze swept across each of them and finally settled on the brunet boy with a nose piercing. Human. No wolf would do that, but the other three were definitely wolves.

Luc said absolutely nothing; he just stared at the boys and waited. Finally Nose Piercing let out a sigh and said, "We're waiting on Eric to pick us up. We were already busted for being out past curfew."

Curfew in Hudson River was a flexible thing, applicable to preteens and those teens without jobs. It encouraged the teens to become more active in the pack and to develop responsibility. The more lackadaisical needed the structure and encouragement, while the more studious were likely to be at home or the library anyway.

Glancing to the other three boys, Luc said, "You all know better, and you've had one grounding in the last six months for this infraction, which makes this your second one. The penalty for that is what?"

"Grounding and community service," the dishwater blond sitting next to Nose Piercing hunched his shoulders and mumbled. Not a dominant one in the grouping—not really. Nose Piercing had it, but he was human. The other three needed more guidance and a firmer hand that was more cognizant of pack hierarchy and rules. Nose Piercing's family might work for Brett, but they weren't full-fledged members of the pack—more protected than included. Willow Bend had humans in their pack.

That might be something to consider, particularly with situations like this. Nose Piercing had the dominance to lead these three around, and he didn't shift. She reached into her pocket and pulled out a business card. Catching Nose Piercing's curious gaze, she studied him, and he tried to look away twice, but she canted her head and kept him pinned while Luc finished dressing down the younger wolves.

She had to give him credit, because he didn't lecture or scold. His tone was downright conversational, and a couple of the boys even laughed. When Luc nodded to them and moved on, she stayed where she was. "What's your name?" she asked Nose Piercing.

"Harris, ma'am. Harris Ryder." Harris straightened under her scrutiny. As with Luc, the three wolves with him went still, as if they could shrink past her notice.

"My name is Charlie Miller, Mr. Ryder," she said by way of introduction and held out the business card. "I'm assuming you do not have work currently?"

"Um…" He fidgeted, and then took the card without looking at it. "Yes, I mean no, Ms. Miller. I don't have a job, but I'm a senior in high school…I've been taking AP classes." He darted a look at his friends, then scowled when all three avoided coming to his defense. "Several of them, and it's a heavy study load."

She could understand that. "How many is a lot?"

Luc had paused two tables away, listening she was certain, but he made no move to interfere.

"Six. Do you want to know the classes?" Yes, if humans were living among them and aware of them, which Harris seemed to be one of them, then they needed more schooling in pack dynamics, and how and when to hold a gaze. The kid was too young to be a challenge, but he couldn't seem to back out of trying to stare her down.

"That would be nice." It wasn't an order, but the kid frowned as he tried to parse it. His friends continued to be less than helpful.

Finally Harris sighed, and said, "AP World History, Literature, Government, Economics, French, and Statistics."

"French language and culture?" She confirmed, but curious to know how fluent he was, she asked, *"Comment parlez-vous couramment le français?"*

"Pas aussi couramment que j'ai besoin d'être, Mademoiselle." The edge of sarcasm returned, but it was more self-deprecating.

"Your accent and intonation are excellent. I might have a part time job you can do. Call my office next week, and have your parents available when you do, and we'll discuss how much work you can handle." It wasn't a request.

Harris blinked, then glanced at her card before looking up at her. *"Merci."*

"De rien." Then she looked at the wolves sitting around him. "Are any of you in AP classes?"

A slow round of headshakes. Somehow, she wasn't surprised, though she was disappointed.

"Pity. Good evening, boys." Then she turned and met Luc's amused gaze, and raised an eyebrow. He shook his head and beckoned her to the round booth in the very back. Wolves had astute hearing, so the location had less to do with not being overheard than to convey privacy to the other patrons.

Luc actually waited for her to slide into the booth before he dropped in on the other side. She set her purse down and then pulled out her laptop.

"We're not going to need that..."

"If we're meeting about the task Brett set before us, I think notes would be an appropriate way to keep us both on the same page." Notes, agendas, and summaries were keys to successful management of all projects and helped to keep expectations in check as well as achieve goals.

Leaning forward with his arms on the table, Luc studied her. "This isn't about the actual task yet—this is about you and me getting to know each other."

Before she could respond, the waitress came over. Rita smiled at them, and Charlie raised her brows in surprise. She hadn't seen Rita Standish in years, but then Charlie didn't linger when she came up for meetings with Brett.

"Charlie Miller, you are a sight for sore eyes. Does your mother know you're up here?"

Maintaining her expression, Charlie smiled. "No, she doesn't, and as soon as Mr. Danes and I finish our meeting, I have to get back to Manhattan. I have a conference call in a few hours."

"So you were just up to see Brett?" This was the other problem with coming too close too home. Everyone was always in everyone else's business.

"As usual," Charlie said, keeping it light. "Could I just have a cup of coffee, please?" What little appetite she'd possessed fled when Rita frowned at her.

"You never eat," the older wolf complained. "And fine, I won't tell your mother…"

"Rita," Luc simply said her name, and Rita's little guilt trip silenced as she looked to him. "Coffee for Charlie, and I'll take coffee and a slice of the apple pie." He cut a quick look to her. "Make it two slices, and then we'd like privacy. Thank you."

As she had earlier with Harris, Luc wasn't making a request. Rita dipped her gaze without even attempting to boss Luc around. She merely nodded and hurried away from their table.

"You didn't have to shut her down," Charlie told him. "I'm used to the disapproval."

With a careless shrug, Luc said, "I wanted you here so we could talk, not so Rita can grind up some beans for the rumor mill. They have more than enough swill passing through it."

Leaning back in the seat, Charlie spared a glance toward the pie case where Rita was cutting out two slices. "She'll be on the phone to my mother five minutes after she brings the coffee."

"Five bucks says she calls mine first," Luc said with a smile that nearly verged on a smirk, but it didn't quite reach his eyes.

"What's your mother going to do to the Second?"

"I don't know, Charlie, what's yours going to do?" The retort actually made her smile.

"Guilt." One word, and Luc pointed his thumb and forefinger at her like a gun. In her case, guilt would be the best-case scenario. It would mean she cared.

"Exactly. So—we have coffee and our pie, and we bond over our mutual need to avoid our mothers." Despite herself,

Charlie chuckled, and Luc's smile grew. "See, I knew you couldn't resist me."

And just as quickly as that, her humor dried up. "You'd be surprised what I can resist, Mr. Danes."

"I told you that I'm Luc, let's save the Mr. Danes stuff for formalities." His eyes narrowed a fraction. It must be irritating that she didn't behave like some besotted young female he bestowed his attention upon. His reputation had been carefully curated and hard won *before* he left the pack. It had only increased in legend since he returned, or so her mother had said on that rare Sunday Charlie had spent following the pack being called in.

"You did," she acknowledged. "My apologies. I often rely on formality in meetings, it keeps everyone focused and less prone to distractions."

Rita returned with their coffee mugs filled to the brim—it smelled fresh. There were some pros to being at home, none of the restaurants would try to get away with serving burnt coffee. The apple pies she placed in front of each of them, along with silverware rolled tight into napkins, were freshly baked, likely earlier that day. She added a carafe of coffee to the table to save them having to call her back over.

"Can I get you anything else?" The tone was polite, as were the words, but a cord of irritation scraped off each syllable. Rita did not appreciate Luc's earlier dismissal.

"No, thank you," Charlie said. Despite her own impatience with Rita's gossip mongering, she was at heart a nice woman, and she meant well—even when she really wanted the latest bit of juicy scandal or revealing tidbit.

Rita's eyes softened on her a moment, but they radiated disapproval for a flash when she glanced at Luc. Then she touched her hand. "Just remember, sweetie, call your mom when you can. You know she worries."

No, her mother really didn't, but Charlie smiled anyway. "I will. Thank you, Rita."

"That will be all Rita."

"Of course, Luc," she said. "Please give my best to Brett and Colby." Then she pivoted and walked away. Charlie didn't miss the tightening of Luc's jaw at the comment, or the way he tracked Rita's progress across the diner. A glance to the window gave her a good view of Rita's reflection, and the small smirk she wore.

"She means well," Charlie told him, not at all certain why she'd need to intercede on Rita's behalf. The old wolf had been around three times Charlie's lifespan, and she'd wrangled all of them at one point or another when they were kids.

"Sometimes meaning well and doing well are two different things," her companion said with a shake of his head, and then scoffed before focusing on her again. "And again, not what we're here to discuss."

"True."

"First of all, let's lay out some ground rules."

"Very well," she agreed, picking up her coffee cup and taking a sip. "I would like to schedule meetings in advance in order to prepare for them."

"Fine, we meet twice a week. What nights work for you? Since I'm assuming you're busy during the day."

"Twice? Could we do one by phone conference?"

"No, I like to see the person I'm talking to."

Of course, he did. It was nearly an hour's drive once she got out of the city, and getting out of the city could take even longer. "Twice a week... if you want to meet that often you'll have to come to me for one of those meetings."

Luc dug into his apple pie and eyed her. "Manhattan's not *that* far."

"And I have more responsibilities than just this project." Not that she wanted to imply he didn't have responsibilities, but he was far more fluid than her. She managed a quick glance at her watch before taking a sip of the coffee. Oh, that was good.

"This will likely become your primary responsibility until we have the kinks worked out," Luc informed her.

"No," she told him, locking gazes. Yes, he was dominant. Yes, he ranked higher in the pack. But he didn't rank higher in the business, and there she was the dominant, and it was *hers* to protect. "The company takes precedence. It provides for the pack, and if we miss a negotiation or fail to meet a deadline because I am having to drive up here twice a week or more…" To be blunt she didn't put it past him. "Then the pack suffers, and I won't allow that."

Nostrils flaring, Luc studied her. Whether it was inciting his wolf or not, he didn't really react to her stare. If anything, his pupils dilated a fraction, and gold bled in to the blue. "What is it, exactly, that you do, Charlie?"

"We do not have enough hours in the day for me to go over the list of duties I take care of," she demurred tackling that particular topic. "Let's just say I've been doing my job longer than you've been doing yours."

A slow smirk curled his lips. "Let's say you explain, particularly if you want me to come to the city for these meetings rather than you coming here. Most of my tasks keep me in the valley." He dug into another piece of the pie. "And I can't say I've ever been fond of the city."

The pie smelled delicious, but she focused on the coffee. As it was, she hadn't eaten a proper meal, despite the fact Brett offered her dinner when she arrived. Their Alpha was a terrific cook, not as good as his father, but he'd definitely become something of an expert. A meal meant more socializing, and that would have extended the time spent on the meeting. Once a month, she drove up from the city to meet with him and go over any of the finer details from her reports or to answer any questions.

Most of the time it was merely a matter of checking in, for Brett to take her pulse, and for Charlie to reconnect with her pack. Then she went back to the city and business as usual, and he continued on here. It had worked for a decade. She made the pack money and protected their business interests, while Brett protected and looked after the pack.

"You don't like me," Luc said, after the pause went long past polite.

"I don't dislike you precisely," she offered, but it sounded weak to her own ears. "But no, I'm not a fan."

He laughed, then shoveled another bite of the pie into his mouth as he shook his head. His scent shifted, a sour note just muddying the cinnamon spice of his flavor. Not that she'd been cataloging his scent. If anything, she'd focused very specifically on *not* doing that.

"What did I do?" Luc asked, washing down the last of his pie with his coffee, then refilling his mug and hers before she could cover it. The offer, once accepted, made it impolite to turn down.

Ugh, how she hated pack politics. So, so much.

"What makes you think you did anything?" she countered, then nudged the plate with her untouched slice of pie toward him.

"You should eat that," he said, his eyes narrowing. "Your stomach is gurgling despite your need to cover it up. If you don't want pie, we can order something else."

Tongue firmly locked behind her teeth, she did her best to avoid grinding them. "First rule of negotiation," she said unable to keep the clipped note buried. "Do not presume you know what your opponent wants."

"You're hungry," he argued. "It's not a presumption."

"It is when I've expressed no interest in eating. I have a

29

schedule to keep, Luc." She almost hated saying his name, and the man in question propped his chin on his hand as he studied her. "I came here because you specifically chose this for our conversation." She was not going to add she'd rather drag her starving carcass over broken glass than eat at this diner. The coffee was more than enough.

"Fair enough," he relented. "So what did I do?"

They were back to that. "Who said you did anything?"

"No one, but you're a very put together wolf. Exceptionally rational, and the way Brett talks about you—probably his favorite lieutenant. So what did I do that made you dislike me so much?"

"You're making another presumption," she informed him, and rather than force herself to drink more coffee, she pushed the mug aside. They weren't here to be polite, so she could take a step to the side for the moment. Except—they really couldn't. They weren't alone.

Luc leaned back in the seat, and his gaze went from her to the diner. "Fair enough." Sliding out of the booth, he pulled out a few bills and set them on the table. Then he held out his hand. "You have a schedule. I can respect that. But we have a task, and I need you to respect me."

Taking his hand, she let him help her out of the booth before she reached for her bag and her laptop. After stowing it away, she slung the strap over her shoulder. "You are pack Second, respecting you comes with the package."

Laughing softly, he motioned toward the door and murmured in an almost sub vocal tone, "Sweetheart, the fact your scent didn't even change when you said that impresses me more than anything else. Let's take this conversation somewhere more private."

Well on that, they could agree. They said nothing as they made their way past the other patrons, and Charlie couldn't miss the weight of their regard. In fact, Rita frowned at their exodus, which made Charlie pick up the pace. If Rita had called her mother, then Adele may already be on her way, and just—no.

Luc frowned at her as they reached their vehicles. "You choose the destination."

It was—a generous offer, and it took her a moment to think about *where* they could go that no one would bother them. Hudson River had vast land, but they also had far flung pack mates.

"Is the old sawmill still standing?" When she was in high school, it had been popular with her year mates. They had more than their fair share of parties out there. Enough that Brett's grandfather—their Alpha at the time—had once sentenced every single one of her year mates to fixing the place up and cleaning out all the rotting wood.

It had been a truly uncomfortable sentence. After, they'd been forbidden from going out there again, because the old river sawmill was a landmark for the pack and should be treated with respect.

"Yep," Luc told her. "It's still protected. Good call. I'll follow you—unless you don't remember the way?"

The question ruffled her fur the wrong way, but there was nothing in his scent that suggested it was a dig. Then again, he'd accused her of masking her own when she'd made her comment about respecting his position. Yes, his position was absolutely due respect. Therefore, he should be respected.

She didn't say she respected him.

The difference might be splitting hairs, but that was where the devil lay in every deal she negotiated for Hudson River International. The details. "I remember," she assured him, then because he'd given an inch even as he tweaked her, she added, "Do try to keep up. I don't want to have to double back."

"Just try and lose me, sweetheart," Luc said with a slow smile. "I dare you."

Her wolf perked up, ears forward, and Charlie let out a dismissive laugh. No, she wasn't biting. Though after she was in the driver's seat and pulling away from the diner, she didn't miss the speculative look in his eyes, or the way he focused on her before he pulled out to follow her with his truck.

Hopefully they could make a quick resolution, she really didn't want to have to take her call with the Japanese executives in her car. That could be a very uncomfortable night.

A flick of a look to her rearview mirror, and the corner of her mouth kicked up.

Luc was right there, on her tail. As promised.

She pressed the accelerator and teased a little more speed out of her hybrid.

If he was going to chase her, she might as well have a little fun before he got bored.

CHAPTER 3

*T*he drive to the sawmill passed almost too swiftly as Luc kept his truck squarely on the tail of Charlie's little hybrid. The vehicle was so innocuous and silent, he could appreciate it. At the same time, it rubbed him the wrong way.

She rubbed him the wrong way. Nothing ruffled her cool, clipped demeanor or seemed to disturb those stunning green eyes. The fact he'd been looking for a way to make them flash wasn't lost on him. Particularly after her deft handling of Harris. That kid was trouble with a capital T. Restless and far too intelligent for his own good, he constantly got his year mates into trouble because in his group, none of them could match his dominance. Throw in charm—other people's assessments of the little punk, not Luc's—and Harris Ryder was a threat in need of a firm hand.

The fact it was a task landing squarely on his shoulders hadn't been lost on Luc. But he had yet to find a method that cowed the younger man, truly, particularly since the human didn't fall under the same rules as the rest of the pack. Dominance wasn't limited to wolves, though their wolves tended to be smarter about it. Human dominance was very much a thing, as was human risk-taking, and Harris pushed boundaries and patience.

That she more or less co-opted the boy for a possible job intrigued him.

The old sawmill occupied a sliver of land down by the river. It used to send all processed wood downriver to the city via barges, back in the day. It had closed some fifty plus years earlier, but the structure remained, and it became a popular hangout for teens in the pack for many of those years.

Luc had spent his fair share of time playing there. Years earlier, the old Alpha had disrupted a party that had gotten out of hand—a fight club—and in punishment, the wolves in that year all had to participate in restoring the sawmill to its former glory, and then they were all banished from playing there.

It had fallen out of favor as a play spot, and Hunters would roust any young gatherings that even attempted to hang out there. So it was an excellent place for some privacy.

He parked next to her again. She was up and out of her car before he could get to her. To his absolute surprise, she'd stripped off her shoes for bare feet before nodding to where the mill waited. The scent of the river was heavy in the air, along with the deeper scents of forest, pine and oak, wild flowers, and somewhere upwind, the faint tease of woodsmoke.

The cooler temperatures allowed them to indulge, even if as wolves, they rarely got that cold. Colby liked fires, and Brett would build one in his patio firepit most evenings when she was home if the weather was too warm to build one inside. There wasn't much Brett wouldn't do for his mate, and they grew more sloppily in love as the months passed. But they also pushed and challenged each other, her with her refusals to be buried and cosseted in heavy layers of protection, while Brett learned to ease back the throttle on self-loathing. She lifted him up, and he kept her grounded.

It worked for them.

Luc couldn't be happier.

The path from the cars to the mill was over grassy earth, the old ruts having long since worn away, and the road had been swallowed by the forest, a bit of aging cracked blacktop appearing here and there. On the wooden planks of the deck surrounding the mill, his quarry didn't slow until she reached the railing overlooking the river itself.

The clear skies revealed a crescent moon, even as the breeze tugged at her hair and surrounded him in her scent. Earlier, her scent had been sweet with a tang—brown sugar and honey—while they'd been at Brett's. At the diner, it had been contained with only hints of fur beneath the earthier taste of crushed autumn leaves to remind him she was indeed a wolf.

Out here with only the river and the woods, his wolf perked up at the bottom notes of amber and musk sharpening the hint of lemon at the top. Smart, restrained, and mysterious, Charlie proved a puzzle he wanted to define, if not solve. What the hell did he remember about her family?

Adele Miller was one of the pack's senior Hunters. She trained their youths primarily, but she occasionally took on apprentices. Usually those Hunters deemed needing specialized training. Tough. Resourceful. Unflinching. Luc respected her, but he'd never much liked her.

Charlie was her daughter.

This pup had not only wandered far from the litter, she'd left for another territory altogether.

The click of her tongue refocused his attention, and he found the wolf in question studying him with unreadable eyes. With only the faint light of the moon, they were both cast in shadows, but it didn't hamper his night vision at all.

"We have to work together," he began without preamble. "That means I have to trust you, and you need to trust me."

"I trust your dedication to the pack, you can trust mine." Clear. Blunt. To the point.

"It's not your dedication to the pack I'm questioning." It wasn't. "You're loyal. But there's more to being a *part* of a pack than loyalty."

She snorted. "Loyalty is the heart of being *pack*."

"For some, maybe," Luc continued with a shrug.

"But not for you?" Folding her arms, she leaned against the rail and met his gaze. She held it longer here, unflinching, longer than she had in Brett's office or the diner. The serenity in those eyes, coupled with her unreadable expressions, made him want to snarl and dishevel her pristine image. Muss her up and remind her she was a wolf.

The urge sparked his wolf's interest. It had been a while since they faced a real challenge, and the longer they spent in Charlie's company, the more he itched to take on the hunt. "No," he told her flatly. "To be loyal, all you have to do is never betray. It doesn't mean you would lift a hand to help, put yourself out there, or take any risks. Loyalty implies trustworthy, it doesn't *mean* trustworthy."

"Actually," she said, one corner of her mouth tipping upwards. "It refers to the qualities of being loyal, which are fidelity, allegiance, devotion—trustworthiness."

"So you would fight for your pack?"

"I do every day."

"I'm not talking corporate politics, or whatever games you indulge in for the business."

Her eyes went flat, a hint of gold at their edge, but it was there and gone again so fast, he couldn't be sure. "The games I *indulge* in?"

"You heard me," he told her, unyielding. "Brett has asked us to enter the territory of other wolves, to meet their Seconds and lawyers, to negotiate the language of the treaties that will define our pack and theirs for the next few generations. Not everyone will be on the same page, and the respect and accord between the Alphas does not mean it extends to every member of their packs. Every pack has its own problems."

"Oh, I'm aware of that. Hudson River has its share of bad apples."

Ignoring her pointed look, he said, "Those situations are open to disagreements and possible repercussions—tell me *why* I should trust you at my back?"

For love of the pack, give him something more wolf-like in a response than the cool expression and faintly arched brows. This wasn't a boardroom or some five-star restaurant at the top of a building in Manhattan. They would most likely *have* to travel to the Yukon, there would be meetings with the Enforcers, trips to Sutter Butte and, if Luc were lucky, at least one trip to the Big Easy. Not all packs were made equal, and some of these situations would be far more volatile than others.

"Because Brett assigned me to the task and told us to work together."

Whatever he'd been looking for in a response, it was most definitely *not* that. "I should trust you because Brett assigned us to the task?"

"I have to trust you for the same reason," she retorted with a careless shrug. "Unless your current circumstances have left you in need of handholding, in which case, I'd refer you again to the Alpha who gave us this task."

The cavalier tone added a layer of insult to the charge he

couldn't handle his position. His wolf roused, and he studied the woman in front of him. Her serenity seemed unfazed, but she'd been almost uncomfortable at the diner when Rita brought up her mother—part of why he'd sent the old busy-body away. Rita was a good woman, and she could be kind, but she enjoyed gossiping far too much. In so many ways, she was who his mother, Babette, would be eventually.

"Yet, you don't trust me."

"I don't *know* you," she countered.

"My point," he almost snarled the words. "That's what *this* is—a chance to get to know each other so we can work together."

"You'll find that in most areas of business and negotiation, we don't have to hold hands and skip in order to reach an equitable and profitable relationship. In fact, more often than not, personal feelings and investment can muddy the waters and compromise our perspectives."

Folding his arms, he ground his teeth together. Impossible woman. "Explain."

She sighed, then loosened the button on her suit coat to let it drape open, giving him a better view of the soft white shirt beneath. After a glance at her watch, she focused on him. "What is the first thing that happens when you introduce two dominants?"

"You establish which dominant is the more powerful."

"How?"

Blandly, he said, "Force of personality. A stare. If necessary, a release of personal power. I'm sure you're familiar."

"What happens to the other wolves in their immediate environs?"

"Nothing, the dominants wouldn't allow it." If she thought he'd allow another wolf to lay a finger on her when he was right there, she had another think coming. "It is possible, however unlikely, that in those moments before the dominance is established or we've both shown our cards, that less dominant wolves might be uncomfortable."

"Accepted." She nodded once. "Now add to this moment, the fact that most of the wolves likely tasked toward this are unmated—as far as I know, only the Seconds of Willow Bend and the Enforcers have mates."

He considered what he knew of them. "You are correct."

"And only the Yukon's Second is female."

"When you arrive at a point, would you let me know?"

With a sigh, she said, "From the moment you met me, you've been trying to pigeonhole me, yes or no?"

"Yes." He didn't hesitate to admit it.

"You can't."

Eyes narrowed, he conceded the point. "No, my dominance doesn't appear to affect you." Considering she hadn't looked away from him once during their current conversation, nor had she roused his wolf with the desire to put her in her place for her belligerence. "At all. Though you played along at Brett's and at the diner."

"How does that make you feel?"

Irked. Aggravated. Ready to punch something—yet not punch her. "What are you doing precisely?"

"My job," she reminded him. "When I walk into a room, dominants take notice, but I slide a glance to the side and they relax. Their fundamental need to respond to a challenge averted. They scent no threat, they disregard me as a potential challenger and leave their reactions open for me to observe."

She wasn't a submissive. She didn't *read* as submissive. The overwhelming urge to protect didn't stir. She was not an Omega. She didn't redirect his own weaknesses back at him. Her dominance, however, it was very present and yet—not.

"What *are* you?" He asked.

"I am the Chief Operating Officer of Hudson River

39

International, I negotiate deals with executives—human and lupine—from all over the world. I work to protect the pack's financial interests and to grow them…"

Shock rippled through him. "You're a Shadow."

Charlie smiled, the first real smile he'd seen her wear. Shadows were rare in packs. Rarer than Omegas, and there were less than one to two of those born to a generation in any of the packs.

As far as Luc knew, there were no known Shadows amongst any of the packs.

In fact… "How is that possible?" Luc stared at her. "How does no one know?"

"Brett knows," she told him, sliding her gaze from his for the first time since the conversation began to glance at the water. "You would have learned eventually, and you're right, in a getting to know you way—you should probably know."

Almost at once, his irritation faded and his wolf settled, even if Luc's concern ramped up. Shadows—Shadows could become whatever they needed in a pack, they had fluid dominance, fluid positioning—and their loyalty couldn't be controlled or demanded. They offered it, or they didn't. But more—they were fluid themselves. Sometimes dominant, other times not. While they could will it, sometimes their wolves demanded it. Unpredictable. Difficult to track and even more difficult to work, with because they didn't always respond as expected.

The shift was almost imperceptible, and he narrowed the distance, his instincts sharpening. The need to protect pounded in his veins and yet…

Intellectually, he recognized the manipulation now that she'd pointed it out. Just as soon as it began, it ended and he inhaled a deep breath, filling his lungs with her scent.

Bad cop.

"That's why Brett gave you the bad cop job."

She nodded slowly. "Negotiation is something I am well-versed in. I trained, I went to school, I have degrees, and I spend nearly every minute of every day putting powerful people at ease and building up those who lack the confidence in their own capabilities."

"And you stay in the city, far away from your own pack, why?" He could guess, but he wanted to hear it from her. Movement pricked his ears. Rushing feet through the forest, distant, but closing and fast.

"You're about to meet four of them."

They came from downwind, masking their scent. Charlie didn't evince any concern, but Luc was less than interested in the potential interruption. "They would be?"

The sound was closer now, and at least the wolves were smart enough not to mask their passage. He was not in the mood for a surprise *or* an interruption. Their guests were almost to the sawmill, and Luc tracked them as they left the cover of the woods. They slowed from their dead run to jogging, one of them shoving the others.

A moment later, their scent hit and his wolf snarled.

Her brothers.

She had four of them. Of course she did, Adele Miller had four sons, and Luc knew them. Irritating bastards every single one, but damn good at their jobs and loyal.

Bishop, Duke, Noah, and Sullivan—two sets of twin brothers. Bishop and Duke being the elder pair, with Noah and Sullivan just two years younger. That would make Charlie the youngest.

"Charlie!" Sullivan bellowed. "You thought you were going to sneak in and sneak out without saying hello?" Unlike Charlie, her brothers were all dark-headed, though the elder pair had green eyes, the younger were brown-eyed.

Sullivan bounded across the deck, shot Luc a bright smile

and a "Hey, Luc!" then swept his sister up into a hug that squeezed the air out of her. Noah was right behind him.

"Hey, Luc, thanks for making Sis hang out long enough to say hi." He dragged her away from Sullivan, and they manhandled her like a doll, definitely rumpling her suit.

"Hey," Sullivan complained and slapped Noah upside the head. "I wasn't done with my hug." He yanked her back. Noah snarled and pulled Charlie to him.

Done with the shenanigans, Luc opened his mouth, but both Noah and Sullivan were suddenly on the ground, clutching their nuts.

Charlie dusted off her hands before smoothing her jacket down.

"I told you idiots to be nice to her," Bishop said without an ounce of sympathy as he stepped over the boys. He held out his hand to Luc. "Luc."

"Bishop." The eldest of all the Miller children, Bishop, as well as his brother Duke, were Hunters like their mother. Both Noah and Sullivan were Hunters, as well as craftsmen who worked part time in their father's shop. They were designers and innovators. The whole Miller family was a credit to the pack, really. But they were private, and they tended toward isolation.

Gripping his hand, Luc nodded to him. "You should also remind your idiot brothers that interrupting a meeting is not a good idea."

"So this is a meeting?" Bishop said with a pointed look at his sister then at Luc.

With a snort, Luc just stared at him. He didn't owe him or any of her brothers an explanation, but Duke nodded to him as he dragged the other two up and shoved them to the side before holding out his arms.

Sighing, Charlie walked to him and gave him a hug. The big bear of a wolf lifted her off her feet, but without the force of their younger siblings, and without squeezing all the air out of her.

Bishop chuckled, but the laughter didn't quite reach his green eyes. He raised his hands and backed off a step. A surrender without submission, then nodded to his sister. "We haven't seen Charlie in months."

That...

Turning, Luc stared at Charlie as Duke set her down. Though her brother didn't say anything, she ducked her head. Everything in her manner went gentler, more submissive, and the racing energy over her siblings settled.

Did they not know...?

"I've been busy, Bishop," Charlie chastised him lightly, though there wasn't an ounce of bite to her tone, and Luc found himself missing those cool, precise intonations.

"We're all busy, Charlie-bear, but we all make time to visit and to see Mom and Dad..."

The quiet submissiveness slipped away, and she narrowed her eyes. "Don't start. I am busy. I have a job."

"That you could leave and come home where you belong," Sullivan complained as he managed to stand upright. Luc might almost feel sorry for him, but almost all of them, save for Duke, behaved like an ass. The last brother had his arm around her shoulders, and she had hers around his waist, not seeming remotely uncomfortable.

"Sullivan, I'm not having this discussion with you."

"Yeah, we forgot," Noah grunted sarcastically. "We're just the dumb hicks who never look past our own noses."

"Enough," Bishop told them, and it shut them up, then he glanced from Luc back to Charlie. "Mom wants to see you."

Nothing changed in Charlie's expression or her scent, if anything it smoothed over. Unruffled or seemingly undisturbed, but Luc would bet everything he owned she masked

43

it. Her reaction at the diner when Rita brought up her mother in the first place promised him that much.

"Yeah, kid," Duke murmured. "Mom knows you're here. She told Dad, who called us."

"Of course he did," she said evenly. "Adele likes her routines. I'm not due for another supper for at least a month, I was here eleven months ago. Once per year is more than sufficient."

"The hell it is," Noah snarled, and took a step forward, but Luc pinned him with a look, and the wolf slowed then stopped. Even Sullivan dropped back a foot, and when Luc met Duke's gaze, the wolf had the wisdom to drop his immediately.

"Enough," Luc said once he had their attention. "Charlie and I have business to discuss, and this family drama is not a part of it."

For a flicker of a moment, her embarrassment soured the breeze, but she blotted it almost immediately.

"You'll forgive me, Luc, but my sister doesn't have any business with you. You're"

"About to remind you what it feels like to lose a tooth, if you keep talking." Luc was done. "Let her go." The order rippled through the air, and Duke dropped his arm immediately. "All four of you go. If Charlie wants to call you, she will. Obviously, she has your number. Ambushing her to say hi and be affectionate is one thing, this..." He motioned to them. "This is not. Now go." With enough command punched into it to make it effective, he glared. Her younger brothers didn't quibble, but Duke and Bishop resisted.

"You don't get to decide when we see our sister, Luc." It was damn close to a challenge, and there was no way Bishop didn't know it.

"At the moment?" And for as long as they were partnered, he absolutely could make that call. "Yes, I do. Particularly because she didn't invite you out here, nor did she seem to enjoy the bullying. Go home, boys."

Duke jerked his head to Sullivan and Noah. The pair shot looks at their sister—while not hateful, they did promise some sibling revenge. Whatever, Luc had siblings. They were annoying, not dangerous.

But even as the younger pair disappeared into the darkness, Duke and Bishop held their ground.

"Charlie," Bishop said, not taking his gaze off Luc, yet not holding Luc's gaze at the same time.

She sighed. "I have to finish this meeting, then I have a call with Japan to take in less than two hours. At this rate, I'll be taking it in the car. I'll call you tomorrow."

"Promise." Though Bishop's tone made it an order, his expression turned it into a request. "You keep your promises."

"I promise." But she certainly didn't like it, and unlike her neutral tone of earlier, she didn't disguise this one. "But if you do this again, you can kiss my ass on getting another promise out of me."

Bishop grinned. "There's the bite. I thought you'd pulled all your claws living in the big city, bratling. Call me tomorrow. I'll hold Mom off, but you need to come out and have dinner. She hates it when you don't call."

"Are her fingers broken?" Charlie challenged.

"No, kid," Duke told her, then with a half-look at Luc, pressed a kiss to the top of Charlie's head and murmured something too low for Luc to catch. The sub-vocal deliberately aimed away from him.

She rolled her eyes. "Go away. Both of you. I have work to do. This is hardly a social call, and you know it."

"Good," Bishop said, and Luc's irritation magnified at her *and* her brothers. "We'll talk tomorrow."

The pair nodded to Luc before Bishop spread his hands as

he gave Charlie an inquiring look. Rolling her eyes, she crossed to him and then gave him a hug. Like Duke, Bishop didn't squeeze her tight, but he did enfold her close. Warning flashed in his eyes when he caught Luc watching them.

Brothers.

He'd been the big brother long enough to appreciate the promise of menace. At the same time, he was very done with this impromptu visit by her brothers. Finally, the older pair left after a couple of quiet words to her while Luc gave them some privacy by glancing at the river.

"I am beginning to understand the appeal of the city," he admitted to her with a sidelong glance.

Charlie tilted her head, the smile curling her lips deepening before she laughed. The rich, husky sound of it rolled over him like a gathering storm.

"They're not so bad. Wait until you meet my mother."

"I have met your mother," he admitted. "I'm not a fan." Why the fuck he chose to say that, he'd never know, but she didn't seem offended by it.

"Neither am I."

The less said about that, the better.

"You have a call with Japan?" he asked after a beat of silence. It was what she'd lobbed at her brothers in her scolding.

She nodded. "I do. A negotiation for licensing software for the new chips the company is employing in our effort to minimize constantly discarding new technology and making it more recyclable."

"If you left now, would you have to take the call in your car?" Her impatience with his demands made more sense.

She checked her watch. "No, I might even be able to change before I had to make the call."

"Then go. I'll come in to the city tomorrow and take you out to dinner."

Surprise flickered across her face. "I have meetings until eight."

"Fine, I'll be at the office at eight-fifteen. If your schedule changes, call me. You have my number."

He motioned her toward their vehicles. But instead of moving, she stared at him.

"What?"

"Why?"

"Why what?" Wasn't she the one who said she had to go?

"Why the sudden about face? Don't tell me Bishop intimidated you with his promise of a shovel to the back of the head for even looking at me."

Luc snorted. "Hardly. I said we needed to know each other to work together. I maintain that. I also said I needed your respect. If I have to earn it, fine... I'll show you and your position respect."

The surprise flickering through her expression before she muted it annoyed him. That she was eminently capable was extremely evident. So why the surprise?

"Thank you," she said, finally walking, and he fell into step with her. "Instead of going out, why don't I have food catered into the office? Then we don't have to deal with the noisy restaurants and the chance of being overheard."

"Your office, not your apartment?"

They were at the vehicles. Charlie gave him another smile. The second real one of the evening, and it made him want to collect another. "This is business, Luc. Not pleasure. Tomorrow, then?"

He nodded. "Tomorrow."

Waiting by the side of his truck, he watched until her taillights vanished, then pulled out his phone and sent a message to Brett.

You're a dick.

A moment later, Brett's response flashed on the screen.

You're welcome. She's a wonderful wolf. If you hurt her, I'll feed you your spleen.

Yeah. Luc believed that.

She said their dinner was business. Not pleasure.

"For now, little Shadow," he murmured. "For now."

He was starting to get the scent of this hunt.

CHAPTER 4

*T*he few hours of sleep she'd managed following the call to Japan had left her eyes sore and her body fatigued. She'd made a larger breakfast than normal, then picked up a smoothie on her way to the office. Debbie Locke, her assistant, was already at her desk when Charlie sailed through the door arriving precisely three minutes before her first meeting of the day.

Executives from all divisions would be reporting in with their quarterly estimates and future projections. Each one was given a thirty-minute window with five minutes in between if she required refreshment. Hudson River International had begun as a shipping company, then expanded to a multi-tiered organization handling everything from research and development to deployment of improved shipping technologies and methodology. Years earlier, Brett's grandfather—their Alpha at the time—proposed to the take the company in another direction just ahead of the tech boom in the 90s.

She'd initially begun this position as Brett's executive assistant. It provided him with a presence at the office daily and got her away from her family. As far as she was concerned, it had been a win-win. For a while, Brett had toyed with the idea of courting her, but neither of them had felt any great pull. In simple truth, they made better friends, which worked to their benefit. Within a year, Brett laid out his ideas to take what his grandfather began and push it toward a green initiative.

A year after that, he promoted her from executive assistant to executive officer. With each successive year, she'd tackled more of the day-to-day, allowing Brett to focus on the pack.

While her work carried the title of Chief Operating Officer, she was every bit Brett's Second in the corporate world as Luc was his Second in the pack. The rank didn't matter; she looked after the pack's interest and the company.

The majority of the company's seven thousand employees were human. Of that seven thousand, six hundred and twelve held management positions. A little over one hundred and fourteen were director-level or higher, with just twenty-seven achieving a senior position directly reportable to her.

The quarterly meetings allowed her to take the pulse of that twenty-seven. They were each encouraged to invite their top candidates or employees deserving recognition for service to these meetings. While Debbie occasionally complained about these days, because the scheduling took a lot of planning, she also admitted that the meetings buoyed morale.

It would be impossible for Charlie to get to know every single person who worked for the company, but she never forgot a name, and she made a point to acknowledge them, whether they were a janitor or a project manager. Brett had joked with her once that she ran the company like it was pack—and he approved.

"You have thirty minutes," Debbie informed her as she

strode into the office following the departure of the most recent executive. She laid a folder on her desk. "These are the contracts you wanted hard copies of to review, they don't require signatures before next week so take them home with you this weekend."

She slid a pair of boxes onto the center of her desk, both boasting over-sized roast beef sandwiches and french fries. Without missing a beat, Debbie settled into a chair opposite her, tablet open. "I doubled your lunch order, you looked a little pale this morning, which means you were up north later than you expected, but I see the call with Japan went well. Do you want to go over your calls?"

Not particularly, she wanted a few minutes to just be, but they hadn't factored those in to today's schedule, so she nodded and began to devour a sandwich. Debbie Locke, in addition to being a most capable assistant, had the added benefit of understanding she worked for wolves. Telling her had been a choice, one Brett approved, and while it had been a risk at the time, Debbie had taken the news gracefully. Though she had killed two full bottles of wine and ended up sleeping on Charlie's sofa for the night. The following morning, she'd woken with a mild hangover and acceptance.

They'd been fast friends ever since, though they maintained a professional distance. Normally the executive assistant would also be a wolf, but Charlie didn't want to deal with those complications, and Brett had agreed. In every way that counted, Debbie was now the highest ranked human in Charlie's satellite pack of the company. One benefit of that was she never looked askance at how much and how swiftly Charlie could eat.

As she went over the list of calls, Debbie ranked them in importance from greatest to least as well as suggested which ones Debbie could handle for her. Charlie agreed with her assessment. "What time did Mr. Esposito call?"

It was unusual for the Alpha of Seven Hills to place a call personally. Fortunately, Debbie indicated he had not been remotely offended at being put off due to Charlie's meeting schedule.

"An hour ago," Debbie told her. "It was late there, and he said as much when he was on the phone."

It was after six in Rome. Salvatore Esposito did not take business calls over the weekend unless it was an emergency. His message didn't indicate this counted as such. "Contact his office, arrange a call for next week, earliest convenience. If he wishes sooner, let me know, and I can call him over the weekend."

Sooner would indicate pack business and privacy. A scheduled call would be purely business. International Alphas contacting Brett via her office was not unusual.

Charlie finished the second of her sandwiches, then washed it down with the iced green tea. "Oh, before I forget, I gave my card to Harris Ryder, he's a teen. I'm going to offer him an internship in my office after I speak to him and his parents. They should be calling sometimes this week, likely a late afternoon call, put them through immediately."

"Even if you're in another meeting?" Debbie didn't judge, she clarified.

"Yes." His parents would be as human as he was, therefore, some special considerations would go a long way in persuading them to let her apprentice the young man and redirect his restlessness somewhere productive.

"Got it. Okay, you about ready for the next run? This will take you up five. A short break. Then you'll have the last four."

After another long drink of the green tea, Charlie nodded. "Also, can you order dinner in from Rangoon's? Enough for two wolves, I have a dinner meeting at eight."

With a gimlet stare, Debbie glanced from the boxes she

was picking up to her. "You scheduled a meeting without telling me?"

"Yes," she told her, tone soothing. "I overstepped the boundaries, I'm aware. Special circumstances. He'll be here at eight-fifteen, his name is Luc Danes. Security will clear him to the private elevator. You don't have to hang out for him, I'll handle the appointment."

Narrowing her eyes, Debbie studied her. "Personal or business?"

Charlie snorted. "Definitely business. Now, shoo, I want the last four minutes for quiet."

"Steaks, baked potatoes, vegetables? Do you want wine and dessert?"

"It's not a date," she reminded her assistant.

But the woman merely gave her a grin. "Then you definitely deserve wine and something sweet after today—or maybe some salted caramel chocolate tort?"

That tort was a personal weakness, and Debbie knew better than to invoke it, and at the same time, Charlie's mouth watered at the idea. "You are an evil woman, and I hate you."

"Should I make it a whole tort or just two slices?"

With her luck, Luc would love the damn thing. "Get a whole one."

"Done. Three minutes." Then Debbie strode out with the empty takeout containers, leaving Charlie to a blissful three minutes of quiet.

Her phone buzzed and Charlie opened the desk drawer to the cell. On the screen was a message:

Should I bring anything for dinner tonight?

Luc.

With a sigh, she considered the message, then sent, *No. It's taken care of.*

Then closed the drawer. She closed her eyes and leaned

her head back in the chair. Two and a half minutes to just be…

Her phone buzzed.

Slitting her eyes open, she pulled the drawer out again.

Do you have a favorite flower?

One eyebrow arched, she exhaled. It wasn't a date, it was business. So she sent back *No.*

Two minutes…

The phone buzzed.

A growl rumbled in her throat.

No favorites at all? Roses can be overpowering, but I bet you like daffodils or daisies. They're sunnier.

Why was he going on about flowers?

No. She typed, and then added, *Meetings.*

Not closing the drawer, she clung to the next ninety seconds she had left for quiet.

Buzz.

She was going to kill him.

Looking forward to seeing you.

Another growl threaded its way up from her chest.

Bringing you a surprise.

She wasn't sure what irritated her more, the messages or her curiosity.

The knock on the door preceding the arrival of her next meeting signified the end of her aborted peace and quiet. She dismissed the messages unread, then closed the drawer and rose.

It was time to work.

John Carr was her last appointment of the day. He was the director of supply chain management and one of the few people she worked with regularly. He'd joined the company four years earlier, and he'd been an asset.

"You always schedule me last because you don't actually need my report," he joked as they wrapped up.

"Not true, I schedule you last because you're usually here this late, and you don't mind when I go over the numbers with you."

"The others mind?" He sounded skeptical and he should, but she shrugged.

"Oddly enough, they seem to think I'm second guessing them. Job hazard, I suppose. But tell me," she threaded her fingers together on the desk as she faced him. "We've gone over the numbers I need, what can I do for you?"

"Go out on a date with me." The man was attractive and had a fantastic smile, but he worked for her. While the playful requests flattered, that was all they could ever be. Playful requests.

Charlie smiled. This little dance was also familiar. "Not this quarter. What else do you have?"

Laughing, John leaned back in his chair, his ankle braced against his knee. "Nothing really. We've got the kinks worked out for the new delivery schedule. The tracking software lets us spot problems before they foul the works. I think we're in good shape. In six months or so, we may want to look at hiring site managers, especially if this Japan deal goes through. You're going to want people there who can be boots on the ground as we incorporate their style and manufacturing into our scheduling."

"Six months." She considered where they were following her call with Japan and the upcoming series of meetings she'd scheduled with factories in both North America and Canada. She hadn't briefed John on the expansion idea—yet. It was still in the nascent stages. "Pull me numbers, relevant requirements, and time constraints. I'm not saying yes, yet.

But I want to know what the cost to benefit ratio would be over the one to five to ten year increments."

"Can do," John said. "Anything else? Or would you like to actually get out of here at an early hour on a Friday?"

"Unfortunately, I have another meeting."

He scoffed, hand to his chest. "You've replaced me as your closing call? How will I survive?"

"Probably snarkily. Go on, get out of here and have a good weekend." She waved him off as she rose and cleaned off her desk. Her tablet went into the drawer with her phone. There were new messages from Luc on it.

Your brothers entertain me.

That was vague.

Pack gathering first weekend of next month. You should clear your schedule.

She grimaced.

I find these little talks stimulating.

A laugh escaped her in spite of herself.

The traffic on the way into the city is unreal. It's worse than I remember.

Well, she didn't drive unless she was leaving the city. It was easier to walk or take the subway. Her wolf didn't object to the close quarters the way so many others did. There was a beauty to the city she enjoyed.

I've been sitting on the bridge for a half-hour. If I'm late, I'm going to blame you.

She arched a brow. A knock on the door pulled her attention, and Debbie cracked it open. The scent of steaks, hot rolls, and dessert teased her nose, leaving her mouth to water. She hadn't eaten since lunch, and the steaks smelled *perfect*. There was something floral beneath the scent of the meat and the chocolate, but she focused on the latter over the former.

"Dinner is here, and your 8:15 is in the lobby. Security

called up to clear his credentials for the private elevator, since he's never visited before."

"Thanks, Debbie. Go on and have a good weekend." Charlie left her phone on the desk. "I copied all the reports over to the server. Put them together in a book for me on Monday?"

"Absolutely," Debbie told her, pushing the dining cart into the office and snapping up the sides to turn it into a table. The food had been set beautifully. "I ordered some wine for you and these came…" She hurried back out to her desk and returned with a wild bouquet filled with roses, sunflowers, daffodils, marigolds, pansies, carnations, and begonias. The stunning array of yellow and orange blossoms with three red roses in the center was amazing. It looked like a sunset.

Debbie set the flowers on the table next to the window overlooking the city. The armchairs and sofa formed a conversation pit where she could hold higher-level meetings with foreign executives in town to be wined and dined.

"These are some 'hot mama is going to get laid tonight' flowers." Debbie's open and frank teasing robbed the statement of any insult.

Rolling her eyes, Charlie pointed. "Go, get out of here. I'll lock up when I'm done. Don't come back in until after seven on Monday morning."

"But you're usually here at six," Debbie argued.

"And I am capable of placing my own calls. Shoo."

"Fine," Debbie huffed. "But I want details on the fine dining and hot flowers dude."

It was just eight, so Luc was early. That satisfied her need for promptness and lacked the typical posturing of arriving when he felt like. She'd had a few wolves pull that crap with her.

They only did it once.

Back at her desk, she finished the messages as Debbie

locked her desk, and the ding of the open elevator rang to announce her exit. She was probably heading down to the lobby to see if she could catch Luc, though if security had just called up, he should be in the private elevator.

She limited it to wolves only. If pack members or foreign packs came to visit—including one of the Enforcers who liked to come see her regularly—they didn't have to share confined space with others and public elevators stunk. There was no getting around it. Charlie sighed, she hadn't had a visit from Adler in quite some time. He was due.

Glancing at her phone, she laughed aloud.

On second thought, I won't blame you, but I will ask you to make it up to me. Tell me something you like to do.

The next message was five minutes later.

Again, I can't get over how much these chats entertain me.

The last message was stamped ten minutes before.

Forgot something in the truck, I'll be up in a sec.

Almost perfect timing, the subtler chime on the private elevator sounded. The scent of him: wolf, snow, and woods invaded the perfume from the flowers and the rich headiness rolling off the steaks.

"Come on through, Luc," she called, tabbing out of his messages to see one from her mother.

Pack gathering next month. Not optional. Your brothers said you were here last night.

Well... that was subtle.

Not rolling her eyes took effort, and she set the phone in the drawer and closed it.

"Good evening," Luc called as he strode in carrying... what the hell was he carrying? It was a table, carved from the stump of a tree. He glanced around her office for a moment, his gaze assessing. A quick grin appeared when he saw the flowers, and he carried his polished stump table over, replaced the current side table with the stump, and transferred the flowers to it. "Better," he commented before glancing at her. "You should always have little bit of home here."

There was warmth glittering in those eyes. Too much warmth.

"You do realize this is business, yes?" They should nip this in the bud, immediately. She had no desire to be pursued by the pack's Second or the wolf earning the most gossip in the pack.

She just did not need that kind of attention, nor did she want it.

"It's a sad comment that you're uncomfortable receiving affection from a packmate." He tsked. "Remind me to knock some heads together."

A deep breath filled her lungs with his scent, not what she needed to focus on. "I'm not uncomfortable, but I also prefer to avoid misconceptions. We're working together."

"I'm aware," he told her. "Did you like the flowers? You wouldn't tell me your favorites, so I went with something that reminded me of you."

Sunsets reminded him of her? The rumors of Luc's charm had not been exaggerated. "They're lovely, hopefully they survive the weekend. I've ordered dinner," she gathered the reins of the conversation. "I think you'll find it to your liking. It's from one of my favorite restaurants."

Not information he needed.

At the table, he pulled a chair out for her and this time, she rolled her eyes. "Knock that off and sit down."

A smirk curved his lips. "No."

Worth the fight or not? The fact Luc was a dominant had a role to play in future negotiations. Neutering him here and now could affect his performance later. The mental image that conjured had nothing to do with business, and she had to bite back a smile before it escaped.

Amused enough to let the battle go, she dropped into the chair and snapped out the napkin. "It occurred to me," she said as he circled the table to sit opposite her, his pleasure at the simple act adding a nuance to his scent. "We need to decide the order in which we want to approach the other packs. Brett didn't indicate any actual schedule or coordinator for these meetings."

"That would be my job," Luc said as he took his seat. It gave her a moment to actually assess him. The night before, he'd been dressed in nice jeans and a button down, the dark blue shirt matching his eyes near perfectly. Today, he'd gone for a crisp golden yellow shirt that shouldn't have worked with his coloring and yet, it did. No tie, but instead of jeans, he wore slacks and a pair of loafers.

Huh, he could clean up.

"Do you have a plan, then?" Because that would be useful in their current circumstances. She lifted the lid off her steak, and Luc's expression became almost blissful when he got a good look at the 64-ounce beauty awaiting him. Not wasting any time, Charlie reached for the hot rolls and flicked the cloth back to free one up. Tearing it open, she added butter as she waited for his answer.

"I figured we'd just wing it. We have a good relationship with Willow Bend, so we start there."

Blinking slowly, she paused. "That's a terrible idea."

"Excuse me?" He cut into his steak, and she lost all of his focus for a few seconds as he took a bite.

After licking her lips, she took a bite of the roll. All of her senses narrowed to the hot, honeyed taste of the fluffy roll and the sweet salt of the butter enhancing it. Her stomach growled in appreciation, and she cut into her steak without glancing at him. "You don't start with the group you don't need time to perfect your message with. We have a good relationship with Willow Bend, in all likelihood, we'll be in lock step on almost every issue. The groups we have the most difficulty with should be the first on our list."

"That sounds like asking for a headache. It could take weeks to hammer out an arrangement with Sutter Butte."

"My point," she countered, glancing up to find him watching her as she took a bite of the steak.

"Is what? We spend weeks on one pack? When we could just as easily close the deal with Willow Bend, and then we can see if we can leverage them for more clout with the troublemakers?"

Charlie took another bite and chewed it thoughtfully as he pulled out the wine and glanced at her.

"Did you want some of this with dinner?"

"Sure," she said after swallowing. "Follow my logic— Willow Bend has strategic relationships with nearly every single pack *including* the Enforcers. The only pack they don't have strong ties to is Three Rivers. We actually have clout there, thanks first to the Reagans, and then to you and Colby."

"More her than me, but I'm listening." The cork came out with a smooth pop, then he filled her glass first before filling his own.

"Any negotiations we enter into in conjunction *with* Willow Bend will favor Willow Bend, that doesn't mean it will favor Hudson River."

"We're allies," he said, as if reminding her.

"Yes, but they have their own needs and desires to drive this. Mason Clayborne may be younger than some of the other Alphas, but he's made a point of building very strong alliances and loyalty with pivotal members of other packs— including ours."

"You're also forgetting," Luc continued. "We have an alliance with the Enforcers. We have Dallas."

"Who is Brett's cousin, yes. But she and her mate are the

parents of Willow Bend's Omega and the grandparents of her child. Children beat cousins when you compare loyalties." Simple facts when it came to wolves. Mates and family earned the first loyalty, Alphas got the next, and the pack came third. For most, it wasn't a stretch to include all three —for others? Well, when it came to keeping a pack happy, Julian and Dallas would be far more interested in protecting the pack where their child lived. "And isn't the Second of the Enforcers mated to someone from Willow Bend?"

"I see your point," Luc admitted after a long moment. He lifted the wine to her, then took a sip before digging back into his steak. "What would you suggest?"

"Delta Crescent and Sutter Butte have ties now, growing ones. We leverage those. While we have relatively decent relations with Delta Crescent, we have almost *no* open channels with Sutter Butte."

"You could argue that about the Yukon."

"No, I have strong ties to Montana, she's the Second of the Yukon Pack, and she handles some business dealings for trade and investments, we speak about once a month."

Shock rippled through his expression.

"And the Yukon has strong ties to Willow Bend. Their Alpha's mate is the sister to Willow Bend's Second."

He was halfway through his steak, but Luc paused to study her. "You know a lot about all of the other packs."

"I believe research is key when it comes to opening a negotiation. When I walk into a room, the more I know, the more I can use." The baked potatoes were near perfect, as were the vegetables. As much as she'd like to tear into the steak, she kept her bites neat and even.

"So you have a plan already?"

"Just the beginnings of one," she admitted. Brett had only assigned her to the task the evening before, but she'd turned the idea over in her head on the way back to the city and in between meetings.

"Tell me," Luc leaned forward, his voice dropping, and for the first time since he'd arrived, he seemed wholly focused on the task at hand.

Smiling, she said, "Sutter Butte is our key. They need a better reputation with the other packs. Cassius has been working diligently to correct their image, as well as their culture. But shifts in cultural paradigms can take generations. Not to mention—Hudson River originally opposed the formation of Sutter Butte, so there's some history to trade on there. By courting them and finding out what they need that we can provide, we can foster ties based on mutual benefit, that then leads us back to Delta Crescent. As it turns out—the mate to the Alpha of Delta Crescent is also a brother to the Second of Willow Bend and the mate of the Yukon's Alpha. Now we have windows to build bridges. In the meanwhile, we talk to Three Rivers about what we can do to help them continue getting their feet under them. They get fewer concessions considering how they formed, but not so few as to be a punishment. If they flourish, then we flourish."

"And the Enforcers?"

"We will need a better enticement, but they tend to be neutral on most interpack politics, particularly since they are now a pack of their own. Their first duty is the security of all packs."

"And I suppose you want to bring all these wolves here? Take the position of strength?"

"On the contrary," she said. "I want to go there. The Enforcers can come to us. They are used to it. But for the rest, we go to them. We become the guests, we rely on guesting privileges to create an open avenue of communication. If we're lucky, they'll show off, and we'll have more information to work with—how we can maximize the relationships and create effective, mutually beneficial treaties that tilt a little more in our favor than theirs. But that will happen when they massage the language."

"You sound very sure of yourself." Luc's eyes narrowed as he studied her.

"I am," she said, picking up her wine. "What's more, those favorable circumstances will be suggested by them."

"How do you know it will work?"

"You're sitting in my office, you brought me gifts, and you're trying to impress me," she said slowly, enjoying the sudden realization dawning in his eyes. "What did you get out of me?"

CHAPTER 5

What did I get out of her? Luc studied her. Her scent came and went, almost impossible to nail down. The masking of one's scent was not a skill all wolves possessed. Luc could, narrowly, though he had to concentrate on it. Most of the wolves who could were higher-level dominants and Alphas. As a Shadow, Charlie defied most cultural pack norms. So maybe masking her scent was part of that, and the teasing bits of her leaking through were due to her variant nature.

Honestly, he had no idea, and to be even more frank, he didn't care. He just wanted to take the time get to know her and peel back that onion. "I got dinner with you out of it," he murmured. A faint smile touched her lips, the barest hint of one, and he savored it. Closer to what he wanted, but he would have to work harder.

"The simple fact is almost all negotiation is a dance. You can have two people or ten, but someone always leads and everyone else follows. If you're very good at it, you can take and give back the lead without the other realizing what you've done, because they are too captivated by the dance."

And he could listen to her discuss this all day. "That's what you want to do when we go to Sutter Butte. You want to invite them to dance?" The idea of her courting other wolves didn't sit well with him. Of course, he would be there.

"Metaphorically, yes. They are… tough. Their culture prizes strength and cunning. They tend toward keeping very strict pack roles, but that paradigm is shifting." She paused as she lifted the wine glass, her gorgeous green eyes considering. At this distance, he couldn't miss the faint flecks of gold amongst the green.

"What is it?" The pitch of his voice deepened, even as his wolf roused. Whatever occurred to her had unsettled her. The sweet scent of amber beneath crushed leaves appealed to him far more than the steak he'd been devouring.

"The strict nature of their interactions—strength is something vital. One of the reasons we rarely did business with Sutter Butte beyond the most cursory is the brutality within the pack." She took a swallow of the wine.

"You won't have to worry about that—good cop or bad cop, I won't let anyone get near enough to you to make that challenge."

The tempting curl of her lips teased him, but still she held back that smile he hungered to release. "I'm not worried about physical challenges. As you may have noticed, I dropped two of my brothers last night."

"They're brothers," he said with a shrug. He'd never strike any of his sisters, not even Sam when she was being a raging pain in his ass.

"Would you *let* one of your sisters hit you in the balls, Luc?"

"Well, no," he admitted, and Sam had tried.

"Then why on Earth would you dismiss my brothers as overbearing idiots who'd *let* me?"

She had a point. "Conceded. You dropped your rather

irritating brothers. But they didn't genuinely mean you harm." Though he'd tired of the way they wanted to bully her, and how she'd refrained from shutting it down, even if he'd tasted her dominance. Maybe she was fluid, easily slipping between dominance and submission, but he couldn't imagine she enjoyed the attitude they displayed, no matter which way she swung. In his experience, most she-wolves just didn't tolerate that bullshit or put up with it, unless they were indulging some other need.

"They run interference for you with your mother," he said aloud, the realization dawning.

A little shrug and what smile she'd proffered vanished. "My mother is not subject for discussion. As for Sutter Butte, I'm more concerned that we will need to demonstrate our strength in a manner that proves we can run with them without humiliating them."

"Fight to first blood, break some bones." He drained his wine and then speared another piece of steak. "There are a lot of ways to do it that are friendly. I've handled my share of fights."

"And if you lose?"

"Your faith in me, sweetheart, is overwhelming." Maybe it was his dry tone or maybe it was a combination of the tone and his words, but she grinned, sudden and bright.

Perfect.

"It's not about faith, Luc. I could likely take on a fight just as easily—" The hell she would. "—as you. But you would be right to question whether or not I would lose."

She wouldn't, because she wouldn't be fighting. But if he thrust that out there, she'd dismiss him, and he'd just earned that smile. "Whatever you say," he conceded. "But this is where being good cop would pay off. A friendly wager, a way to break the ice. You can disapprove and treat me like the boorish idiot you think I am."

"I don't think you're an idiot or boorish," she stated categorically. Then rolled her eyes when he grinned.

"Don't be like that, I'm glad to know you find me intelligent and interesting."

Her snort would probably deflate a lesser wolf's ego, but there was another smile flirting with an appearance, and he wanted it. "You think highly of yourself."

"Someone has to," he told her with a wink. "I think pretty highly of you, so be careful what you say. Being protective of my friends is something I excel at."

Instead of an immediate response, she studied him and took another bite. They'd nearly eaten all of their steaks, and she'd cleared her baked potato and vegetables. "Luc," she murmured setting her wine glass aside. "There will not be any sex at the end of this flirtation."

"Well," he told her cheerfully. "If I had a dollar for every time a wolf has told me that lately, I'd be wealthy." Boundaries were fine. He needed to know where hers were. But if she thought just telling him that there was no chance of sex would dissuade him from getting to know her, she needed to spend more time researching him.

He certainly planned to learn what he could about her. The person to ask, of course, was his mother. Babette Danes knew *everything* about *everyone*. Irritating quality, but useful in this case. He hoped.

The smile peeked out. "I apologize for being so blunt."

"You shouldn't," he told her, nudging his plate aside as he finished the steak. "I'd much rather you were blunt with me. Dancing with words and intentions we can save for our meetings. Between you and I? I'd prefer absolute honesty, even if it's painful."

Oddly enough, he meant it. Whatever the reasoning for her declaration, he doubted it had anything to do with the rumors. She might not be interested in him, and that was fine. It just meant he needed to work more diligently to snag her interest. He did like a challenge.

"That's an unusual attitude for someone in your position to take."

"What? Preferring to be told the truth?"

"Well no, truth can come in many forms. Most don't want brutal truth. They want honesty and integrity, but brutal truth can be challenging."

"Are you interested in challenging me, Charlie?" He liked saying her name. Probably a little too much, so he would use it judiciously.

"No," she said, her tone almost as thoughtful as her eyes. "But I'm not rolling over and showing you my belly either."

"Then we know where we stand—or in this case sit." He winked. "Now, is that chocolate I smell?"

"Salted caramel chocolate tort," she exhaled those words like she would a lover's name. And suddenly, he had a new goal to add to his collection of smiles. He very much wanted to hear his name on her lips with a similar sigh and exhale of breath.

"Smells divine. Do you mind if I…?" He motioned to the plate.

"Help yourself, I had Debbie order a whole one, because sometimes a single slice is just not enough, and I wasn't sure I could entice you to share."

He snorted. She could entice him to do a lot of things. "I'm going to applaud your forethought. Chocolate is a weakness." Come, little Shadow wolf, take the bait.

With a groan, she tilted her head back and the action tossed the smooth lines of her red hair, even as it revealed her slender throat. "Mine, too, unfortunately. I'm pretty sure that's why Debbie ordered my wine. This is what I get when I've had a long week and need to unwind."

"Has it been that bad?" He soaked up the information like

a sponge while he sectioned them both large pieces effectively quartering the tort.

"Not particularly, but it has been a long week." She accepted the plate with her piece and smiled, though it was more polite and less the one he wanted. "I've been very busy with meetings, and today was the quarterly assessments. I'll put together a report on those for Brett next week."

"You were able to make your call with Japan though, right?" Part of the reason he'd shifted strategies was to meet her needs and not demand she conform to his.

"I did, and thank you," she said, then reached for the wine. After she refilled her glass, she eyed his. He held it out to her. The wine was good, not that it would do anything to them with their metabolisms. "The call took a couple of hours, but it was nice to be at home and in my pajamas, rather than in the car at a rest stop."

He grimaced. "Have you had to do that often?"

Instead of answering, she took a bite of her dessert, effortlessly capturing his whole attention as she savored the chocolate and sweetness. Most of his blood fled southward, and he bit back a growl before dragging his attention to his own dessert. A bite of it had the taste exploding on his tongue, but no matter how sweet it was, it was not the flavor he wanted to lick up at the moment. Washing down the bite with a swallow of wine, he kept his scent masked as he jerked his mind off following that particular path.

"Again, probably more than I care to admit. The meetings with Brett are regular. It's good for me to come up once per month to see him, go over reports, and make sure he has everything he needs. Most of his work can be done from there, and he sits in on a number of my calls, but it's still better for him to hear it from me."

It also reinforced her pack bonds, bonds that would strain with her living so far away. "I imagine that was difficult for a few months." It had been a difficult time for everyone after the murder of Brett's grandfather and the other deaths. Having a wolf go mad... that was bad enough. Having them kill those under your protection? Brett had been a difficult and different Alpha after.

Bringing Colby to Hudson River was the best thing Luc had ever done. She'd brought his best friend back, and Luc found a new friend in her. It didn't hurt that she turned out to be latent and a healer, even if she'd discovered her latency rather abruptly when Trent called her wolf out.

Charlie cleared her throat. "It was not unpleasant specifically, but I am grateful that he seems more himself these days."

"What does that mean? Not unpleasant specifically?"

Brett's warning flickered through his mind. He called her a wonderful wolf and threatened to feed Luc his spleen if he hurt her.

"I'm not going to talk out of turn," Charlie told him before taking another bite.

"It's not out of turn if something happened you weren't comfortable with. Brett would want to know." While Luc definitely wanted to know, he wasn't kidding. His best friend had been harder on himself than anyone else when it came to the malaise and depression he'd suffered from. His distance from his own pack had nearly cost him his pack.

"Stop growling." The chastisement brought him back to himself abruptly. He hadn't even realized he had growled.

"My apologies." It wasn't a grave offense, but it was rude. "The entire incident and the following months are a source of aggravation."

"Why? You weren't even here."

"No," he said bluntly. "If I had been, maybe Brett wouldn't have gone through Hell. Maybe I could have sniffed that bastard out."

"It's arrogant to believe your mere presence would have made all the difference." She pointed her fork at him. "What happened—when it happened—no one scented on Marco. No one identified *him* as the threat. Everyone trusted him. His scent didn't betray him. He was as protective and solicitous as any dominant might be. But when the coin turned, he was a ruthless killer with no soul or conscience. They call it madness for a reason, Luc."

She'd both slapped him down and buoyed him in a few short sentences.

"Then at least he wouldn't have been alone."

"He was never alone," she said, almost gently. "You came back at the right time, when he was ready to hear someone and see them. There is no telling if it would have worked had you been here. And if you'd been here, would you have met Colby and lured her to the pack by asking her to drive you?"

Now that surprised him. Until he thought about it. "My mother," he said slowly.

"Yes, she speaks to mine, and it was conversation in those first few weeks after you arrived. Most thought Colby was yours, and then she turned out to be Brett's and a healer to boot. But now everyone thinks there is more to it than just the two of them."

He groaned. "It's not," he stated flatly. "I love Colby, I'd die for her. But that's because she's Brett's *mate* and our healer. She's also my friend. I love Brett like a brother, but the man does not share what's his."

Charlie laughed, the sound transcendent and her eyes glittering with mirth, even as it lit her whole face. "I know he wouldn't, not where his mate was concerned. I knew long before last night's rant," she continued, reminding him of his arrival at Brett's house.

"Well, I wish everyone else did."

"Colby doesn't smell like you," she reminded him, not that

he needed the reminder. "You'd think wolves would be better at this than they are, but they love good gossip. The meatier the better. It's sweet to think two lifelong friends could find a mate in the same woman."

"Sweet?" He couldn't help the snort of derision as he scoffed. "It would be an uncomfortable bond to settle. Not to mention the competition for who is more dominant."

"Only if the males—or females as the case may be— weren't comfortable with each other. You are comfortable following Brett, if Colby was your mate as well, then he would be the dominant and you would find that bond settling."

The dessert forgotten, he studied her. "How do you know so much about a three-way bond?"

"I told you, I do my research."

"You know someone…" Three-way bonds happened.

"Now, who is gossiping?" Raised eyebrows dared him to contradict her.

"Absolutely, because I'm curious. Especially since it's what we're being accused of."

"You don't approve of three-way bonds."

He blinked. "Where the hell did that come from?"

"Accused."

Luc turned the word over in his mind.

"When someone accuses you of something, it implies that it's bad. If you said that's how we're being described or perceived, it wouldn't be laden with disapproval."

"I'll concede half that point," he said slowly. "But when I'm being *described* as something I'm not, and it's passed through the pack like fact, it's not a slight so much as…"

"A cock block?" There was that trace of amusement.

"Fine, a cock block. I enjoy women. I'm allowed to— except now I'm not." He rubbed the back of his neck. "This is not where the conversation was supposed to go."

"I kind of like that it took a more natural turn. You're trying to impress me, Luc Danes, and I'd much rather you just be you. After all, if we're supposed to work together, we need to know each other, right?"

Everything about her defied expectations. She turned his words, his ideas, and even his assumptions back on him.

His little Shadow wolf tantalized him like no other. This was going to be so much fun.

If he survived her... it would definitely be fun.

"Yes," he promised. "We do need to know each other. So tell me about this research into three-way bonds." Who knew, it might be useful.

DINNER WITH CHARLIE HADN'T GONE REMOTELY THE WAY HE expected and yet, he'd enjoyed himself. Even more when she consented to let him drive her home after he found out she planned to take the subway. Every day, she told him.

Why?

Because driving in the city, as he learned, heading across the bridge to her brownstone in Brooklyn, was a bear—an unmitigated, raging bear that needed to be taken down. Her laughter at his comments kept him grousing at the roads and the people all the way until he pulled into her neighborhood and she directed him toward her brownstone. She would have a near perfect view of Manhattan from the roof, but there was a distinct lack of green.

Even as he eyed her front door speculatively, he didn't ask to go inside. That was territory he would have to earn. What did she say? A concession she would offer him rather than one he asked for...

Time.

Double-parking, he slid out of the truck and moved

around to scan the street. He couldn't stay in the truck while she was out the open anymore than he could have let her take the damn subway home.

"Where is the subway around here?" He didn't see an entrance, and the competing scents of water, car exhaust, and something that suspiciously smelled like garbage—there, a can overturned at the end of the street. He'd stuff it back in there and put the lid on before he pulled away.

"About two blocks that way," she said, pointing. She had a strap of her laptop bag crisscross over her body and a back-pack over her shoulder. In the backpack, he'd discovered, were running shoes. It satisfied something in him that she didn't walk to and from the subway or even venture into the subway on those heels. They did fabulous things for her legs, but not so much for her speed.

Then again, she was a wolf. She could just kick them off.

"Huh." He scratched his jaw as he examined the neighbor-hood. There were a *lot* of humans. In fact, he would hazard a guess they were all humans.

"Something wrong?" She had her keys in hand but made no move to ascend the steps to her front door.

"No, just—getting a feel for it." His wolf disliked it intensely. Too closed in and crowded. They liked leaving her there even less.

"The city isn't for everyone. But I like it," she said, then tilted her head and took a deep breath. It was late. Nearly eleven and yet, activity hummed. A jogger up the street. An older gentlemen out walking his poodle. Cars weren't racing by directly, but they were on the other streets. There was a couple returning from dinner—and from the direction she'd pointed. They were a little inebriated, but holding hands and laughing together.

There was a hum, and almost vibration in the ground. The subway.

The smells were not pack. Not familiar. Except...

He faced her. "Thank you for having me for dinner tonight."

"Thank you for driving in—for the flowers and the table." He'd offered to bring the flowers here, but she wanted to leave them in the office and likely to deny him a reason to enter her place.

"I'll call you tomorrow," he said. "If you're not busy. We can work more on your Sutter Butte plan."

"Sunday."

"Excuse me?"

"Tomorrow is *my* day. Call me Sunday. If you're busy, we can talk next week."

Her day.

Intrigued, he wanted to ask, but that would be pushing it. "Sunday it is. Next month is a pack gathering—technically in two weeks."

"I know," she said with a sigh. "I'll see if I can find an AirBNB nearby."

"A what?"

"A place to rent for the weekend. I used to stay with Brett or his grandfather, but it's a little close there with Colby, and I don't want to make her uncomfortable."

Nothing about Charlie would make Colby uncomfortable. The little spitfire probably loved Charlie.

"You can stay with me," he offered. "My place is new, but it's got more than enough space, and you can have your own room."

"That would send the wrong message."

"To who?" He challenged.

"To anyone."

"Think about it," he offered, backing off. "And look at it this way," he continued as he motioned her toward her door. "Your family isn't going to bother you there."

Surprise flickered in her eyes, and he didn't smile.

Gotcha.

"One perk of being Second, I can send them away and they will go."

"That really shouldn't sound that attractive."

"I'm yours, Charlie. Use me. I don't mind."

That got him an exasperated smile and a roll of her eyes. "You had to go and ruin it."

She was at the top step and had unlocked her door.

"I didn't ruin anything," he murmured. "You're already thinking about it. You have to be up there for the weekend, we can get work done, and I can run interference with your family. I say it's a win-win."

"I'll *think* about it," she conceded, and Luc spread his arms.

"That's all I'm saying. Goodnight, Charlie."

"Goodnight."

She hesitated in the open doorway, and he'd just put his hand on the driver's side door, when she said, "Luc?"

She didn't need to call out, he could hear her just fine. "Yeah?"

"Be careful of my mom. She's—just be careful of her. If she thinks you're sniffing around me or pursuing me... let's just say you'd prefer all four of my brothers to her."

Leaning against the truck, he studied her. There was a genuine worry in her eyes, brief, but there nonetheless. "I can take care of myself, Charlie. Don't worry."

"You haven't ever had to deal with my mother." It wasn't a question, and while he knew Adele—or at least knew of her, he couldn't say they'd had any direct dealings. Not since he'd been back.

He had dealt with the younger pair of idiots she called brothers earlier in the day, when they decided to drop in on his lunch and interrogate him for spending time with their sister.

They both had extra details on distant loops and would for the next seven days. Pierce promised him he'd take care of it. Brothers were supposed to be protective. But there was something off about the family.

"Goodnight," he told her firmly, and waited until she let out a huff and muttered something about warning him before she ducked inside and closed the door. The locks engaged, and he swept his gaze over the street again. Why didn't she have at least one Hunter down here to keep an eye on her back? In a city with more than 8.6 million people, she was far too alone.

Once in the truck, he got it started and headed out of the borough and for the road to take him north. He had an hour's drive ahead of him, maybe a little longer if he ran into issues.

It was putting him too far away from her, and his wolf fidgeted. He would talk to Brett about this. There had to be a reason, and he just wasn't seeing it. If there wasn't, he and Pierce were going to make a few changes.

Something was up with the Miller family, and he planned to tap his number one resource for pack drama first thing in the morning.

Mama always did like when he dropped by for breakfast.

CHAPTER 6

*C*harlie hit play on her voicemails while she stepped into the shower.

"Charlie, Salvatore called. There will be representatives from Seven Hills coming to negotiate the new shipping contracts in person. Giovanni and his mate, as well as one other. They'll notify us of the name within the week. You'll be dealing primarily with Giovanni. Can you have your assistant arrange accommodations for them? An executive suite. Our expense account." Brett's tone was all brisk business, then it softened. "There's also a pack gathering in a couple of weeks. I know you're not a fan, but I *want* you to attend."

Translation, she was not allowed to find a more pressing matter to skip the event. She'd done that a couple of times. Seeing Brett regularly renewed her pack bonds, she didn't need to see anyone else.

The call clicked. Next up was Debbie, and Charlie sighed as she ran the shampoo through her hair.

"Before you say *dammit, Debbie*, I wanted to make sure

you had all the books on your desk before next week. I just got word the Italians have moved up their visit, and you needed the full book on shipping and transport. We also have the trucking schedules to review, particularly with the added routes."

Sighing, Charlie shifted her head from side to side. Debbie wasn't wrong. She dunked her head under the water and rinsed out the shampoo.

"As soon as these are done, I'm out of the office. Also, love the new table. Did you get lucky last night? Inquiring minds want to know. See you Monday."

She snorted. The message beeped.

"Charlotte."

The muscles in her back went stiff at her mother's voice.

"You did not answer my message, so I am making it clear. Pack gathering in two weeks. Don't embarrass me by making us send someone to the city to retrieve you. Your room will be ready. I expect you by seven on Friday, not a minute later."

The call ended, and she considered hitting her head against the wall until she knocked herself out. Not a successful coping technique.

"Rabbit." Adler's voice had her twisting. "I'd hoped to catch you answering, but I forgot how late it was. I was passing through. I should be back up to the city next weekend, if you're free on Saturday, we could catch up."

Oh. She'd like that very much. She made a mental note to call him and tell him when she'd be free. The problem with Enforcers. They didn't keep an actual schedule. So it was fly by night, even when they made arrangements, they didn't always show up because they could be needed anywhere.

After rinsing off, she reached for a towel as the message rolled over to the next.

"Charlie." Luc's voice drawled out of the speakers, and she paused at the cheerful note in his voice. "I enjoyed dinner last night. I'd like to do it again. I'll come to the city later this week, just let me know when you're free, and if you're amenable, I'll take you out somewhere rather than eat in your office. Then we can go out for dinner up here when you come up for the pack gathering. Anyway, I know you said this was your day. I'll call you tomorrow, and we can brainstorm our approach to Sutter Butte. Sound good? Talk to you then."

A shiver raced up her spine. Not from the invitations. She'd expected him to ask again. Something in his demeanor warned her, he hadn't been dissuaded. Luc was a virile, healthy wolf being cock-blocked left, right, and sideways because of pack gossip. They had to work together, which created forced proximity. It was a natural reaction.

But they had to work together, and she didn't need the pack focus on her for consorting with the pack's Second. With a sigh, she toweled off. It would be easier if he weren't so interesting.

Shuttling that thought to the side, she dressed and grabbed some breakfast, then reviewed her email over coffee. There were three that required a response from her immediately, including a request from Hatch Garrett. There was a name she hadn't seen in a while.

And she couldn't ignore it.

Hitting Brett's contact on her phone, she placed it to her ear. It rang twice before he answered. "What's wrong?"

"It's a sad comment on how often I call you that your initial greeting is what's wrong?" Her wolf settled almost immediately. She always did when she heard Brett's voice. Or when they went to see him. Her Alpha didn't trigger the fight or flight in her wolf, the need to rise for dominance or submit depending on her mood. He was her Alpha, and she was safe there.

"It is, you should fix that," Brett said, a smile in his voice.

"I, however, know better than to call you on a Saturday. This is supposed to be your day, Charlie, so let me repeat my question. What's wrong?"

"Hatch Garrett."

"What the fuck did he do now?" From relaxed to impatient in the blink of an eye. Hatch had a gift.

"Nothing, yet. But he's requesting to return to Hudson River and asked if I'd broach the topic with you."

Brett's snort echoed over the phone. His silence wasn't worrying, but the long breath he exhaled was. "Why did he want *you* to broach it?"

"Because he would like to invite two wolves to join him. They were the wolves he came with when they were all sent home during the incidents."

The incidents. The attacks. Dead Enforcers. Dead pack wolves. Very messy. She'd spent three months with two Hunters at her back full time because Brett wouldn't let her stay in the city by herself.

Uncomfortable didn't begin to cover it.

At least Pierce had shared some of the duty and kept her brothers out of that particular loop.

"He thinks I'm going to say no," Brett wasn't asking. "They haven't settled their bond."

"No," she admitted. "Apparently, it's proving a struggle. They've been in Delta Crescent for the last few months, but they aren't happy there. Robyn doesn't want to go to Sutter Butte, so Hatch is hoping if they come here, it will work better for them."

"A bond doesn't need a location to settle," Brett said drily.

"I know," she admitted. Hatch was one of the reasons she'd studied three-way bonds. They were trying to settle a mating, and it wasn't working. She had her suspicions as to why, but she was hardly an expert.

"Is there any hope he spoke to Serafina about this before reaching out?"

"I don't know," she admitted. "His note didn't say. I can email him back and ask him…"

"No." His tone grew firm. "Let him stew for a couple of days. You go enjoy your day off. Luc said you were getting together tomorrow to work on the treaties, and you have meetings next week. Hatch can wait." Before she could dispute the Luc piece, Brett said, "Go on, enjoy your day. I'll talk to you soon." Then the call ended.

She stared at the phone for a minute. Brett had made it an order on purpose. Though her wolf paced a little at the fact she was being essentially told to go and relax. On the other hand, relaxing meant a run, and a run meant heading up to the Delaware Water Gap. Far enough out of the city for fresh air, and far enough away from the pack to avoid running into others.

Win-win.

It was a short subway ride to the long-term garage where she kept her car. Traffic was light on the bridge and decent when she reached the tunnel. She was making good time, an audiobook playing and her mind leaving the office, the pack, and the myriad of duties behind.

On a bad day, it could take two and a half hours to reach her destination, but leaving early and on a weekend? Ninety minutes. She rotated her destinations, better to not be spotted regularly anywhere off pack lands. But the Water Gap boasted miles of trails, some of them closed for *work* that didn't happen on the weekends, which meant she got isolated areas free of humans where she could run, play, and even hunt if she were in the mood.

In the winter, the absence of deciduous leaves gave way to stunning views on the trails, and hidden stone walls and foundations—remnants of the past. In the spring, she savored the wildflowers and flowering trees. There were hemlock forests to race through in summer, but autumn brought the stunning oranges, reds, yellows, and crisp air.

It was her favorite time of year. She stood out against most natural foliage, but in autumn? She found her perfect environment. Once she'd parked, she sent a message to Brett with her location and the time—the required check-in before she went wolf and disappeared for a few hours. She'd send another one when she got back to the car. In the meanwhile, she secured the phone inside and grabbed her backpack with its book, change of clothes, some protein bars, and a couple of water bottles. After locking the car, she headed out.

The trails all had different access points. But she didn't have to check in with anyone, and she looked like any other hiker, right down to her windbreaker and baseball cap. It took her an hour to reach the first blocked trail and another twenty minutes to penetrate the closed area. Her nose told her she was alone long before she found a place to secure her gear. The backpack was waterproof, and there was a poncho inside. Stripping, she stuffed her clothes away and dropped the GPS tracker on the ground before she worked the backpack into a hidden location between some rocks.

Rolling her head from side to side, she stretched and then reached for her wolf. It was always a rush, the change as it rippled over her, contorting and reshaping her. Sure there was pain, but at the other end of it was a bliss that was the closest she could get to an orgasm she'd ever found without a partner.

As her fur settled, she gave herself a good shake then rolled in the crispy leaves carpeting the ground. The scent teased her nose and made her sneeze, but also spread her scent closer to the bag. Any wandering predators would leave her stuff alone. She'd encountered a couple of black bears up here once. They'd gone out of their way around her, but she'd shadowed them for a while, more curious than anything.

She'd seen them again another time, and they hadn't been as wary. Charlie wasn't going to trust that she'd made *friends*, but she hadn't made enemies, and bears fascinated her. They were never in a hurry, they just glided through life and seemed to relish playing. The last time she'd seen the pair, there'd been a couple of cubs with them and those, she'd given a wide berth.

Even the friendliest of wild animals could be vicious when it came to their young.

Finally, she rubbed against the tree. The bark felt good against her fur and skin. Satisfied she'd made her mark, she rooted up the GPS tracker and stepped her foot into it. It took a little skill to get it up her leg without losing it, and then she gripped the end with her teeth and pulled.

The only problem with them was while she could secure them, she couldn't loosen it. That meant she had to rip it off. So, after every trip, she had to replace the band.

Small price to pay.

The tracker was Brett's other requirement for her wandering alone. *"Just call me paranoid,"* he'd told her the night he'd dropped it on his desk. *"But you go out there and something happens or you don't check in, at least I have a starting point to find you. Once I'm there, I know I can, but I don't want to waste time if you're in trouble."*

"What trouble do you honestly think I'm going to get into?" She'd risked it. From the beginning, she and Brett had gotten along. She'd been very fond of his grandfathers—both their former Alpha and the healer. In fact, Hatch had been named for his grandfather, Hatcher. Another sore point, not that she'd asked.

"Hopefully none, but with that, I know I can find you. Wear it, or you can only run here. Take it or leave it."

Of course, she'd taken it, and once it was secure, she tested her steps. It wasn't in the way. That had taken more practice. Enough that she actually had extra bands in her backpack if she had to tear it off and try again.

There. Done. With a huff, she lifted her nose to the breeze. The sun was shining, but there were clouds in the sky. The forecast had a twenty percent chance of rain, but she wouldn't melt. Flicking her ears, she set off to parallel the trail through the woods. There was fresh water not far, and that was definitely deer she could smell.

Hmm, venison for lunch sounded good.

The next few hours passed in a pleasant haze as she raced the trails, stalked a few rabbits and flushed them out just to see them run. Then she began to actively hunt the deer. Twice she came across does with fawns, while not dependent on their mothers, she wasn't going to go after them.

She found an older one, nursing an injury and a little lamed. That one wouldn't survive hunting season, and she took her down swiftly. Fed and pleasantly relaxed, she dealt with the remains, dragging them off deeper into the woods for a scavenger to have before she headed upwind to a cliff where she could sun herself and listen to the water.

When she told Luc she couldn't do anything on Saturday because it was her time, this was the moment she referred to. Life was far more basic in her fur. Especially when she was alone. If not for her job, she might have gone Lone Wolf years earlier. She'd been tempted, but it had been Brett's grandfather, Hatcher, who talked her out of it.

She'd discussed it with Brett on his advice, and Brett asked her what she wanted to do. She had both law and business degrees from NYU.

A week later, she started at Hudson River International

and moved into the city. She'd never felt the need to leave the pack again. Unlike most other wolves, she didn't mind the congested city and the millions of human occupants. They were her neighbors, her employees, the people she purchased items from, and the people she rode the subway with everyday.

They weren't pack. But she was never alone, not even in that huge crowd that couldn't begin to know her. They weren't wolves, and that made them safe. Still, she craved solitude, which these runs let her achieve.

The crunch of leaves and deliberate footsteps pulled her from her doze. The interloper approached from downwind, hiding their scent, but they weren't being stealthy. Not with such determined footsteps.

Lips peeling back from her teeth, she rose. There were a few places she could vanish to, especially if some human hiker had stolen her idea to wander one of the closed trails.

Then again, this little bluff she'd found wasn't exactly on the trail. Ears flicking forward, she caught the half-whistled tune, and a growl rumbled up from her chest.

"Now, now," Bishop called. "Don't be snarly. I just came to talk."

Her brothers.

She loved them, but some days she could just eat them.

As promised by the nearness of his voice, he appeared through the trees. He'd dressed in jeans, a t-shirt, along with a windbreaker and hat, just like she had earlier. There was a backpack on his back and a pair of hiking boots on his feet.

At least he hadn't invaded her space in his fur. That would have been complicated—even with Bishop. He and Duke handled her nature far better than Noah or Sullivan did and leagues ahead of their mother. Only their father was better, and she had to avoid him to avoid her mother.

Not fair. She knew.

Bishop and Duke had darker hair than she did, but it had strands of red amongst the brown. They were both tall and broadly built—thicker than Noah and Sullivan, who'd taken their lean builds from Mom. All four, however, had become Hunters like Mom. A path her mother intended for her, if she weren't so *warped*.

It was an old argument, and a terrible voice to hear, so she shoved it aside to concentrate on her brother. He'd slowed his steps, giving her time to acclimate. Her wolf was of two minds, he wasn't supposed to be here. The fact he'd tracked her at all said either he had access to her GPS, which would be in violation of her agreement with Brett, *or* he'd spoken to their Alpha and received permission to locate her.

Which was it?

"Okay, you're pissed, I get it." About six feet away, he dropped to sit on the browning grass. "I asked Brett where you were heading today and endured the thirty minutes of interrogation on why I wanted to bother you. So trust that I have a good reason, okay?"

If that was the case, then yes, Brett had given him her location. Or at least the general area and, thanks to the GPS, he had a solid lock on where she was. Unfortunately, it still left her disgruntled. Sitting with a huff, she lashed her tail and stared at her brother.

"Okay, so silent treatment. Got it. Fine, I'll talk. You listen."

Since her brothers often preferred to get their words in first, she usually listened to their rants. Most of the time, she listened anyway. Sometimes, she'd just tune them out.

Bishop wasn't so bad, though. Not by comparison. At least, he, in turn, would listen to her.

"Pack gathering is coming."

If she could roll her eyes, she would. As it was, she just flopped down and opened her mouth to pant.

"Luc informed me that you would be staying with him."

Oh, did he?

"That's an epically bad idea, Sis."

Well, it wouldn't be the first one she'd had. Even if she hadn't had the idea herself.

"Not only does it send the wrong message to the pack, it's going to send the wrong message to Mom."

The first was a real concern. As for the second, she couldn't bring herself to care. Nothing she did or chose was ever good enough for Mom, so this was not exactly new territory.

"And I know, you don't care about Mom."

That wasn't entirely true, either. She'd stopped trying to care about her a long time before, because it did absolutely no good for any of them. It was why she also stayed away.

"But I want to offer you an alternative. You can stay with me."

Nope.

No.

Uh-uh.

Never.

Nyet.

Non.

Pfft.

She sneezed.

Bishop quirked his lips. "When you're done insulting me in your head, just give a little yip, okay?"

Oh, to have a middle finger.

Good to his word, he said nothing as he waited her out.

Fine. She wanted to go back to her solitude. She yipped.

"Thank you," he said. "You apparently have added to your repertoire, if it takes you that long to get through the list. Staying with me has its advantages. One, I'm not Mom."

True.

"Two, I'm not Luc."

Also true.

"Three, I can give you cover with Mom *and* Luc. It's not like we can't movie marathon when we're not running with the pack."

She sneezed.

"Yeah, I know you never run. If you're staying at my place, you can *pretend* to head out on the run and just divert back to it. I bought the Carlson's old cabin out past the sawmill on Junction."

That was definitely out of town and a decent distance. Getting to it from Brett's, where the run would start, would actually require a good distance through the woods. He was right, she could mask her scent and slip away.

"Ahh, see, not a bad idea, is it?"

She couldn't shrug, so she just sneezed and Bishop looped his arms around his upraised knees.

"There's another perk."

She tilted her head, she was listening.

"I'll cook for you."

That was laughable, and she rose to her feet, dancing sideways as she barked at him.

"Rude," he commented. "I don't actually burn food anymore."

She snorted.

"Or put too much salt on it."

Another sneeze.

"*Or* add too much garlic."

Mouth open, she grinned at him, tongue lolling. Bishop was a horrid cook.

"Fine, you sussed me out. The perk would be for me. I get to hang out with my baby sister, and she can cook for me."

Uh huh. That was what she thought.

Of the five of them, only she seemed to have inherited their father's patience in food preparation—and taste buds.

Cocking his head to the side, he grinned. "Just think about it? I can't imagine you want the pack gossiping about you, and that's going to happen if you stay with Luc. Everyone knows he's the third in the Alpha's triad."

Yep. Couldn't roll her eyes, so she just peeled her lips back from her teeth. It was a really stupid rumor.

"You don't think so?"

She just stared at him.

"Huh. Okay, you have to tell me why you don't think so. The guy's not so bad, when he isn't interested in my sister."

She sneezed. Because yes, she'd already figured that part out.

And now, she was done with talking because he'd interrupted her alone time. She lunged at him then darted away. A half-dozen steps away she wagged her tail as she stared at him.

"You sure you want to start that?" But he was grinning.

Sidling, she danced a half-circle then charged him again, switching directions at the last minute before he could grab her and raced toward the woods. At the edge of them, she paused and looked back.

"Last chance," he warned as he rose to his feet and dusted off his hands.

She huffed a laugh and charged him again before dashing in a circle through some crunchy leaves. Movement from the corner of her eye sent her streaking away as he chased after her. He stayed on two feet while she was on four, but it was the best game of tag she'd played in a while.

The sun was beginning its descent in the west when he called it, and she bumped her nose against his hand. When he gave her a good scratch behind her ears, she tilted her head a little so he'd get that one spot—there it was.

"C'mon," he said. "Let's go get you changed." They ran together, not rushing, back to where she'd left her bag. With Bishop there, he could remove the GPS for her, which saved her another ruined band, then he pulled her bag open and nodded toward the woods heading to the trail.

"I'll meet you out there."

Then he left her to shift. The bliss of the day made the transition easier. As dominant as her brother was, he didn't spark the need to challenge in her, particularly if he stayed on two feet. If anything, she leaned more on her submissive side around him. Except when he got bossy.

She found him after she was dressed, leaning against a tree and staring at his phone.

"There's no signal."

"That's the point," she said in the same tone she'd say *idiot*. He chuckled and held his arms open. She walked into them for a hug and tucked her head under his chin. He ran his hand up and down her back in a soothing motion.

See, he got it. Didn't judge. It was nice to lean on him, when he wasn't being a pain in the ass.

"So, can I buy you dinner?"

"Hmm, I had venison for lunch."

"And you didn't share."

She snickered. "You weren't here, and I wasn't expecting you to ambush me."

"True. Dinner?"

"Sure," she agreed with one last squeeze. "Provided you don't spend all of it trying to tell me how bad Luc is for me or my reputation."

"Done—though you do need to tell me why you think the rumor is bullshit."

Leaning away, she stared at him. "He doesn't smell like them."

"Huh." Bishop grinned. "Keep that to yourself. I'm going to make a killing on the betting pool."

Charlie rolled her eyes and hooked her arm around his waist as he settled his on her shoulders. "Do you know who has the largest wager on they aren't?"

He stared down at her. "And you didn't cut me in on the action?"

"Learn to use your nose and not your ears."

"He's around them a lot," Bishop complained. "Sometimes Colby does smell like him."

"Colby smells like Trent and sometimes Gillian, depending on how much time they're working together, and they aren't mated either. Stop stirring up trouble." Luc didn't deserve it.

"Uh oh, does Charlie like Luc?"

She punched him, and he winced backward with a laugh and muttered, "Ow."

"I'm hungry," she told him.

"Yeah, yeah," he said, rubbing his arm. "Damn, you've gotten mean with your left."

She just grinned.

"Steak," he offered. "That place off 80."

She knew it. They'd eaten there before. They had prime rib to die for.

Big brothers were good for some things—like punching and food.

When he wrapped his arm around her shoulders again, she leaned into him, and he kissed the top of her head. "One last thing, kid, and I'll leave it alone."

She sighed.

"If he hurts you, I get the first shot at gutting him."

Oh for the love of... "You know what, fine. If I haven't, you can, deal?"

He grinned. "Deal."

"Can we let it go now?"

"Yes, we can. Do you want to talk about Mom now?"

Her groan carried, and Bishop laughed.

Asshole.

She loved him.

But he was an asshole.

CHAPTER 7

$\mathcal{H}$e hit the button on his phone to call Charlie before he backed out of the driveway. "Charlie," he said, heading for his mother's. "I enjoyed dinner last night." Understatement. He'd had a hell of a lot of fun. "I'd like to do it again." That slipped out without a second thought. Then again, he'd already decided he wanted more before they were halfway through the meal. "I'll come to the city later this week, just let me know when you're free, and if you're amenable, I'll take you out somewhere rather than eat in your office."

That had been fun, but she lived in the city and made it clear she enjoyed it. If he was going to actively pursue her, he wanted to see the world she enjoyed. Admittedly, he wasn't a fan of any large city, much less New York.

"Then we can go out for dinner up here when you come for the pack gathering." He had more than enough room for her to stay, and while he was more than willing to open his bed, he also had guest rooms. Having her closer was more important. "Anyway, I know you said this was your day. I'll call you tomorrow, and we can brainstorm our approach to Sutter Butte. Sounds good? Talk to you then."

Better to also include actual business. She hadn't been particularly encouraging, though clearly she understood his relationship with Brett and Colby did not follow rumors. He loved her reasoning—"*Colby doesn't smell like you.*"

Short, simple, and to the point. No, Colby and Brett wore each other's scents, as it should be. Luc swung down the block toward his mother's house and kept an eye out for the kids who might be out playing. The weather had turned chillier, sure, but it was a Saturday, and most of the kids didn't have places they had to go.

The front screen door opened with a creak. Hands on her hips, Babette Danes stared at him as he climbed out of the truck. "What's wrong?"

"Why does anything have to be wrong?" he asked, crossing the yard to the steps leading up to the porch.

"Because you're here early on a Saturday, and you didn't call first." She tipped her face to the side as he dropped a kiss on her cheek.

"Can't I want to come over and have breakfast with my mother?"

"No," she said firmly, slapping his chest with a grin. "You can't. Because my son is such a busy and important wolf, he doesn't have time for his mama these days."

There was just the barest hint of an edge to her teasing. She wasn't entirely making fun of him. At the same time, she gave him a measuring look.

"You got me," he admitted. "I heard a rumor that you've been baking, and as the favored son, I've come to demand tribute."

Snorting, she patted his cheek. "You're lucky I love you. Get in here."

Yes, he was, even when she frustrated him with her

meddling. Babette Danes cared about people, and the pack knew it. She could be trusted as someone always willing to listen. That she loved to gossip like it was the national pastime could be overlooked.

Mostly.

Unless you were, in fact, her favored son and thus topic. He trailed her into the house. The alluring and rich scent of coffee drifted out to tease him, beckoning him to track into the kitchen. As his nose had warned him, she had indeed been baking, and there were stacks of hot croissants and muffins lining the sideboard.

"Having a party?" he asked as he snatched a couple of croissants on his way to the coffee pot.

"Bake sale at the new school." New school. It had been there twenty years, but it was still considered new. Not that his mother had any children attending the school, but it hardly limited her participation. If anything, she probably went more.

"Nice," he murmured, taking a bite and sighing. Buttery and light, it was the perfect blend of decadent and basic. "Did you want coffee, too?" He already had his mug down as she hustled around him to the oven. Apple something—oh, apple dumpcake. He paused and stared at the oven.

"Luc Danes, you touch the apple dumpcake, and I will tear your ear off."

His mother was a cruel woman. "You know how I feel about dumpcake."

"I do, and this is for the *bake sale*."

After pouring the coffee, Luc had to know. "How much?"

Exasperated, Babette gave him a look. "Fifty dollars."

"Damn, Mama." Didn't stop him from pulling out his wallet and unfolding a couple of crisp twenties and one slightly ragged ten. He set the payment on the counter.

She scooped it up with a smile. "The school appreciates your support. It should be ready before you go."

"Thank you." He refilled her coffee mug before picking up his own. They toasted, and his mother's grin widened.

"Now I really know you want something." Despite the light tone, her blue eyes appraised him. "Spill it."

Instead of talking, he took a sip of the coffee. It was a good blend, a lighter roast and one of the Columbian brands he often acquired for Babette, since sending her the gift from his wanderings. There were notes of lemon, brown sugar, and honey in the blend itself. While Luc wasn't a coffee expert, he did know what would appeal to his eclectic mother.

"Just came to see you, Mama. Gonna get busy over the next few weeks, and I'm not likely to be around much." Besides, if he wanted access to what she knew without answering an interrogation himself, then he had to come at it sideways.

"Oh?" She studied him a beat. "What's going on?"

"Brett's asked me to tackle a task with the other packs, and no, I'm not giving you the details. When he's ready for the pack to know, he'll tell you himself. Until then," he said, adding just the barest hint of command. "Let's keep the speculation to a minimum, and no sharing."

Exasperation flooded her scent. "Child, what have I ever done that makes you think I can't keep a secret?"

"Do you want that in chronological or alphabetical order?"

With a roll of her eyes, she pointed him to the table. "Sit. You're cluttering my cooking space."

Obediently, he moved over, dropped into a chair, and slung a foot up into another. Coffee in one hand, and his second croissant in the other. She hustled to the fridge and pulled out bacon, eggs, cheese, ham, and more fixings for an omelet.

"So busy means traveling?"

"Possibly," he said. "It may also mean hosting. Working on that schedule now."

"You aren't missing the gathering, are you? I heard tell Brett is going to make an announcement," she fished openly, and then muttered, "and about time, too."

"Mama," he said, keeping his patience fisted. "I wouldn't miss the gathering." No matter what their plans for Sutter Butte, Luc would make sure he and Charlie were both present. "Which reminds me, Charlie Miller will be staying with me for the gathering, so can you help me make sure the house is stocked in case I forget?"

Most days, his mother would see right through that ploy. He never invited her to just let herself in and restock his fridge or pantry. She often did it regardless, but it wasn't something he requested. Part of having his own place was to have privacy from his nosy family and pack. Being back home definitely had its perks, but it also came with its fair share of detractions, too.

"Charlotte Miller?" She frowned as she whipped the eggs in a bowl.

"Yep, she works at Hudson River International," Luc said, keeping it light and talking around the croissant. "Anyway, she'll be in that weekend, and since I've a long list to tackle myself, I don't want her to find the fridge with expired milk and some moldy takeout."

His fridge *never* had takeout in it. But according to his mother, he'd never mastered keeping a home and wouldn't until he finally settled in with his mate. Since she was convinced he belonged with Brett and Colby…

"Of course, I'll take care of it. You'll probably be at Brett's anyway. I heard we've got the Italians coming in as guests. That could be exciting."

Italians? Luc raised his eyebrows. The visit was a business negotiation and to address some issues directly related to Three Rivers. Brett was running interference for Rayne and Luciana while Julian and Dallas did a little more investigation. Right, wrong, or indifferent, the North American packs were *done* with foreign interference.

"Wouldn't it be nice if you could introduce your sister to some eligible wolf?"

He snorted. "Sam knows plenty of eligible wolves, Mama. She's not interested in them." And until she got her own anger management issues under control, she likely wouldn't be. She'd been close with some of the Reagans, though. Maybe he could recommend Sam to spend some time in Three Rivers with them at some future point.

The moment that weird thought occurred, he turned it over in his head. Three Rivers had definitely leap-frogged in his estimation, despite his severe doubts about them. Colby's experiences there, and getting to know the Alpha pairing, had changed Luc's mind, somewhat. The pack wasn't bad, inexperienced and maybe being bitten in the ass by their own optimism, sure, but not so bad.

Besides, Luc had a few bones to pick with the Italian Centurions. Rodrigo Mazzanti had been one of theirs. His actions had cost Three Rivers on several levels.

Setting the omelet in front of him, she added another pair of croissants. "It doesn't mean you can't help your sister out. I know she's struggled for a while, but she's making a real effort."

Yeah, okay. He wasn't having this argument. Nor did he want to focus on Sam's love life. At. All. "Most of the pack will be here for the gathering, so she can visit with old and new friends. The omelet's good, Mama. Thank you."

"Charlotte Miller—wait that's Adele Miller's daughter, isn't she?" His mother was already moving to the oven.

"Could be, got a couple of brothers—Bishop and Duke."

"She has four brothers," his mother corrected him. "Seriously, Lucas, you're the pack Second, shouldn't you know everyone?"

"Knowing them and knowing who they are related to are two entirely different things. Pierce does most of the work with the Hunters, I supervise only when needed." Delegation worked when trustworthy people were allowed to do their jobs. Pierce reported directly to Brett, but he often looped Luc into those updates the same way Luc kept Pierce in the know on issues Luc tackled. That way they didn't step on each other's toes or create a situation Brett had to solve.

Their job was to make Brett's life easier while protecting the pack at the same time. The best way to accomplish that was coordination. He tore a croissant in half.

"Adele Miller is the longest serving Hunter in the pack, she comes from a full line of them." His mother put her fists on her hips. "She began her service decades ago, and the only months she's ever taken off were when she was pregnant. How do you not know her?"

"Didn't say I didn't know her, Mama." All true.

A huff. "I swear, Luc. I actually sent you to study with Adele, and you act like you don't know her whole family."

Consternation raked through him. "I was—ten." He'd spent three months with the Hunters, as had Brett, and it wasn't Babette who sent them, but Brett's grandfather. "And we didn't study under Adele, specifically."

It wasn't unusual for youths in the packs to study under all the disciplines to find what appealed to them most. As he and Brett both had Alpha potential, Brett's grandfather insisted they be exposed to all aspects of pack life, from teaching to protecting to healing, and everything in between.

Their summer jobs from ages nine to sixteen had been anything but glamorous. On the other hand, Luc and Brett understood Hudson River from the ground up, and his grandfather had been right—leading was about more than just having the dominance to assert authority, it required the wisdom to know when to assert it and when to listen to others.

"I suppose I shouldn't be surprised you don't remember working with her, you had so much going on that summer, but Adele supervised that training. She also did your assessments. She thought you would both make fine Hunters."

"A fate I would gladly have embraced, were I anyone else," Luc said cheerfully. As it was, he was only Second because Brett needed him, and he wanted to be there for his best friend. The time spent roaming had been good. The restless edge had begun to invade him again, however, so his latest task might be good for that.

Babette chuckled. "I suppose. You know, it occurs to me that Adele raised all of her children to be Hunters, unusual enough I guess, for all of your children to follow you into your calling. Well, all but the youngest one."

"Hunter to high-powered executive…still, she's Brett's lieutenant, that has to count for something."

The skeptical laugh his mother release decried that answer. "Not if you're Adele Miller. Her children are a reflection of her success. Charlie's a failure as far as she is concerned. The fact she stays in the city so much just emphasizes the point."

Though he lasered onto the fact, he had to keep his demeanor nonchalant and uncaring. "Sounds wretched for her." Detached or not, he couldn't keep the sarcasm out of his voice as he finished the last bite of his omelet and drained the coffee cup. "You'd do cartwheels if that was Sam."

"I'd do cartwheels if Sam found anything that made her

happy," Babette admitted. "But for now, she's working with your father, and we'll have to call that good."

"Do you need me to talk to her?" Rising, he carried his dishes over to the sink and rinsed off the plate before beginning to systematically wash off and load the dishwasher with the stack she had going in the side sink.

"You're a doll to offer," his mother said as she took the dumpcake out of the oven. The combination of apple and cinnamon had his stomach growling, whether he'd just had breakfast or not. "I may take you up on it, but she'll just get defensive if you corner her. It would be better if she asked for it herself."

Mom was not wrong. He loved his sister, but they tended toward the incendiary side of things.

"Just let me know." It couldn't hurt to offer, and he made a mental note to actually check on Sam while he was at it.

Pivoting to face him, his mother smiled. "You might be stubborn to a fault, sweetheart, but you're a good brother. You know, maybe that's Adele's problem, she made her children too competitive with each other, much less the rest of the pack."

Having met all five of said children, Luc doubted that. Charlie's brothers adored her, even if they were overbearing little shits. Just the way they should be when it came to their sister.

"At the same time..." She paused, as if editing herself, and that was a first. "I don't know. I have enormous respect for Adele, but I can't say I like her very much."

Okay, now *that* surprised him. "You know you can't say something like that and not have me ask why."

Wiping her hands, Babette seemed to consider her answer. "Children are the point."

"Of?"

"Of—life. I know not everyone wants to be parents. But

for those of us who do, children—raising them, guiding them, helping them discover who they are, and seeing them grow into who they can be? That's—that's everything. Even when we don't agree with their choices." She gave him a look. "Not once, even when you decided to roam and stayed gone for so long, did I feel like it reflected on me as a mother. Your success is yours—am I proud of you? Absolutely. But you could have…" She took a deep breath. "You could have chosen to leave after you healed, to not stay and join Brett and Colby."

Oh for the love of…

"But you didn't, you made the right call for you. I wouldn't have liked it if you left, because I would have missed you, but it still wouldn't be making your choices about me."

"I appreciate that Mama, and side note, Brett's my best friend and my Alpha, I am not now, nor have I *ever* been involved in their relationship."

"Of course you're involved, maybe you're not mated, but they wouldn't even have each other without you. You train with Colby, you found her, you brought her to us. You could have claimed her."

Luc closed his eyes for a moment, then shook his head. "No, I couldn't."

"Of course…"

"Mother," he said firmly, and she snapped her gaze to his. "No, I *couldn't*. Colby is a dear friend, and I love her like a sister. I would die to protect her because she is our healer *and* Brett's mate, but she is not *mine*. She has never been mine. She will never be mine. For the love of everything, please stop talking about us like we're at the centerpiece of some Greek tragedy."

Lips compressing, she frowned. Finally, she let out a

breath. "Fine, but that does not in anyway let you off the hook for giving me grandkids."

He didn't roll his eyes. He thought about it, but he didn't. "You do realize telling everyone and their Great-Aunt Mary that I'm bound to the Alpha's pairing wasn't getting you any either, right?"

"But you could be," she argued. "You're all so close, and you"

"No," he barked. "I can't. Enough."

Fisting his temper took every ounce of his effort. While some in the pack might have the good damn sense to look away, or at least let it go, his mother just gave him a measuring look.

"If all you want is for me to be happy," he managed in a civilized tone. "It would make me *happy* if you would dispute that rumor and put it to bed."

"Fine," she said, tilting her head as she pulled a fresh tray out and uncovered the cookie dough she'd been hiding. "Does that mean there's potential if Charlie stays with you for the gathering?"

Shoot him. "She's a guest, Mama. Brett's lieutenant? I'm doing her a favor. Nothing more."

His mother studied him a beat longer, then nodded. "Probably easier on the girl than staying where her mother can pour disapproval all over her."

While he was happier to change the subject, he wasn't thrilled with that revelation. "Her disapproval?"

"She's not a Hunter. She had skills, incredible skills according to everyone I know, and she walked away. Didn't say a word to her mother, just enrolled in college at eighteen, then law school, and avoids the pack like the plague. Adele... Adele felt it reflected on her poorly. Watch her when Charlie is here, she has never forgiven her for straying from the family business." Then with a quick shake of her head, she dispelled the sudden gloom over her expression. "And bring her for dinner. I'd love to see her, it's been ages since I saw that girl. I don't even know if I could pick her out of a crowd."

Luc would have no problem. If Charlie was getting hell from her mother, why the fuck hadn't Brett done something about it? He lingered for another hour, managing to purchase a dozen of her cookies to go with the apple dump-cake. She wrapped those up for him, and then he loaded all her sweet treats in the car so she could carry them over to the school.

Apparently, whatever sale they were doing was later that afternoon. Once he'd waved her off, he slid into the truck and checked his phone. A couple of messages from Pierce, the forest and public land was looking good. They'd begin the ground clearing shortly. Cleaning out the tangles of roots and bushes entwining the trees. Made for better runs.

No messages from Charlie. Not that he expected any. She'd been clear about taking the day to herself. Still, be nice if she'd been inspired to reach out after his message. Hitting Brett's number, he waited for him to pick up.

"I could have been in bed," was how he answered the call.

"If you were in bed with her, you wouldn't have bothered with the phone."

"This is true," Brett said with a chuckle. "I'm standing outside while she and Trent are wrestling." In other words, he wasn't going anywhere. The younger wolf had responded well to Gillian's training, but Colby and he had become fast friends, and when she wasn't training to defend herself, she worked to grow more comfortable with her wolf and it happened more and more.

Trent, of all of them, relaxed her. Made sense. Healers needed soothing. Even feisty ones. Now more than ever.

"What's up?"

"Tell me about Adele Miller."

"You know as much as I do. Longest serving Hunter in the pack still active. Tough, determined, and a definite asset. She was on outer loop swings when everything went down with Marco, but she beat herself up about Marco for a while. It's only in the last year, she's finally begun to let that go." Sobriety gave way to amusement. "I wouldn't recommend approaching her about Charlie if you want even a snowball's chance in Hell with Charlie."

"No, I've gotten that impression. What I want to know is why her mother is pissed at her? She's a Shadow. That's biology, no different than Alpha potential."

"Not everyone sees it that way, Luc. Lot of wolves still think you're dominant or submissive—Omegas are the rare exception, and most of the time, they're treated like crap. It surprises you that a Shadow would face similar prejudice?"

No, but it pissed him off. Brett had a younger cousin through Dallas that was an Omega. Sweet kid. And she was the child of two profoundly dominant wolves. Still, Hudson River hadn't had an Omega in a long time, they were probably due one sooner or later.

"So, she blames Charlie for not choosing to become a Hunter?" Because fuck her mother, really. There were *other* ways to serve the pack, and she was doing that.

"It's lot more complicated than that."

"And you're not going to tell me any more..."

"Nope, love you like a brother, but you're all mine to protect." That was the end of that.

"You're still an asshole."

"And you like her." The grin in his voice translated easily. "Be patient. Get to know her. Don't pick your battles now."

"That's your advice?"

"Hey, you want to open a door into your face a few times

before you figure out how to get through it, you can do that, too."

Luc chuckled. "I've been known to resemble that remark."

They talked for a few more minutes, and when the call ended, Luc drummed his hands against the steering wheel. With a glance at the boxed cake next to him, he debated his next move.

Work first, he decided, after he dropped the cake back at his place. He'd take it into the city for Charlie. Hopefully, she enjoyed apple dumpcake. He could probably send her more flowers… Closing his eyes, he pictured her office. She definitely needed more plants. Everyone deserved a piece of home.

Eyes open, he sent a message to Pierce that he'd be out to meet him in thirty minutes before he reversed out of the driveway and headed back toward his place to drop off the cake.

He had a plan.

He just needed to tweak it.

A little.

CHAPTER 8

*S*unday dawned with a call from Giovanni Conti. She talked to him for nearly an hour, hammering down details for the business side of their visit. Twice, he tried to swing the conversation to more political matters, but she managed to dance around those. For one, she handled Hudson River International and two, political issues were not the candy she wanted to take a bite out of. Negotiating treaties was going to be one thing, but the issues currently on the table between Seven Hills—the Italian pack—and the North American packs were far above her pay grade.

Too far.

Fortunately, from a business perspective, they were in good shape. She promised to have legal vet the contracts, and then she'd present it to Brett ahead of the upcoming meeting. This particular contract was only one of the items on that agenda. Hopefully, she could do her part and avoid the rest of the drama.

Done with the call, she flopped back on her sofa. She had an actual office in the brownstone, one she used when she had to work from home for any length of time. The idea being work stayed in the office and didn't invade the peace in the rest of her home.

But she and Bishop had stayed out far too late the night before. After dinner, they'd gone for a walk and then drinks. Finally, he'd followed her all the way back into the city —*brothers!*—and she'd invited him in for coffee before he went back to Hudson River.

The sound of a thudding footstep on the stairs reminded her the last part hadn't actually occurred. Bishop's scent reached her just as he hit the last step. "Your shower needs fixing in the guest bath," he told her as he wandered into her sitting room. "You want more coffee?"

She smiled. "I don't use that bathroom often, but I'll have someone…"

"I'll do it," he offered. "I'm here. I can find a hardware shop and pick up the new showerhead and change out the cartridge, then tighten it all up."

Was it really worth the fight? She debated it, but Bishop grinned. The fact she hadn't just told him no immediately was a good sign in his book. She waved him off. "Fine, but I'm paying for the parts." When he opened his mouth to argue, she straightened her spine. "I pay for the parts, or you don't get to fix it."

Eyes narrowed, Bishop glared at her. "Fine. You can pay for the parts."

"Thank you for your cooperation," she said with a smile, and he snorted. "Yes, I'd like more coffee. I started a fresh pot before I got on the phone."

She flopped back on the sofa and reached for one of the binders. She had seven of them to read. About ten pages of her skimming later, Bishop returned with her oversized mug of coffee and his own. He bumped her legs so he could sit next to her, and she pulled herself up and resisted the urge to kick him.

"Thanks for letting me stay over."

"It was two in the morning, and you were still talking. I assumed you would have talked until dawn unless I shoved you in the guest room."

His smirk didn't deny the charge.

"So who are you running away from?" She sat cross-legged and perched the binder in her lap so she could sip her coffee and flip the pages. Speed-reading was a necessary skill. She'd always been a fast reader, but she could devour reams of data in short order, which kept her ahead of the curve with all the various departments she managed.

"What makes you think I'm running away from someone? Can't I want to hang out with my baby sister, whom I *never* see?" The reproach in his voice irked, but she refused to let him bait her off the topic.

"You saw me a couple of nights ago…"

"For five minutes *with* Luc Danes. Not the same thing," he countered. Dressed in jeans and a t-shirt, he'd left his shoes upstairs. Not that she was commenting on the casual wear, she'd opted for ripped denim shorts and a tank top. Other than working at home, she had zero plans for the day. The run the day before had taken the edge off, and she could focus.

Glancing at him over the rim of the mug as she took a sip, she considered Bishop. "Are you planning to stay all day?"

"At least long enough to fix the shower in the guest bath. Anything else need tinkering with?"

Charlie hid a smile. His wolf drove him at the moment, the dominant-needed-to-look-after-baby-sister wolf. It was easy with Bishop to just let him have his way, but this was her space. She didn't have to roll over or snarl, or at least she shouldn't have to.

"Probably," she told him. "But I'd rather you didn't make it a thing, Bish, just—fix the shower if it will make you happy."

The grumpy look on his face gave way an abashed grin. "That obvious, huh?"

"Only for the last thirty or so plus years," she reminded him. "You got your pride poked the other night, and then you decided you needed to protect me. That protecting me also involved tracking me down during my much-needed quiet time, and then tagging along so that you could stay over and make sure I was safe? I forgive you." She poked him with a toe, and he caught her ankle lightly.

"You are my favorite sister."

"I'm you're *only* sister, don't try to pretend that is some lofty title."

"Okay, fine," he growled. "Favorite sibling."

"Oh no, Duke will be heartbroken."

There was a pause, and then they both cracked up. Duke would have cheerfully flipped him off and then decided that Charlie was his favorite sister, and thus the squabble would have begun.

"He'd get over it," Bishop said, grinning. "Now, what will you feed your starving brother? I can't work on an empty stomach."

She snorted, and then took a long swallow of her coffee. "I'm already working, and now you want me to feed you, too?"

"Yes," he replied without an ounce of shame. "I could go for some steak and eggs."

"Hmm… then I'd have to jog down to the corner market and pick up steak if they have it." Though she was due a trip to the butcher's.

Bishop gave her the equivalent of puppy dog eyes, and she raised her brows.

"Really?"

"Pretty please, Charlie? For your favorite brother."

Hand against his face, she pushed him away. "I don't have a favorite brother."

"Wounded," he gasped, hand against his chest. The playfulness wrapped around her and beckoned to her to join in. More, delight suffused her at the fact he wanted to play. Damn her nature sometimes, she wanted to cave immediately because it would make him happy.

"You're cheating," she chastised him, and he sobered.

"Not totally on purpose," he admitted. "But I am hungry, and you haven't cooked for me in forever. If I had to live on my own cooking, I'd have died long before now."

Another indelicate snort escaped her, even as her wolf whined and pawed at her. Brother, pack, and, at the moment, the dominant in the room, and she wanted to just roll over. "You could hunt."

"And I do, but your food is better," he tossed the compliment easily, but it wasn't just charm, there was genuine warmth and sincerity layered into his words and his voice.

She groaned. "I hate you."

"Yes!" He lifted a fist. Because, of course, he got his way.

After draining her coffee, she flipped the binder closed and returned it to the stack on the table. "I'll go get my shoes."

"I'll pay for the steaks," he called after her.

"Shut up, you can do the dishes."

"I'll try, might have to leave…"

"Bishop." She paused on the steps up to her room and growled.

"Of course, I'll do the dishes!" His laughter chased after her.

She dragged out a pair of running shoes and socks. The shorts and tank were fine. It wasn't super warm outside, but it also wasn't cold. Nothing suspicious, and she was too comfortable to change. She did pull her hair up into a ponytail and snag a hat along with her sunglasses before fishing a credit card out of her wallet and sliding it into her back pocket.

Downstairs, she found Bishop with his feet up on her coffee table and the television on, tuned to a sports channel. At her look, he grinned. "Did you want me to go with you?"

"No," she said bluntly. "I can do it." She loved him all the more because while he might wheedle and tease and occasionally take advantage, if playfully, of her, he also recognized the limits he could push. "But get your feet off my table."

With a roll of his eyes, he took them down. "Better?"

"Hmm. I'll be back." No doubt ten seconds after she let herself outside, he had his feet back on the table. It was still early on a Sunday morning. Just a little before eight. The sun offered the promise of warmth, and the air was still cool. The scent of the river carried, along with hints of someone grilling on a rooftop the night before, most likely. The Daileys had been by with their pair of German Shepherds, she loved those dogs, and Ms. Mahoney must have had her poodles out.

Charlie absorbed all of it. The street was quiet. Some of the families would be off to church soon, if they weren't already getting ready to leave. More would be at the park in a few hours, letting the kids run off their energy. Traffic was quiet on their street, but it would pick up for a while and then slow down again.

The weekends had their own pulse. It was why she liked working from home on Sundays, she could focus and still enjoy that sense of community beyond the doors.

The closer market wouldn't be open for another couple of hours, so she'd have to go with the one a mile farther. That was fine. They had a better meat selection anyway.

The honk of a horn caught her attention as she reached

the first corner, and she glanced back to find Luc slowing to stop on the other side of the parked cars.

Oh.

Joy.

"Hey," he called, the passenger window open.

"Good morning," she said, keeping her tone polite as she moved between the cars and up to the door. No sense in shouting, not that they needed to. Better not to look weird.

There was an appreciative gleam in Luc's eyes. "Heading somewhere fun?"

"Well, I have a breakfast companion who is demanding steak in trade for services he hasn't rendered yet," she answered. "Course, he'd probably have done the services without the steak, he'd just whine a lot."

The easygoing expression on Luc's face fled, and his eyes narrowed. "Excuse me?"

"No need to excuse you," she teased him. Truthfully, he shouldn't even be here, so if he got tweaked, that was on him. "What brings you to my neck of the woods? You're a little far to just have made a wrong turn."

His eyebrows tightened together. "Mom sent something for you, so I had to deliver it."

The bald face lie surprised her, but she didn't call him on it.

"And I wanted to see you. Thought we could start planning our Sutter Butte approach, and you could sit in on the call to Trask." But his eyes remained narrowed, even as he fought to make his tone easier. "I didn't realize you'd have company. Saturdays were your days, weren't they?"

Guilt pricked her. "They are, and it was a good day." She glanced down the street, he wasn't blocking traffic, and he had come all this way... "You know, I have to go pick up the steaks. You want to park and come with me?"

His eyes brightened a fraction. "Are you sure your guest

won't mind?" The hints of anticipation in his scent gave him away, and no amount of nonchalance could cover the intrigue in his blue eyes.

"Tell you what, you can ask him yourself. Go park," she told him. "There's no rules on the street for Sunday, so you can park anywhere."

He grinned. "Stay right there."

Oh, she wouldn't dream of going too far. Bishop was going to kill her.

Well, he wanted to be her favorite brother, he could put up with Luc. Besides, it served him right for inviting himself over. While she probably shouldn't tease Luc, her wolf brushed against the inside of her skin, tail lashing. He'd lied to her, maybe with all the best intentions in the world, but he'd still told a lie.

They both wanted to know why.

He actually reversed down the street and parked two brownstones down from hers. Waiting for him on the sidewalk, she tipped her head back and let the sunlight warm her face. She scented him a second before she caught the faint scrape of his shoes against the sidewalk. He moved so quietly.

Slanting a look at him, she gave him a faint smile. The crisp scent of his soap combined with the woodsy notes reminded her of the valley. "You must have left early to come down this morning."

"I had some work to do," he admitted. "Getting things ready for the gathering, did a run, and when I came back it was almost sun up, and I decided to indulge myself."

"With work?" She dared him to dispute his earlier fabrication.

"And a little pleasure," he retaliated. "I enjoy your company. Sue me."

"You've barely spent any time with me," she countered as

she set off. Luc fell into step with her easily, moving to her left so he was between her and the street.

"And I'm rectifying that oversight. Give a guy a break," he teased.

"You don't need a break." He didn't. Luc Danes might be getting a ration of crap from the pack right now, but they'd get over it, and then the females would be lining up. His very well earned reputation had been the grist of rumors for years. Enough that even she, who didn't tend to gossip, heard enough about it.

Even if she hadn't, then Bishop's and Duke's reactions revealed a great deal. Bishop played up the rumor, but he'd caved on it when she'd pointed out the stupidity. No, he didn't want Luc around her. Big brothers were such a pain in the ass.

"Do I get to ask what you do on days for you?"

"You can ask," she told him.

"But that doesn't mean you'll answer."

"Nope," she said, popping the "p."

He chuckled. "Do you like being difficult?"

"Am I being difficult?" She tilted her head as their gazes locked briefly.

"To be determined," he answered slowly.

"Nice," she said with a grin.

The walk to the store was companionable; Luc didn't try to fill the silence. Definitely a mark in his favor. The grocer was open, fresh fruit in the stands outside, and the interior smelled like coffee and fresh bread.

Luc snagged a basket and followed her back to the meat counter, where she examined the steaks. He seemed to prefer the ribeyes, but she was much more into the New York strips. She loaded six of each into the basket, and Luc frowned.

"You don't have to get ribeyes just for me." The hint of pleasure in his voice decried the protest.

"Didn't say I was getting them for you," she countered, and his smile faded a notch. But her lips twitched as she turned, and he was a half step behind her as she headed for the bakery and the fresh bread. The fact her stomach had been snarling since she caught the first whiff told her she'd need a few of the crusty loaves.

He added another two loaves to three she'd chosen, and when she angled toward the eggs, he grinned. "Do you want anything else to go with it? Potatoes or fruit?"

Charlie considered her options. At this point, she was salivating. Her normal breakfast had been three hours earlier, and the anticipation of the meal turned her stomach into knots.

"An onion and some potatoes, I think. I can do fried potatoes."

"On it." He scooted toward the produce while she glanced over the egg selection. With three of them, an eighteen count would make plenty of scrambled eggs. She grabbed some cheese while she was at it, and then snagged some picante sauce on her way to meet Luc by the register. He already had their items stacked up and then helped take the ones from her.

Before she could pull out her credit card, he'd already offered his. At her scowl, he grinned. "The least I can do for the ribeyes that aren't for me."

Rolling her eyes, she spread her hands. "Thank you."

"No," he murmured, giving another of those speculative looks. "Thank you."

Her wolf shivered from nose to tail, and all but wanted to roll over. Pivoting away, she clasped her hands behind her back and dug her nails into her palms. No, they weren't going to lie down at his feet. Enough of that.

Luc was the pack Second. They had a job to do.

That was *it*. They could get along, and he seemed to be making a real effort. Nothing more.

Bags of food in hand, Luc joined her and concern had replaced his speculative expression. "All good?"

"Yes, just starving."

"Well, we have the food. I don't suppose you'll let me help you cook."

Seriously?

A growl teased at the back of her throat. "Do you know how to cook?"

"You might be surprised," he informed her. "You know Brett's father is a chef."

True. She did know that. "If you burn one of my pans…"

"I'll replace it."

"Agreed."

The street was still relatively quiet, though she caught sight of the Emerson teen jogging with his golden retriever. Big dumb dog—sweet as hell, but dumber than a box of rocks —always barked at her like mad. Today was no exception.

Luc rumbled next to her, and the retriever shut up. She smacked his arm, and he raised his eyebrows.

"Be nice, he's a sweet dog."

"Uh huh. And you definitely have more dominance than him, don't let them do that."

"It doesn't bother me." It never had. Most of the dogs in the area liked her, even the big barky one. "It's actually kind of funny."

Luc snorted.

A half-a-block from the brownstone, he asked, "Is your company going to object to you bringing another man in for breakfast?" His tone was light. Too light.

"It's my house," she reminded him. "But I do expect you to be polite."

Yes, she was being a bit of a snot. Bishop and Luc both deserved it.

At the steps, she said, "Do you want me to take the bags so you can get whatever your mother sent you down here for?"

He blinked once. "What?" The surprise lasted all of a split-second before he went. "Oh. Yeah. Okay." He handed her two of the bags. "One sec."

So it wasn't a lie? She tilted her head, tracking him as he went to his truck. He opened the passenger door and lifted out a cake carrier. His mother sent a cake.

Guilt swarmed through her. If she'd actually sent the cake, then what had been the lie?

When he joined her, he said, "Apple dumpcake—my favorite."

Her stomach grumbled loudly, and Luc's smile grew.

"All yours for the bargain basement price of a breakfast invitation."

Laughter bubbled up through her. "Since you were already invited to a breakfast you purchased the items for, I think I'm getting off cheap."

"You're having me for breakfast," he said slowly. "That's invaluable to me."

Uh huh.

Their gazes locked for a moment, and her wolf bristled. She held his stare, but his smile grew lazy. "We can stand out here all day, or you can invite me inside. The dumpcake isn't going to eat itself."

True.

She dipped her lashes, but didn't miss the deepening of his smile as she led him up the stairs. Unlocking the door, she pushed it open. "Come on through."

He waited for her to open the mudroom door after she relocked the front door, his expression steeled. Poor dear, he was determined to be on his best behavior. Once she pushed it inside, Bishop called, "You took your sweet—what the hell is he doing here?"

"Your morning guest is your brother?" Luc growled.

"Yes," she answered as innocently and earnestly as possible. "Is that a problem?"

Bishop was on his feet, and he and Luc split a glare.

Oh.

This should be fun.

CHAPTER 9

*C*harlie had four brothers, and Luc wondered how much she would notice if he removed one of them permanently while he finished dicing up the potatoes. She had the onions grilling on the stove, and the steaks were loaded onto a tray, the broiler heated and ready to go. While she whipped eighteen eggs for scrambled, Bishop leaned against the counter with his arms folded.

"Move," she ordered him, and bumped him with her hip after she dropped one whisk in the sink. "If you're not going to help, go sit at the table." The kitchen was one huge square with a four top walnut cherry table in the corner next to two tall windows looking into a boxy garden.

What surprised Luc even more was the fact there were herbs growing in that garden in long earthen tubs along with a small table and two chairs, probably for those days when she wanted to sit out there. It was still small and cramped. At least the walls were thick, since there were brownstones on either side of them. He couldn't hear the neighbors.

That would drive him mad.

With more than half the potatoes chopped, he carried the

cutting board over and scraped them into the pan, where they began to sizzle almost immediately. She danced around him and set the mixing bowl to the side before adding another round of seasoning to the steaks. He peered the container, but it didn't have a label.

Bishop grunted. "I guess I'll make more coffee." Luc had taken great pleasure in pouring himself the last cup *after* he made sure Charlie didn't want it.

"Being useful would be good," Luc told him over his shoulder.

"I'm often useful," Bishop countered. "I've been useful for far longer than you've been around."

"I don't know about that, maybe you need some extra circuits if you have time to come harass your sister." Specifically after Luc told them to lay off of her.

"I made time for *my* sister," Bishop stated, his tone edging toward a challenge. "What's your excuse? Don't you have a gathering to prepare for?"

Charlie nudged Luc away from the pan and used a wooden spoon to stir the potatoes. "Can you finish the rest? I can watch these."

"Of course," he murmured, letting his hand linger against her back as he moved around her. There was something about seeing her in the cutoff denim shorts and tank top with her bare feet that made her all the more accessible. The armor she wore in her business suit was absent. The hair up in a ponytail bared her gorgeous neck and at the same time, gave her a more innocent and youthful air. The rest of her though? It was all sensuous curves and smooth skin.

He set the cutting board back on the island and met Bishop's stony glare. Oh, big brother really didn't like his presence.

Too. Fucking. Bad.

"Speaking of the gathering, since you have so much free

time, I'll let Pierce know you can run extra circuits at the national park. We need to mark the trails so the kids don't venture into the open areas."

After sliding the coffee pot in and hitting the button, Bishop nearly glared at him. A vein throbbed in his forehead. Irritation discolored his scent, but he couldn't quite hold Luc's eyes. Though, he was trying. "You still didn't explain what you're doing here."

"At the moment, I'm cutting up potatoes because your sister is cooking us breakfast."

After clearing his throat, Bishop said, "You know that's not what I meant."

"Boys," Charlie said, a warning invading her cheerful tone as she padded over to pull another pan down. Probably for the eggs. "Behave. Or you can both leave."

The light reminder had Luc smirking. "I'm just answering your brother's questions."

"Uh huh," she retorted, raising both of her eyebrows. "You're also baiting him. Play innocent with someone else."

"Ha," Bishop chortled.

"Shut up, Bish. You're worse."

He growled, and Luc glared at him. Sister or not, Bishop didn't get to growl at Charlie.

"Fine." Her brother lifted his hands in surrender. "I'll behave. Thank you for making breakfast, Charlie. Coffee is almost ready."

The last of the potatoes were ready, and he made it over to where she was scraping out the crisped first round into a paper towel lined bowl. Then he tossed the rest in and snagged the wooden spoon from her before she shifted to slide the steaks into the broiler.

The food smells beginning to wreath the room made his mouth water, especially when the steaks began to sizzle. It was almost no time before the scrambled eggs and cheese were loaded onto plates and the steaks came out. Luc spooned generous amounts of potatoes to her plate and his. Bishop could get his own. At the kitchen table, he waited for her to sit then took one of the chairs next to her. Amusement filtered through him when Bishop sat opposite him.

Yes, big brother really didn't want him here.

Charlie was an excellent cook, and the steaks were close to perfection. He gave it a few beats before he asked, "So what services are you supposed to be rendering for your sister that required a steak breakfast?" If Charlie needed help, he'd be glad to take over.

"Apparently the shower in my guest bath isn't working right," Charlie answered, her tone indulgent. So was it really broken, or was she just letting Bishop do something to be useful. It wasn't that unusual for dominants to need to help the more submissive wolves. Caretaking was just another facet of their personalities.

But Charlie wasn't totally submissive or dominant. Shadows switched, though when and how wasn't always clear. They just did it. She could probably explain it to him, but that might be a rude question so early in their acquaintance.

"Water pressure isn't great, and the showerhead leaks," Bishop admitted. "I'll go pick up the pieces and get it repaired after breakfast."

"Thank you, Bish," she murmured, and the softness in her expression and tone pulled at his wolf. He cut a look toward her brother who sighed a little. It was the most submissive Luc had seen Charlie be, and he couldn't determine if he liked it or not.

More toward not, because her behavior seemed triggered by her brother. The face he frowned as he focused on his plate, and the wolf across from him, quieted. Submissives could do that, too. They could quiet irritated dominants.

Keeping that in mind, Luc and his own wolf settled. If nothing else, they could contain their reactions.

Fighting with her brother was not what he'd come here to do. "Let me know if you need a hand," Luc said instead. "Though we have work to do, as well."

Charlie's green eyes held a tint of gold around the edges, and he could almost scent the fur of her wolf, even though nothing else about her changed. "Yes, a phone call to make." She glanced at her watch. "It's still early there."

"Time to go over our game plan." Then with a nod toward Bishop, he added, "Privately."

"I know," she acknowledged before finishing the last bite. Her expression was replete as she rose with her plate. After setting in the sink, she refilled her coffee cup. "I also have work to do for tomorrow. So I'll let you two chat, and I'm going to do that. When you're ready, Luc, we can move into my office."

He was ready right now, but she gave him a look and then her brother. Fine, he'd make nice with him. Still, he couldn't quite get over the picture she made balancing her coffee cup, long legs on display and the cuteness of her toes.

What the fuck? Toes are not cute. The thought stealthed its way through him as he tracked her path, until she vanished down the hall toward her sitting or living room presumably.

"Stop looking at my sister like that," Bishop ordered in a near sub-vocal voice. It wouldn't carry far, but Luc heard him loud and clear.

"Like what? She's a beautiful woman and an elegant wolf," he replied in a similar tone. There were still a few more bites of steak on his plate, and he took his time with them.

"She's not for you." Bishop set his knife and fork down and leaned forward. "She doesn't need the kind of problems you bring."

That was a new one. "What kind of problems do I

bring?" He kept his tone as idle as he could, even as his wolf bristled. Bishop was really pushing his luck. Protecting his sister was fine, constantly trying to get in Luc's face wasn't.

"You know the rumors."

"I don't care about rumors," Luc told him flatly. "Nor should you. Bullshit gossip is what packmates do as an answer to idle boredom. Which means they need more to do than spread that crap around."

"Your own mother believes it."

Didn't he know it. "*That* has been dealt with. Next."

"Luc," Bishop sighed. "Look, you're—a decent guy and a good Second. But you're everywhere, and you're vital within the pack structure, Charlie stays as far away from it as she can. Do you expect she'll be able to do that with you in hot pursuit?"

"That's a decision for her to make."

"So you're not denying you're interested."

"Only a fool wouldn't be interested," he retorted. "She's charming, intelligent, and beautiful. At the moment, however, she and I have a job to do." Anything else would just be a perk.

That didn't mean he wasn't going to give chase, but he'd already begun to get the scent of this particular hunt. He'd have to be patient. She needed to be caught before she realized she had been.

"She's not like other wolves," Bishop warned him. "You could do damage if you're not careful."

He narrowed his eyes. "Did someone hurt her?"

"Everyone has hurt her," her brother said, and he glanced toward the doorway she'd vanished through.

Frowning, Luc leaned back in the chair. "Explain."

"Not my story to tell," he answered. "That's my point. She's isolated herself here for a reason. You coming down regularly, pulling her back to the pack—that's going to force changes and confrontations."

Her mother, for one, Luc imagined. "I'm not letting anything happen to her." Period.

"That's an easy thing to say…"

"No," he said slowly. "It's not. I've never known a Shadow before. I can imagine it takes some getting used to, but then I'm not always sweetness and light either. Right now we're just Luc and Charlie. We're getting to know each other. I respect your desire to protect her, but I'm not one to be scared off easily."

Her brother sighed. "You might be Second, Luc, but she's my sister. You hurt her…"

"I have no intentions of hurting her." He'd allow the threat. Bishop was her brother. "Though I have a feeling if I do hurt her, she can more than get her own vengeance."

Bishop snorted. "That she can."

They finished their meals in silence. When Luc would have helped with the clean up, Bishop waved him out of the kitchen.

"Clean up was my job, so I'll do this, then head to the hardware store."

Fine by Luc, he left him to clean up and poured himself another cup of coffee before following his nose through the brownstone. The kitchen was all the way in the back, and a long hallway connected toward the front door and stairs that went down as well as the stairs going up.

He thought she'd be in the sitting room, but when he reached the room closest to her foyer, it was empty. The binders that had been stacked on the table were gone. Glancing around the room, he gave himself a moment to admire the layout. It was simple, but elegant. One wall had bookshelves while another boasted a fireplace. There was one long sofa and a love seat. A third wall—a half wall really

—featured a forest scene that was so visceral and real, he tried to identify it. The fact some of the trees actually looked familiar told him it was somewhere within pack lands.

The scent of her lingered in the room, but she'd likely gone to her office. He debated—up or down? Up was likely a more private domain, so rather than invade, he backtracked up the hallway and headed down the steps.

Following the sweet notes of amber and musk with hints of lemon, he traced her all the way to a corner of what was likely a basement, but she'd transformed into a perfect little study down to the desk, book shelves, and plants. Actual plants under plant lights. Probably to dissuade the gloom. She sat curled up in her desk chair, a binder open in front of her while she hugged one knee to her chest.

"There you are," he said by way of greeting.

"Yes," she murmured. "Here I am. I thought I would give you and Bishop some privacy so you could beat your chests and snarl at each other without worrying about me."

Heat licked at his face.

Amusement grew in her smile. "Never been so transparent before?"

"No," he said slowly. "And not sure I'm enjoying the feeling." Though, it was kind of sweet that she'd given them the opportunity to get it out in the open.

"Well to be fair, you're not that subtle."

That almost sounded like an insult.

"And my brother is very protective. The fact you're male and here would set him off."

"So a female sniffing after you wouldn't get the same reaction?" He meant to tease, but her slow smile intrigued the hell out of him.

"Not so far."

Yeah, his jaw might have hung a little lower. "Seriously?"

"A lady never kisses and tells, Luc. You should know

better than to ask. Would you like me to check on your previous lovers?"

He opened his mouth and then snapped it shut. Maybe that was a conversation they never needed to have. Suddenly, Bishop's warning about someone hurting her flared to mind. "If you ever want to know," he said quietly. "I'll be an open book."

"Hmm, I think on that subject, we should both remain illiterate," she said, and almost at once the playful twinkle in her eyes went guarded. "We do have to work together, and we'll do much better if we don't muddy the waters."

"Muddy waters don't frighten me, Charlie," he said, aware of the barriers she had thrown up. "But I won't make you wade into them." No, she'd leap in of her own accord. Glancing at the binders she had open, he said, "Do you need more time to finish those up before we get started?"

She gave him one slow blink, her nostrils flared and for a moment, he worried he'd pushed too far too fast. It was like she was torn between reactions. Finally, she said, "I'd like to finish this one," she answered him a slow, very deliberate tone. "I have about thirty pages left. Then we can discuss Sutter Butte."

Lifting his coffee in salute, he said, "I can do that. In fact..." He glanced at her nearly empty mug. "Why don't I get you more coffee and my notes from the truck?"

Another slow blink. "You brought notes?"

He grinned. "I'm not a total boob. Yes, I made notes. Did some brainstorming. I roamed pretty far, and I ran into my share of Lone Wolves out there, including some from Sutter Butte. Trask was a distant wolf out there, he didn't really get involved with the pack dynamics until the big upheaval Cassius instituted. He followed Claire Buckley—before she was Claire Buckley."

"The Willow Bend wolf." Gradually, Charlie relaxed.

"Exactly. He's also a pretty straightforward guy. Either way, I worked up some notes and made a few phone calls to friends. We might consider looping in an Enforcer or two, need to find someone who knows the pack well…"

"Adler might," she mused. "He's pretty much free-roaming these days as they alternate their regions."

Adler.

Suspicion prickled him. She knew an Enforcer to call right off the top of her head. Granted, Luc knew several, but he'd been a Lone Wolf. Their acquaintance was part of being on your own. Then again, she was Hudson River's business liaison and located in the city. There was a safe bet Enforcers checked in with her if they were here for any length of time in addition to checking in with Brett.

"I can call him, he said he might be in town next weekend…" She trailed off, leaving unfinished whatever she'd been about to say. "Yes, I'd like some coffee and to see your notes. I've made a few of my own."

Torn between wanting to press her for more and understanding that he skirted real boundaries here, he reached for her mug. "Well, let me go get that so you can work."

Her expression relaxed minutely, and she smiled. "Thank you."

The softness in the curve of her lips hit him like a hammer blow. He wanted to be able to do that for her all the time. Snagging her cup, he carried his own as well and got his ass out of her way. His own reactions were now all over the place.

On the one hand, he wanted to challenge her. How well did she know Adler? When she teased about females, was she being serious? Was she actually seeing someone? She didn't carry the scent of another wolf on her, and the only other wolf he could scent in her whole place was her brother.

Thankfully, said brother had absented himself by the time

Luc got to the kitchen, he rinsed out her mug and drained his own before leaving them on the counter while he ran out to the truck.

Leaving the front door unlocked, he scanned the area as he descended the steps. There was more activity and fewer cars. It looked like people had begun to get moving on their days. Sound reached him from above, and it occurred to him folks were out on their roofs, eating or spending time. The air had warmed, but it was hardly hot. If anything, it was a nice day. The perfect kind to go for a run—except he was stuck in the city where the smell of fuel and exhaust seemed pounded into the pavement.

At his truck, he pulled out the two legal pads he'd brought with them. He'd jotted notes on both, largely cause he couldn't find the first one when he went to add notes to it so pulled out the second. Then he flipped out his phone and stared at it.

Who the hell could he call to get answers?

He'd already asked enough about her to his mother. If he pushed even an inch more, they'd be pack gossip before sundown. Brett wouldn't tell him. As he'd already said, she was his to protect as well. Her family wasn't going to reveal anything. Bishop didn't even want Luc around.

The internal debate had him tossing the ideas back and forth. Finally, he texted Colby.

Luc: *Think you have time this week for a lesson and a chat?*

Colby: *You know, you better offer to buy me a nice meal or bring me flowers if we're really going to be dating.*

He snorted.

. . .

133

Luc: *I LIKE MY BODY PARTS WHERE THEY'RE AT. BUT I WILL BRING you chocolate.*

Colby: *Oh, you do love me. And sure, I've classes tomorrow, and Brett's got some stuff to do, but I should be free after lunch. How much pain is my lesson going to cause?*

Luc: *That depends. Have you been practicing since our last bout?*

THEIR LAST REAL BOUT WAS TWO WEEKS BEFORE, AND COLBY hadn't been able to shake him. The whole point of the exercise was for her to cover her scent and vanish. It was a difficult trick for natural-born wolves much less latent ones. Still, she needed the practice because in the event of a real threat—healers shouldn't be fighting. They fought and covered her exit.

Colby: *PAINFUL THEN. GOT IT. I'LL BE SURE TO DRESS FOR THE occasion.*

Luc: *I'll try to go easy on you.*

Colby: *No you won't, but then I don't want you to. Any clues on what you want to talk about?*

Luc: *Tomorrow. See you at 1?*

HER RESPONSE WAS A COUPLE OF THUMBS UP EMOJIS AND ONE sticking its tongue out at him. Chuckling, he pocketed the phone. Colby might not know anything, but she noticed far more than they sometimes gave her credit for—largely because she didn't just pay attention to moods through scent or based her interactions off general pack dynamics. She listened to everything they said, the nuances of their behavior, and she was observant as hell.

Probably because she'd spent so much time working toward being a nurse and had hospital experience. She'd certainly been able to read him when most of the morons around her fled. Then again, she'd soothed his wounded wolf, too. There had been something about Colby from the beginning. Literally... it was her scent he'd been tracking when he'd gotten hit by that car.

Stupid curiosity on his part, but then he found her anyway, and she took him back to Hudson River where she met Brett. The rest, as they say, was history.

Coming home hadn't been high on his priorities before the accident, and after he was home, he couldn't imagine being anywhere else. Even the restlessness invading him now had less to do with wanting to be gone than wanting some new challenge.

Brett had given him one.

Shaking off the distractions, he headed back inside. He locked the door up and retrieved the coffee before making his way back to her office; she had a phone to her ear as he circled the brick column.

"No," she said. "When I spoke to Giovanni, he was very explicit on the terms of the contract—but they are fishing for information about what happened in Three Rivers."

"Are they now?" Brett's voice carried, but Charlie waved Luc toward the chairs opposite her desk. "What did he ask you specifically?"

"What, if any, changes were we considering in light of the unfortunate, unsanctioned actions of a wolf who was clearly not in his right mind."

Well, that was direct. Luc shook his head. The wolf in question had nearly killed Luciana Barrows, the co-Alpha of Three Rivers. Another unheard of rarity. A pack could have *two* Alphas if they were closely bonded, but it hadn't happened in Luc's lifetime, and as far as he knew, there wasn't a wolf alive currently who'd seen it before.

Three Rivers had been downplaying it for the moment while the packs decided on what they would do with regard to the rogue Centurion. The troublesome wolf was dead, however, so they had time.

"I take it you told him those are not concerns he should be discussing with you," Brett sounded certain of that answer.

"Quite," Charlie answered with a faint grin. "I'll handle the contracts, you do the politics."

"My kind of girl," Brett said with a chuckle. "If you run into that again, conference Luc in. They shouldn't be doing that to you in the first place. If you can't get him, get me."

"I can do that, but it was early…"

Luc raised his brows.

"I don't care," Brett assured her.

"Agreed," Luc said, and there was silence from the other end of the phone.

"Well, I see you made it into the city." Brett's voice held all kinds of speculation.

"We're going over our Sutter Butte approach," Charlie said, covering for him. "You seemed eager for us to get started on the project."

"True," their Alpha mused. "I did. You are returning later this evening, Luc?"

"That was the plan," he said drily. Brett was well aware where Luc's interests lay. Had already delivered his warning.

"Huh, be gentle with him, Charlie. He prefers the fist to the back of the head approach to negotiation."

She laughed. "He'll be fine. He's already learned a few things about coaxing."

Though she was smiling, it didn't quite reach her eyes. One step forward, two steps back.

Patience, he counseled himself. Patience.

His wolf clawed at him. They didn't want her to be uneasy around them. But the only way they earned her trust was to let her be herself and to not push. No matter how aggravating.

"Glad to hear it. You kids behave. Oh—and sorry about yesterday."

"Hmm," Charlie hummed. "You're lucky I like you."

"Yes, I know. But he was worried, and in all fairness, he promised he wasn't going there to pick a fight."

"He didn't, we actually had fun. While I would prefer to not have my runs interrupted, it was nice to see him."

"Good," Brett said. "Glad to hear it. Keep me updated."

"We will."

"Later," Luc said a beat before Brett hung up. "All good?"

She set her phone down and nodded. "Yes… so… let's see those notes."

Business. It was what would keep them tied together, so he settled his wolf and nudged her coffee toward her before setting the legal pads on the desk. "Keep in mind, this is really just some free thinking on my part…"

"Don't challenge to a battle of wits? It's not fair to the unarmed wolf?" She read from his first two lines.

"Like I said, free thinking."

"Oh, boy."

CHAPTER 10

Sunday proved a longer day than Charlie anticipated. Luc and Bishop spent most of the day at her brownstone. Long enough for Bishop to run out and fetch lunch when he went to the hardware store. When he worked on repairing the guest shower, he broke a few pieces of tile and ended up having to run out on a second trip for new ones. The fact he couldn't find matching tiles meant he ended up purchasing a whole new wall pattern and had to replace all of it.

Luc got involved, determined to speed her brother along, or maybe just irritate him into leaving. However, the hilarity of it all kept her in stitches. They were a pair of grumpy wolves snarking on each other while getting in the way. Luc and Bishop seemed to be building an antagonistic relationship, but they were so alike in so many ways that they kept agreeing with each other. Which in and of itself amused her. Still, the fact those little moments of accords seemed to frustrate them entertained her even more.

By the time dinner rolled around, she conceded that her guests weren't going anywhere anytime soon. They were mostly done with the repairs to the tile that now apparently involved a discussion on changing the floor tile so that it matched the shower tile better.

In self-defense, Charlie ordered pizza. It was an indulgence that she didn't allow herself that often. When she'd gone the college route, she ate pizza five times a week. She'd been addicted to the stuff, though she wouldn't admit it to anyone under pain of death.

So now when she ordered pizza, it had to be for a special occasion, or, as in this case, because she had work to finish and didn't have time to fix a meal for all three of them. Paying for the pizza almost turned into another fight, until she informed them she'd paid for it when she ordered it. That earned her twin, disgruntled glares and raked the fur on her wolf backwards.

Protective she could indulge, but the bossiness grated. After the pizzas finally arrived, they settled into the sitting room, and the guys turned on the sports channel, which to be honest, was never on in her brownstone. Fortunately, all she had to do was eat pizza and read through her binders, which she did and gleefully ignored them while they yelled about sports.

Shockingly, they didn't like the same teams. It was all she could do not to roll her eyes.

IT WAS LATE WHEN CHARLIE FINALLY THREW THEM OUT. Entertainingly enough, and without any kind of subtlety, Bishop and Luc kept trying to make the other one go first. On the one hand, Luc's attentiveness was sweet. On the other hand, Luc's attention was also dangerous.

Bishop's protective instincts told him to not leave her alone with Luc. While she appreciated the fact that her big brother was *being* her big brother, she didn't need, or frankly want, his protection. The struggle to maintain a balance between the two while they were present grew more and more aggravating. That frustration tainted her entertainment.

"It's late," she told them both firmly. "Why don't you both leave together?" It wasn't a question. In fact, she had already opened the mudroom door to encourage them both to leave.

"I know it's getting late, but..." Bishop began.

No, it wasn't getting late. "It is late," she said. "I have work tomorrow. I have meetings tomorrow. I have more binders to finish reviewing. You've both taken up enough of my time today, and while I thank you for fixing the bathroom — after you broke it — I really need you to go now."

Luc went curiously silent. He glanced from Charlie to her brother, and then back again. Finally, he nodded. That was it. He went and grabbed his things and came back and motioned Bishop towards the door. Bishop still resisted, until Luc made it in order.

Charlie had never been fond of that particular piece of hierarchy, even though she accepted it because they were wolves. Dominance meant something. Typically, they didn't try to throw it around at each other and force the issue. The higher up you went in the pack, the more likely it was to happen.

Resentment simmered in Bishop's eyes, and Charlie shook her head. The need to soothe over the rough edges eddied out from her wolf. "Come on, we had a good time today. I don't even hate the fact that you were here all day. Or that you came and interrupted my run yesterday. But it's time. I'm fine. I will *be* fine. You have done your due diligence and duty."

A pained expression crossed his face. "Charlie, I didn't just come here to do a duty. You do realize that, right? You're my baby sister. I'm allowed to worry and care about you."

Luc glanced between them again and this time, he said, "She's fine. And you did get to spend time with her. I got to spend time with her."

"Yes, and you interrupted my day with my sister," Bishop added with fresh displeasure, even as he walked towards the door.

"I didn't know you were going to be here. And I didn't intend to be here all day. I stayed because you broke the bathroom..." Luc defended himself, and her brother immediately reacted with a scowl.

Charlie gritted her teeth and clenched her fists. Her wolf bristled. The growl that escaped jerked both men up, and they turned to stare.

She was well aware that her eyes had likely bled gold as her wolf glared out at them. And while she may wax back and forth between submissive to dominant, the dominant side was in full ascendance and as aggravated as she was with the continuance of this argument.

"Get out."

Bishop was very familiar of this side of her personality, and he had dealt with it probably the best of any of her siblings. Frankly, he dealt with her better than anyone in her family or pack. He lifted his hands nodded his head.

"Sorry, Charlie. You're right; I'll call you later this week. I love you." And then he was out the door.

Luc on the other hand paused. Head tilted, he studied her. Her wolf glowered at him, and realization swept over her that his wolf met her glower and simply stared back. The blue in his eyes gave way to gold, and the measuring look weighing in them sent another frisson of awareness along her spine as woman and wolf refused to back down.

What she was doing was openly challenging, she was well aware of it, however, this was *her* house. They had invaded it and spent their day filling it with noisy arguments and repairs. While she had enjoyed herself, it was time for him to go.

"Okay." That was it, one word from Luc, and he inclined his head, though his wolf never backed down. Hers fully expected him to answer the challenge, and when he didn't, it undercut her irritation and anger, and she settled almost immediately.

When Charlie lowered her eyes, she said, "I'm sorry..."

"You don't have to be. You are absolutely right. I'm being selfish, I enjoyed myself here today. We got a good plan for dealing with Sutter Butte. And you're going to have your assistant look into setting up a call for us this week?"

She nodded once.

"Then I'm gonna wait for that. I'd like to do the call with you here or have you come back up to Hudson River, which-ever is easier for your schedule."

Surprise flickered through her. This wasn't what they discussed.

"Why do you want me with you? We can just conference the calls together."

"We could. But that's not what I want to do. I think we work well as a team so far — we still don't know the little things. Like just now when I pushed too far too fast. I need to know when to pull back, and I need to know when to push forward. I can just do it my way, but that runs the risk of upsetting you. Or if I'm not going far enough in your opin-ion. At the same time, you need to learn to use your words."

The reproach in his voice snapped at her like a rolled towel being used to score a stinging hit. "Excuse me?"

"Your words, Charlie. You're an intelligent woman, and you're very gifted speaker. You could simply have said, I'm done, gentleman. I need my space back. It is time for both of you to go."

She pretty much *had* said that.

"You waited until you were so thoroughly frustrated that it became an issue. You need to do it *before* it's an issue. Now, I'm going to work on understanding when you aren't playing anymore. I'm going to listen and try to hear you better."

Her earlier surprise turned into shock. He wasn't getting angry over the fact that she gone from docile, friendly, and conciliatory to aggravated and challenging. Instead, he made plans. Luc Danes confused her, and that was not a good feeling.

"I'll do my best to be more explicit next time when I need you to go," she told him. He nodded, gave her a smile, and then left.

It was only after she got up to get ready for bed and lay soaking in a hot tub with her head back in the room scented of vanilla and wildflowers, that she realized she just committed to having Luc return to the brownstone and spend another day. Because she promised him next time, she would be clearer when she was done.

Sneaky little bastard.

Monday and Tuesday flew by. Charlie spent most of it in meetings, going over changes from the quarterly reports and dealing with the delegation of her duties. In light of the upcoming travel she faced to help Luc with the negotiations, she needed to have people in place to handle the day-to-day she would be missing. Not that she couldn't do a portion of her job from the road, but her focus would be split. Better to have someone on the ground here that she could direct.

Debbie was amazing. There was no doubt about it. But Debbie couldn't do *her job*, which included helping Charlie manage all her tasks while also doing Charlie's job. So that meant she had to pick someone from her senior staff. A task more daunting than she expected.

In fact, by the end of Tuesday, she hadn't determined who she wanted to tap for the job and was beginning to think she might end up involving Brett.

That would thrill him. While Brett was more than capable of handling the day-to-day, he had tapered back his duties severely since meeting Colby. And why shouldn't he? Taking care of his mate and then the pack were tied as his first priorities.

Colby had her own issues that required Brett's attention. Not the least of which was that she was a latent turned full wolf and still becoming accustomed to her wolf, while also proving to be a capable healer. Making a note on her calendar to bring this up with Brett, Charlie also listed the three top candidates for filling in for her while she was gone. He'd have to sign off on her choice anyway.

This might all end up being moot, as she didn't have firm plans in place to travel *yet*. The call with Sutter Butte had been scheduled for Thursday. She would drive up to Hudson River, and Luc promised her dinner. She told him that wasn't necessary, however, he insisted.

While his continued interest in her was sweet and very flattering, she worried he was beginning to expect more from her than she would be able to offer. Worse, she worried about the fact that she was even considering *what* she could offer him.

Speaking of troubling issues, Duke had been calling her. He was annoyed that she spent so much time with Bishop and not with him. So he was demanding his equal time. Twins for brothers was aggravating. She told Duke she would see him at the gathering, but she really did have a huge workload.

He asked about joining her for her run on Saturday, but

she insisted that she preferred to go alone. If Adler was in town, she would likely take him with her, and the last thing she wanted or needed was her brother showing up. Duke said he might be able to swing coming by and picking her up for dinner after, and she groaned. It took her an hour to get Duke off the phone, and no amount of placating was changing his mind. She was going to kill Bishop. All she could do was ask Brett to *not* tell her brothers where she went this time.

Her mother was also a growing concern. Adele Miller had left her another message.

"Charlotte, when I call you, I expect a response. I do not call to speak to your voicemail. I do not call to leave messages that go unanswered. Respect, young lady, I know I taught you respect and consideration. The gathering is coming, your brothers insist you are aware of this, but I would like to hear it from *you*. I would like you to participate in the run. *Don't* make me send your father."

On the one hand, the inherent warning in every single word of her mother's message just made her shake her head. The fact that she threatened to send her father to get her, however, made Charlie laugh. The simple truth was it tempted her to not answer the message at all, just so Mom would send Dad up to get her. Then she could spend time with Daddy without Mom breathing down her neck.

Sometimes she wondered if she was being unfair to her mother. Sitting in her kitchen, drinking a cup of tea and eating a piece of the apple dumpcake that Luc brought her, she turned over in her mind the idea that Adele really did want what was best for her children — Charlie included. But Adele was very set in her ways. In Adele's world, there was one way to do something. Everything else was wrong. It didn't matter if Charlie was happy, or if she was very well suited to her job, or if she pursued it with a great vigor and enjoyed the day-to-day running of the company. What mattered to Adele was her persistent belief that Charlie was wasting her talents.

Charlie had studied and apprenticed as a Hunter. All of them had. It was impossible not to spend time learning the profession—not with Mom calling the shots and so dedicated to her calling. Granted Dad wasn't a Hunter — he didn't need to be. He was more the nurturer in the family, while Adele took on the more aggressive energy. Daddy was content to let Adele set the rules. Bishop and Duke thrived as Hunters. They were born to look after the individual members of the pack and to provide security. Sullivan and Noah were little different, and a little more fly by the seat of their pants, but being Hunters was better than being unemployed in their world, so they went for it. Charlie didn't hate it — in fact, she'd proven capable to the task of it. She was meticulous, and that meant she covered every base.

But she never *wanted* to be a Hunter. She never wanted to serve that way. And it was difficult to explain to Adele that while she could be dominant, she also needed the time to be submissive, and as a Hunter she *couldn't* be submissive. She would always have to have her dominance in ascendance, and that would drive her wolf mad.

She would be forever grateful to Hatcher for putting her on the path that she was on. A path that led her serve the pack and remain true to our own nature, while not having to deal with the fallout when wolves around her realized the discrepancies in her behavior. More than one had figured out they could manipulate her by manipulating her wolf. Freeing herself from those bullies had been an onerous task, and since Brett became Alpha, none had dared to try it. That didn't mean someone wouldn't.

It was that type of manipulation that worried Bishop and Duke. They'd seen it happen before, and they'd beaten the wolf within an inch of his life. In fact, he'd gone Lone Wolf not long after, and she hadn't seen or heard from him since.

And enough of that...

She had plenty of work to do, and she didn't need to be focusing on the dark past right now. The gathering was growing ever closer. The call with Sutter Butte was right around the corner. And there was every chance that she and Luc would end up having to fly there, which meant more time with him in enclosed spaces. The forced proximity was going to be enough to juggle...

Then again, his reactions on Sunday suggested he could handle it.

The big question was, could she?

THURSDAY, SHE LEFT WORK EARLY ENOUGH TO GET TO HER CAR and head out of the city. Debbie had been shocked when she'd had her clear the afternoon. Leaving early for her monthly check-in with Brett was one thing, but she had done that last week. Pack business was all she told Debbie.

"I'll be on my phone, but I have that conference call, so if I am slow to respond"

"Don't worry about it," Debbie told her. "Go, and try to have some fun while you're up there, yeah?"

Charlie snorted. "I'm going to be up there late most likely." Luc wanted to fix her dinner. "When is my first meeting tomorrow?"

"I moved it to ten," Debbie said with a smirk. "So you can come in a little late if you need it."

"This is why I love you," Charlie replied, her smile growing. "Treat yourself to your favorite lunch deli on me."

"I usually do," Debbie called as Charlie headed for the executive elevator. "See you tomorrow."

She took the subway to where she parked, and it took a few minutes to get the car out of the garage. Once she was in the driver's seat, she sent Luc a message that she was on her way.

His response was swift.

LUC: *HAD TO DEAL WITH SOME HOOLIGANS. WILL BE ONE HOUR late. Key under mat. Let yourself in.*

SHE STARED AT THE MESSAGE FOR A BEAT THEN SENT: *ARE YOU sure? We can reschedule. Call if problem.*

LUC: *VERY SURE. I WANT TO SEE YOU. I HAVE DINNER PLANNED. Just need a little time to crack some heads.*

SHE CHUCKLED AT THE NOTE.

CHARLIE: *ALL RIGHT, I'LL TAKE MY TIME THEN. IF YOU'RE GOING to be later, let me know.*

LUC: *IF THEY MAKE ME ANY LATER, I'LL CRACK MORE THAN THEIR heads. Drive safe.*

THE CORNERS OF HER MOUTH CURLED HIGHER, AND SHE SET the phone in the holder on the dash and queued up the Bluetooth so she could listen to some music. She could probably dictate notes or listen to a recitation of a report, but she felt like music today.

She and her wolf were both a little on edge. Whether it was for the impending call or dinner, she didn't know. Hell, it could be about her mother and the gathering, or even Duke's insistence he wanted to run with her.

The latest Pink song blaring out of the radio had enough beat to help soothe her wolf. Maybe it was Luc's insistence on a specific time frame for being late.

He could have just said late, but no, he was clear. An hour. He intended to be no later than that, and that kind of attention to detail ruffled her fur for some reason.

It was a *good* thing. Why would it agitate her?

Ugh, at this point, everything agitated her.

Enough. Focus on the music and the drive.

It gave her and her wolf something to do.

OF ALL THE DAYS TO SAIL THROUGH TRAFFIC, SHE MADE THE drive in almost record time. She followed the GPS directions to Luc's address and pulled into his empty driveway. The house itself was tucked back away from the road, surrounded by trees with a small creek audible through them, it was —perfect.

It offered the picture of isolation, but it really wasn't that far. As she retrieved her duffle with her change of clothes, she tilted her head and listened.

Birds chirped, and there was the usual scamperings of smaller forest dwellers. Another curiosity, you'd think the little beings wouldn't want to be so close to so many predators. Then again, very few of them hunted squirrels.

She'd had one once.

Blegh.

Never again.

After slipping the strap over her shoulder, she tugged off her heels and tossed them back in the car. Luc didn't have any kind of pathway to his front door, and she didn't feel like cleaning grass and dirt off the shoes.

Thumb hovering over the lock on her keychain, she hesitated. It was a habit to lock it, even when she was on pack lands. Yet, Luc was right to give her an odd stare. What made sense in the city was not necessarily ideal for here.

She made it all the way to the porch before she clicked the button. She couldn't leave it unlocked. It just—ugh—it would drive her nuts. The key for the house was under the mat, and she pulled it out, but when she tried it on the door, she found it wasn't locked.

Why would he...?

Then the corners of her mouth turned up. Of course he didn't lock his doors. The pack wasn't going to just wander into his place without invitation. Jerk.

Still, she chuckled as she tucked the key back under the mat and went inside.

The scent of him wrapped around her like a blanket, and her wolf and she went still.

The whole house smelled of him. Of course it did. This was his home. After forcing herself to take several deep breaths, Charlie and her wolf continued into his place. It was done with rich hardwood floors everywhere. The furniture was leather in his living room, but his kitchen had a cozy little nook with an L shaped bench around the table. The kitchen itself was done up in sunshine yellow, and it was so bright and warm, her earlier trepidation fled.

His kitchen was nice.

She set her purse on the table and then pulled out her phone. No new messages from him. Giving herself some time to acclimate, she checked her email. Then she checked in with Debbie. All told, it took her about twenty minutes to deal with one minor issue.

Finally, she texted Luc.

CHARLIE: *I'M HERE. DO YOU MIND IF I MAKE COFFEE?*
   Luc: *Make yourself at home. Already on my way back.*

OH GOOD, HE GOT DONE SOONER THAN HE EXPECTED. IT TOOK her a minute to locate the coffee and the filters, but she got a pot of coffee going, then snagged her duffle and ventured deeper into his place to find somewhere to get out of her business suit. She'd be much more comfortable with this whole thing if she were in jeans and a t-shirt.

CHAPTER 11

*H*e pulled up in front of Harris Ryder's house, the young man was the last of the teens he had to drop off. Ryder didn't get out of the truck right away.

"Are you waiting for an invitation?" Luc asked him pointedly. "Or for me to physically throw you out?"

"I'm trying to work up to an apology," the kid admitted. The fact he owned his actions didn't surprise Luc in the slightest. Ryder might be stubborn and determined, but he wasn't an idiot. "I know I messed up."

"Do your friends know?" Now, Luc was curious. If the boy was genuinely working his way up to an apology, he wanted to know why.

"Probably not," Ryder admitted. "They don't tend to ask a lot of questions."

"Then maybe they aren't the right kind of friends for you." It bore some thinking about. "You need people willing to challenge you. If those guys aren't, and they are following you like sheep, then you have two problems."

Squinting at him, Ryder raised his brows. The nose ring

drove Luc to distraction. The flash of a gold piercing made him want to rip the damn thing out. Shrapnel was not a fashion statement. No wolf would ever do that to their body. Then again, those holes would heal up too quickly, so even if a wolf wanted to give it a shot, they wouldn't have to live with the mistake for long.

"They're not bad guys," Ryder defended them. "They're fun to do things with."

"But they never stop you, even when you know you're making a stupid decision." This was a guess, but a pretty solid one based on the way his pupils flared.

"Not really," he admitted. "Most of the time, they just go along with it. We make a game out of it and have fun…"

"Until you get busted, and everyone gets grounded—again." Because they'd been busted at the sawmill, adding *art* to it. Some of the pieces were actually impressive, the problem lay in the fact it had been marked off-limits and they knew it, as well as being a historical landmark they defaced.

There were at least four wolves who were about to find every hour of their free time occupied by the Hunters, when they weren't in school or with their parents. Ryder, however, was an altogether different problem. He was human. His parents were human. They were not officially pack. Hudson River didn't have human packmates, not officially, but they had humans under their protection.

Maybe that should change. Willow Bend had human packmates.

As it stood now, they had to trust his parents to enforce his discipline. The Hunters couldn't, and short of Brett having a chat with them, there wasn't much Luc could do to enforce it either.

"So I've probably screwed things up for them, haven't I?"

"They screwed things up for themselves. They weren't

supposed to go to the sawmill, they certainly weren't supposed to hit it with graffiti."

"But it was my idea..."

"I don't care," Luc told him, and he kept his tone even and blunt. Ryder needed to face facts. "You made a bad decision. That's on you. They made a worse decision, not only did they not try to stop you, they followed you into that action. Now, you'll see them at school, but they have lost all privileges. There will be no more escapades, because they will be too busy..."

"What about me?"

"That's a question you should be asking yourself." Luc was at a loss. He had suggestions for Brett, but he had little authority here.

"Why don't I get the same punishment?" The kid was tapping a foot while drumming his hands against his thighs, there wasn't much sound—yet it was still present. A swishing pop of noise. "I *did* it. I'm the reason they were there."

"And it's eating you up that they are going to be punished, and you're not?"

The kid twisted to stare at him. "Yes. I'm seventeen, not stupid. That makes no sense."

"You're also human," he reminded him.

"Which means I'm nothing to the pack..."

"No, it means you are under our protection. But you are *not* pack. If you were pack, Ryder—your ass would have been sent to the Hunters six years ago, and you would have spent every summer training under them."

Ryder's eyes widened. Then he scowled. "So why haven't I? Because I'm human? That's racist."

"Yeah, kid," Luc agreed with him. "It is..." Because he was a dominant, in every way that counted save one. "Have you called Ms. Miller?" Charlie had given him her card.

He sighed. "It's some stupid office job opportunity. That's not what I want to do"

"It's an opportunity to work with a highly placed lieutenant in the pack and to do work *for* the pack. Or are you too good to do that kind of work?" He glared at him.

Hesitating, Ryder shifted sideways in the seat to look at him. "Seriously? I thought—you know—just some accountant or something."

He took one look at Charlie and saw accountant? Was the kid blind? "It's your choice. You have an opportunity. You can take advantage of it and prove yourself productive and worthwhile, or you can keep acting out and isolating yourself as the wolves who want to follow you are left strewn in the wake of your decisions."

Head down, Ryder swallowed hard. "Do you think—I mean I know that there might be some process to go through that—I could really be part of the pack someday?"

"I don't know," Luc told him honestly. "Do you think you can be a part of the pack?"

"I want to be."

"Then prove it." He held his gaze for a beat before the kid glanced away and nodded. "Now get out, I'm going to be late, and I have a date."

The little snot laughed. "Now you sound like the white rabbit."

"Well you're not Alice, so off with you…"

He pushed open the door and then climbed out, but hesitated another beat before glancing back. "If I wanted to go back to the sawmill and help clean up the damage and fix it, do I have to get permission?"

"Yes."

"Can I have permission?"

Drumming his fingers against the steering wheel, Luc debated it. "I'll call Pierce. When he picks the crew to clean it,

I'll tell him you want to be a part of it. Don't fuck up." Pierce wouldn't put up with it, and if he screwed off on the Hunter —well, there went that particular opportunity. "Call Ms. Miller."

"I will. I promise." The kid shut the door and started up the walk toward his door, and Luc sighed.

After lowering the window, he called, "Harris?"

"Yeah?" The kid glanced back at him.

"Stay out of trouble, pull your weight, and be respectful with Pierce and Ms. Miller, and I'll take your case to Brett."

"Really?"

"Yeah. But you gotta prove it to me, kid. That won't be easy."

Shoulders squaring, Harris lifted his chin. "I can do it."

"We'll see."

After the boy was inside, Luc headed for home and called Brett.

"Oh, someone better not be dead at that sawmill." The growl in his voice warned him Brett wasn't in a good mood.

"No one's dead. They made a mess. The four wolves in question are going to be missing their social lives for the next six months, but I'm calling you about Harris Ryder."

The deep sigh echoed his own feelings. "Luc, he's human. We tell his parents and we work out a reparation…"

"Right, cause that's what we've always done. So think about this, Colby was human, too. But she proved vital to the pack."

"She was also latent."

"Right," Luc agreed. "But we didn't really know that. You would have turned her in a heartbeat if it was the only way to keep her."

"Well, since she's my mate, that would make sense. Luc— turning humans is usually limited to mates for a reason."

"Yeah, but it doesn't have to be. We have you, and you're

mated to a healer. We have a kid with dominant enough tendencies to lead wolves astray because he's bored and is desperately seeking purpose. Kid's got intelligence, but he's not being used in the pack, and I'm pretty sure all of this is just his way of challenging authority to get us to notice. Well —what do we do in response?"

Brett sighed. "You want me to offer to turn a kid?"

"He's seventeen and no. I want him to prove his value to himself and to the pack. I want him to feel like he belongs to the pack."

"He's human."

One of the benefits of being his best friend and on the phone, Brett might break his bones, but he wouldn't kill him. At least not right away. "Willow Bend has humans in their pack. Why don't we?"

"You're an asshole."

"Yeah well, that's why you pay me the big bucks."

"That's not a little shift, Luc."

"Doesn't have to happen overnight. Doesn't have to happen with all of them. You can even say we need a test sample to see how it works."

Brett groaned. "I hate you."

"Yeah, buddy, I know. Now, I have a date with a very sexy wolf…"

There was a beat of dead silence. "You and Charlie have a date?"

"Strategy session over dinner at my place, so—if you squint and look at it sideways, it counts as a date."

A long, heavy sigh. "You know, I'm going to take your suggestions under advisement because I think you are due a break."

Luc chuckled. "Well, I'm almost home, so I'll let you know how it goes."

"Just remember what I said about hurting her."

"Damn, have a little faith in me." He shook his head.

"Luc, I have all the faith in the world in you." Then just before the line disconnected, he added, "You're gonna need it."

As the call ended, a message popped up on his screen.

CHARLIE: *I'M HERE. DO YOU MIND IF I MAKE COFFEE?*

GRINNING, HE DICTATED HIS RESPONSE. "MAKE YOURSELF AT home. Already on my way back." After Sunday, he'd been looking forward to her coming up, particularly because her brother wouldn't be here. He wanted the time with her without outside interference or company.

More, he wanted her in his house. He'd gone to hers and the charm of the place hadn't been lost on him. Yes, too much city around it—way too much. But inside? It had been as beautiful and charming as she was. It told him a lot about her —she might choose the isolation of the city, but she craved connection to the world around her. It was in her art, her decorations, and the feeling of warmth infusing every room.

When he reached his driveway, he followed it up through the trees to where his house sat tucked away and comfortable. Close enough to Brett and the rest of the town, he could be anywhere in fifteen minutes or less. Far enough away, he could enjoy the feeling of being on his own.

Life as a Lone Wolf had given him a craving for solitude that wasn't always found in a pack. Yet, he couldn't bring himself to leave the pack again. This let him satisfy both urges.

Charlie's car sitting neatly next to his garage made him

smile. After parking next to her, he picked up the basket of bread from the back and carried it all inside. The house was quiet, save for the hissing of the coffee maker. The rich scent of the dark brew teased his nostrils. He half-expected to find her in the kitchen, but it was empty save for her bag, which likely contained her laptop and other notes. Leaving the bread on the counter, he followed his nose.

She was definitely in the house, and he pushed open the door to his room and paused. Charlie was visible through the guest bedroom door crack, stepping out of one of her sexy pencil skirts and revealing a skimpy lace pair of panties, and the visibly bare skin of her back suggested she had no bra on —at all.

His nostrils flared, and his whole body stilled. A split-second was all he got before she glanced over her shoulder, that tumble of vibrant red hair moving like a living flame against her back.

"Fuck," he said, jerking his attention off of her. Nudity was nothing new to wolves. They shifted between bare skin and fur. It was natural. Ogling was something else altogether. "Sorry," he said. "Just going to get changed myself."

Inside his bedroom, he exhaled a harsh breath. She was probably one of the single most graceful and beautiful women he'd ever seen. The smooth skin of her back revealed the ripple of muscle—perfect.

Just perfect.

"Luc?" Her voice wrapped around him from the far side of the door, and he grasped the handle and yanked it open. If she wanted him, he was damn sure available.

Dressed in a t-shirt that hugged every curve perfectly and a pair of jeans that admittedly emphasized her hips and looked fantastic but also hid that gorgeous skin, she studied him with a small smile.

"Hey." He exhaled the syllable and focused on the green of her eyes. "Sorry about being late, but I'll change and then get dinner started. I can smell the coffee."

"You weren't that late," she said, sliding a duffle bag over her shoulder. Probably how she'd brought in her change of clothes. "I'm just going to run this back out to my car, but I'm not leaving."

That—no actually it made total sense why she made a point of telling him. He'd just been rude, she would have been well within her rights to slug him in the face, much less just walk out and take off.

"I am sorry," he said quietly.

"I could have closed the door all the way," she said with a shrug. "You stopped staring."

But he'd never stop imagining it. Being caught on uneven ground was not a typical sensation for him. He wasn't entirely sure how to respond at the moment. Particularly when he noticed the red polish on her toes. She'd been barefoot at her place on Sunday. Feet weren't the most attractive feature on a person.

They just weren't.

At the same time, she had the most adorable toes, and they were delicate and sweet...

"So, I'm going to put this in the car, and I'll meet you in the kitchen?"

Mentally kicking himself, he nodded. "I'll be the one getting dinner started."

She laughed. "I'll be the one pouring coffee."

"Good to know what we're going to be doing." But she was already disappearing down the hall. Luc stared at the door for a moment and considered hitting himself in the head. Talking to women had never been an issue. Charming them, even less of one.

When the hell had he begun tripping over his own tongue?

With a half-snarl, he stripped out of his clothes and washed up before dressing in a fresh t-shirt and jeans. Her toes were delicate and sweet? What the fuck was wrong with him? Waxing rhapsodic about her feet?

Finally getting his ass in gear, he found her in the kitchen with a mug of coffee, her laptop open, and two legal pads stacked next to each other. Her sexy little feet were tucked onto a chair, and she'd made herself at home.

Perfect.

Warmth settled in his chest, because Charlie looked like she belonged there at the old repurposed farm kitchen table with its ancient wood and recently carved wooden chairs. He'd spent a lot of time stripping, resurfacing, and then adding new legs to the old accessories. His mother found them on one of her antiquing trips to Vermont, and they were exactly what he needed.

"What's for dinner?"

"I picked up some short ribs, and I've had them marinating for hours." He pulled the tub out of the fridge. She leaned forward, the faint narrowing of her eyes one of the first real predatory signs he'd seen out of her. "You approve?"

"I might," she told him, then lifted those gorgeous eyes to meet his gaze. "I just hope you got enough."

Some of the earlier tension eased, and he grinned. "Sweetheart, if I don't have enough, I will get you more."

"Sweetheart?"

Dammit, there he went pushing again. Even when he told himself he wouldn't. For now though, he just shrugged. "You are one. Deal with it." Then turned away and rolled his eyes at himself.

Her soft laughter followed him as he headed for the

French doors leading out to the back. And he allowed himself a smile.

"Gonna get the grill on. You can hang out in here..."

"Did you want coffee?" she called after him.

What he wanted was a long taste of her sassy mouth. What he would settle for, however, was a beer. "Not right now," he said. "Thanks."

Setting the sealed tub with the marinating ribs on the outdoor table, he got the grill fired up.

The sweet hints of citrus tickled his nose, and he glanced over his shoulder to find her leaning in the open doors. The evening air was cool, but far from cold. The faintest scent of honeysuckle lingered in the air, but with the turn in the seasons, that would be gone all too soon.

Her gaze wasn't on him, but the woods beyond his little stone patio. The place needed more work. At some point, he'd do a real patio out here and add some tubs for more plants. The outdoor table and chairs weren't that comfortable, but they were serviceable. He wanted to set up a conversation pit, kind of like what Brett had, but more intimate.

For one, he didn't intend to entertain the whole pack out here. He didn't have to.

"This is nice," she said, almost musing aloud.

"I like it," he admitted. "It's quiet. Don't get a lot of visitors. Can hear myself think."

Another flash of a smile curving her lips. "I didn't take you for the isolationist type."

Closing the lid on the grill so it would heat up, he headed back inside for the vegetables. He'd put together a salad that morning, but he wanted to grill some veggies. Baked potatoes would take too long. She turned to make room so he could re-enter the kitchen.

Careful not to brush up against her, he said, "I went Lone

Wolf for a reason. Spent years out there on my own. Got a taste for it."

"Still, you came back to the pack."

He shrugged as he pulled out the veggies and carried them to the sink to wash them before he cut them up. "It's pack. It's home. But sometimes…it gets claustrophobic."

Not something he admitted to many people.

"They mean well," she murmured, almost too low to be conversational.

"Meaning well can be its own problem," he said as he chopped up the onions, mushrooms, and the last of the summer squash and zucchinis. "They mean well by gossiping about your accomplishments and your failures. They mean well when they want to interfere to smooth things over, or to get you involved in something important to them. They mean well when they expect you to take on tasks that have nothing to do with you, but at the same time, they think you can solve."

"Are you so put upon, Luc?"

He shrugged. "Yes and no."

"That's very clear-cut."

"Of course, it's not. Part of being pack is being involved in each other's lives. Secrets are not encouraged, except by those who want to ferret them out. Sometimes, I just want to come home, have a beer, make dinner, and not worry if the next time I hear my name in conversation it will be dipped in the concern that I'm spending too much time alone, I must be pining."

Abandoning her post at the open door, Charlie rinsed out her coffee mug, then opened the fridge. After retrieving two bottles of beer, she popped them open and offered him one. "Fortunately for you, I don't gossip. Well—most of the time I don't."

Beer in hand, he eyed her as she tipped the bottle up and took a long drink. "So you've gossiped recently?"

"Hmm-hmm. Unfortunately."

"About what?" Curious, he took a swallow of the dark and bitter brew. It went down smoothly. It was the perfect thing for what ailed him. Well—for one of the things anyway.

"You." The admission startled him, and he frowned.

"Why would you be gossiping about me?" Considering his track record of late, he *really* didn't want her gossiping about him at all. Even his own mother was in on the damn conspiracy to keep him celibate or intruding on a pairing that not only *wasn't* his, but he didn't want.

Her shoulders dipped a fraction as did her eyes. "Bishop was being a pain in the ass about you."

A growl worked its way up. As unsurprising as that revelation was, he wanted to punch her brother all the same. "What is his problem?"

"He's a big brother," Charlie said, her gaze sliding away, and Luc had to bite back another growl. "He worries. Needlessly most of the time...then again... he had to deal with a couple of wolves courting me before."

A little shrug.

Wolves had courted her before? A fresh log landed on the flames of his aggravation. "How did he deal with them?"

"It's not important," she said, then took another drink of her beer as he finished with the last of the veggies.

How was it not important? The fact she shied away from the direct question, particularly involving her brother *dealing* with them, lit another match. "It's important enough to get your brother involved. What did they do?"

For a split second her gaze rested on him, the gold bleeding into the green as her pupils flared, and then she dropped her chin. "They were a little too aggressive, and

Bishop didn't like it. It's done, so don't worry about it. I can take care of myself."

Except that she hadn't then. Apparently. Fisting his temper, he made a note to talk to her pain in the ass brother and get some names. "So, why were you gossiping with him about me? Assuring him I wasn't too aggressive?" Because he was damn well trying not to be, but the growl punching up his words did a piss poor job of proving it.

With a scowl more for himself than her, he pulled out foil to wrap up the chopped veggies, seasoned them, and then sealed them in.

"He didn't want me to step on Brett or Colby's toes," she said softly, and Luc dropped his head.

Goddamn the person who came up with that rumor.

"And I told him, you weren't part of their pairing and never would be."

She was a foot away from him, and he glanced at her sideways. The ragged edge of his fraying temper calmed as she all but leaned into his side.

"I told him you didn't smell like them." She set the bottle on the counter and when she pressed against him, he wrapped an arm around her. Warmth flushed through all the irritation, banishing it, and his wolf settled, taking the need to gut some idiot with it. She fit perfectly under his arm, the lift of her chin didn't quite bring her gaze up all the way, but it put her at the ideal angle for a kiss. He zeroed in on the parted lips as she moistened them. "Besides the fact I don't like Bishop bossing me around, even when he means well, I don't think the gossip is fair to you. I told him that."

"Yeah?" That was—fucking thoughtful as hell. "Thank you."

Her smile backed up all the air in his lungs, and the hug she offered him had him abandoning any pretense of the vegetables to wrap his arms around her.

"Seriously, Charlie. Thank you. That rumor is making my life crazy."

"I know," she whispered against his shirt. Whatever Luc had done right in a past life to earn this moment, he swore he'd keep doing it. Her scent eddied around him, sweet and decadent, and his wolf and he both just wanted to roll around in it. Leaning back a fraction, he nudged her chin up and dipped his head. The first stroke of his lips against hers was a test.

If she pushed away, even a little, he would back off, but she didn't. Her mouth opened in an almost welcoming fashion, and he swept his tongue against hers. The heat racing through his veins rose to boiling, and he lifted her, deepening the kiss as she offered him almost perfect surrender. Want and desire collided with need in his system as the distinct notes of arousal—his and hers—began to filter in the air. A little moan vibrated from her throat, and he traced his tongue against her lips before kissing along her jaw.

She tilted her head back, baring her throat fully as his wolf rose. Rolling over for him, metaphorically and literally. His wolf sensed it before he did, the perfect surrender, and Luc groaned, his lips locked over her pulse point, and the longing to suck a deeper kiss there or just sink in his teeth. Mark her and make it clear to everyone she was protected.

Shadow... His brain whispered. Charlie was a Shadow. Submissive and dominant, dual natures she could shift between, but that could also submerge her, and she'd just sunk beneath him.

His irritation and anger...

He suddenly understood what she meant by they were too aggressive. It about killed him, but he released her throat after a gentle nuzzling kiss, then raised his head.

Blown pupils stared up at him as he gazed into her eyes, and he carefully set her down on her feet, keeping her steady until she found her footing. Then another kiss to her lips, just a gentle feathering touch.

"Thank you, sweetheart," he murmured, ignoring his body's very visceral demand to show her his thanks in every way possible. "You don't know what that means to me."

The heart-stopping smile on her face rocked him. Pleasure radiated off of her. Submissives loved to please, not so much in just giving in, but their gentle nature wanted to care for the ones protecting them, as much as those who protected them did. There was no greater pleasure for a submissive.

This—this right here was what he'd always wanted. A beautiful, submissive mate he could protect and tend to, but Charlie wasn't just this. This Charlie would likely fall right into his bed with little provocation, but the other Charlie— the one with teeth and claws.

She'd kick his ass sideways for taking advantage, of her and fuck if he wouldn't deserve it. So, no, as much as he wanted to sink into her body until they were both mindless from it, he wouldn't.

Both sides of her had to choose him.

He wanted all of her.

Even in his decision to pursue, it hadn't hit him just how much he wanted her before. He thought he understood it, the pure carnal lust and the need to know her, they were almost equal in their intensity. But there was something more, something deeper. The need to protect her and meet her on common ground, it overwhelmed everything.

"I need to make dinner now, sweetheart," he told her, and kept his tone gentle and coaxing. She'd done not a damn thing wrong, and the stiffness threatening to snap his cock in two wouldn't kill him. He pressed her beer back into her hands as he backed away. "Want to join me outside while I cook?"

Another brilliant smile, and for a moment, a flicker of gratitude. Maybe her wolf had rolled over for him, but the woman hadn't, and that was all right.

"I'd love to," she said. "I'm starving."

Fuck, so was he.

"Then let's get you fed, hmm?"

CHAPTER 12

*T*hankfully, Friday passed uneventfully, and Charlie escaped the office and back to her brownstone without the further humiliation she'd put herself through at Luc's. If he'd pressed that kiss, if he'd demanded anything—even in cheerful lust—she'd have given it all to him. Even after he'd moved back to preparing the dinner, he kept a careful and distinct distance between them.

The ribs had been to die for, the call with Trask brief, and the evening wound to a very pleasant and polite close, with Luc putting her in the car and pressing a kiss to her temple. What shocked her even more was he didn't insist she stay, if anything, he asked her about everything. Not a single order issued.

As she climbed the steps from the subway, she ignored the hustle of humanity swelling upward on their own journeys home while more flooded down in a rush to get to the nightlife in Manhattan. Or maybe to their own jobs.

Shuttling back and forth between dominance and submission was a fact of her life, a fact of her nature. She could lean into either, but sometimes... sometimes her wolf decided, and those were the times that worried Bishop most. When her wolf caved to a stronger, more dominant one. One even more dominant than her dominant side.

Instead of pressing that advantage, Luc had been blessedly kind and solicitous. All he ordered, the only one he issued after that kiss, had been for her to call or text him once she was home. An order she gladly followed, even as her wolf roused from the blissed-out state to something closer to herself.

She'd texted because the humiliation of that particular moment stung. Not because of what she'd done, no—it was her. Love it or hate it, she would shuttle between her natures for the rest of her life. It was just who she was.

No, his need to show absolute care and the seeming utter awareness of what had happened left her unsettled in the worst way. That he needed to take care of her because she'd been incapable of taking care of herself in that situation grated. How was she supposed to prove invaluable or his equal when clearly, she wasn't?

Ugh.

She covered the walk from the subway to her front door easily, but thoughts of the night before chased themselves around in circles. Inside, she set her purse and bag down on the entry table, hung up her jacket, and kicked off her shoes before walking into the kitchen. She'd deal with all of that later. For now, she opened the fridge and pulled out a bottle of wine and got it open to breathe, then opened the drawer and pulled out her favorite takeout menus.

A long hot bath, take out, and a bottle of wine were exactly what the doctor ordered.

Someone ringing her doorbell was not. Growling under her breath, she debated ignoring it.

Then it rang again.

Her phone vibrated in the same breath, but she'd left it by the front door—in her purse.

The mudroom door was still open, so she walked to the front door and checked through the viewer. The familiar wolf on the porch was a very welcome surprise. Pulling the door open, she stared up at him and shook her head. "You didn't call."

He held up the cell phone in his hand, and her phone ceased buzzing. "I was just about to leave you a message, Rabbit," Adler said with a grin. "You free tonight?"

"I'm tired tonight," she admitted, but leaned into him for a hug, and he wrapped her up tight. The scent of him washed over her, and he burrowed his face against her hair. It was a soothing comfort.

"I can go," he murmured. "I'm only here until tomorrow. Julian needs me down in Florida for a few days."

"Oh, the hardship, Florida means sunshine and surf."

"Swamps and gators," he chided, but gave her a careful squeeze when she didn't let go. "Hey... what's wrong?"

"I had a moment," she confessed, and he lifted her off her feet and walked inside with her, kicking the door closed behind him before he set her down. His deep brown eyes had gone pure gold as he studied her.

"How bad?"

"Just wanted to roll over and give it all up. Haven't done that in a long time." Admitting it sent heat to her face, and she shook her head. She possessed so much more self-control than this. Accepting her status had gone a long way toward finding a balance. Or it had prior to the night before.

"Did someone take advantage of it?" A warning growl rumbled in his words.

"No," she assured him, then smoothed a hand against his arm and over his chest. The vibrations stilled. "He was —wonderful."

Straightening, Adler raised his eyebrows. "Was he?" His tone took on an entirely different meaning. Stripping off his jacket, he hung it next to hers and offered his arm. "Tell me everything."

With a groan, she bumped his hip as she threaded her arm through his and leaned her head to his arm while they walked. Adler was—and would always be—one of her favorite people. In some ways, he was one of the only wolves she'd ever known who didn't react to her dual nature with suspicion or unease, or even needed a lot of time to get used to it. Those wolves were so few and far in between, she clung to them when she found them.

"I'm guessing it must be interesting. You already have the wine out," he teased.

"Hush." She smacked his arm as she let go of him and retrieved the stack of take out menus while he pulled out glasses from the cabinet and retrieved the wine.

They retreated to her sitting room, and he patted his lap after he poured the wine. As much as she hated to admit it, she kind of needed the cuddle, so she crawled onto his lap and let him wrap around her. Nuzzling a kiss to her temple, he pressed a glass of wine into her hand.

"We're getting Thai if you're about to go through that stack." He shifted her enough to pull out his phone. "What temp do you want?"

"A four," she admitted, and he gave her a squeeze.

"That's my girl."

He had the app open, and he placed the order for both of them, paid it, tipped the driver and hit send.

"Thirty minutes." Phone down, he picked up his wine and then stared at her. "Details."

"Edited for pack business?"

"Accepted," Adler agreed, and took a sip of the wine.

"Assigned to work on a project with the pack Second..."

"Luc Danes?" Adler narrowed his eyes.

Why would…? "He was a Lone Wolf for a while. So, you know him?"

"Yes, Rabbit. I know him. Go on." The dead neutral tone betrayed nothing of his thoughts.

With a grumble, she said, "He's overbearing and kind of bossy. But he's also sweet and seems to have matured a great deal from when he was younger—at least if you go by all the stories about him. He's—he wanted to get to know me because we have to work together, and my brothers are…"

"Being your brothers," Adler said with a slow grin. He knew her brothers very well. Duke had found him here once and had been less than thrilled to find out she had invited an Enforcer into her bed. That had been a glorious fight, one Adler had cheerfully stayed to the sidelines of and simply applauded her when Duke finally backed down. Her older brother had kept his word and his mouth shut.

Charlie was allowed to have lovers, and Adler could never stay more than a night or two. They scratched a mutual itch, and he got her on so many levels, but they would never make for a long-term pairing. However, he had been and would remain one of her dearest friends.

"More or less. Bishop invited himself along last week for my run—showed up about halfway through my day, and it worked out. Then he slept over…"

"Before or after he found you working with Luc?"

"After," she admitted.

"So, was Luc already triggering you then?"

"I don't think so, I had no problems telling him no, and I certainly didn't want to roll over for him. Bishop's just got to play big brother—and he likes looking after me. He and Duke do get it for the most part, and they back off when I've had enough."

"But sometimes you just have to let them get it out of

their systems." He tipped the glass back and took a long swallow. "You really have improved your wine selection."

"Bite me," she retorted, but he wasn't wrong. Over the years, he'd been trying to cultivate her taste buds to enjoy a wider variety than her dessert wines, and she had actually developed a taste for some. "I still like beer more."

He laughed, nipped her chin. But it lacked the same heat of earlier interactions. Normally when he showed up, they were half-naked by now and waiting only long enough for the food to arrive so they'd have something to eat after. Snuggled against his chest, she would be intimately aware of an erection, and he was barely half-there, and that just might be proximity.

"It's okay, Rabbit," he soothed, rubbing slow circles against her back. "Sooner or later it would fizzle out, we always knew that would happen."

She made a face.

"Tell me what happened when you submerged."

Because that was what it was like. Her wolf rose, and who she was would vanish beneath it, leaving only a shadow of herself. In those moments, she and her wolf didn't always agree, but her wolf got what she wanted. "Nothing," she admitted. "We were kissing... it was... a *good* kiss. Then, he set me down and fixed dinner, made sure I ate, took point on the call we had to make, and looked after me until he put me in the car to come home."

"Huh," Adler mused before taking another sip of the wine. "How do you feel about that?"

"Are you trying to analyze me?" She shifted so she sat more sideways and could look at him as he curved his arm and kept her close.

"Him," the wolf holding her said. "I want to know he's worthy of you."

"Nothing happened."

"That's my point," he said. "Nothing happened. If you submerged, then he could have taken you to bed without an ounce of battle. You would have given in to everything, and you would have enjoyed it. You might hate yourself later, especially if the rest of you wasn't onboard, but you wouldn't have blamed him."

No. She wouldn't have.

"But that didn't happen. Danes took care of you and treated you with respect." Adler raised his eyebrows as if wanting her to confirm the statement, and she nodded slowly.

"It was still humiliating."

"Rabbit, you should never feel ashamed of who you are."

"I don't, but…"

"The fact you're saying 'but' suggests you might be. You showed him part of your true self, and he didn't reject or take advantage of it."

No. He really hadn't.

"Did he call you today? Ask you questions? Look for an explanation?"

"No, he knows." She bit her lower lip as Adler's smile softened his mouth, and his brown eyes gentled. "Don't look at me like that."

"You *like* him."

"Don't *say* it like that either."

"Like what?" He gave her another squeeze. "You like him."

"I barely know him," she admitted. "He's—he's different. He and Brett are very close. He was gone for years, but he came back, and he's very involved now. He's pack Second, he will always be in the middle of everything."

"Exactly where you don't want to be," the Enforcer said slowly. "But that's not a reason to reject him out of hand."

"It's not a reason to leap into something either. It's not just my wolf he has to deal with, it's me. I'm not always going to back down. There are times I just want...he showed up here Sunday *while* Bishop was here. I didn't expect either, and I had to deal with both."

"How does he handle your brothers?"

She made a face and took a sip of the wine.

Adler chuckled, and even her elbowing him didn't make him stop.

"Oh Rabbit, you have to promise I still get to visit, even if I don't get to make love to you anymore."

"Stop it," she said with a scowl. "I don't know that anything is going to change."

"Of course it is," he told her. "You're just not ready to stop rabbiting yet, but you're going to." He reached up to loosen the bun she'd tied her hair into and then scraped his fingernails gently against her scalp. "One side of you has already decided, or she wouldn't have submitted herself. The other side is intrigued, or you would be a lot more angry than you are."

"Doesn't mean I'm not angry." God, was she pouting? Ugh.

"But you're not angry with him."

Rolling her eyes, Charlie sighed. "Adler...I don't know what to do with this."

"Well, you may get yourself a nice lover who is local," he said, as though musing aloud. "One who can be here far more often than I."

"I've never minded that it has to be infrequent, I know the rules."

"Rules change," he reminded her. "Something I hoped to talk about on this trip, but no worries."

Talk about...Crap. "Adler..."

"Rabbit," he said, his voice deepening. "We are worrying about *you* right now. Everything else can keep."

She sighed.

"And *none* of that," he didn't quite growl the words, but she felt the intonations regardless. "This is important, Rabbit. Do you like Danes?"

"I think so… but again, I barely know him."

"But you know enough to know you're attracted." It wasn't a question.

"It's not a good idea," she admitted, because at the crux of it all lay what she was. "I would not make a good pairing with him, he's always going to have to put the pack and Brett first."

"You put Brett first now, and the company, that's not so different because the company is important to the pack."

True. "But I live *here*," she reminded him.

"Are his legs broken?" The dry tone pulled a reluctant smile from her. "No? He was here on Sunday. I'm assuming he has the capacity to get here on his own."

"Yes, just like I can go home—but his life is there and mine is here, and we are getting *way* ahead of ourselves. He kissed me, and then he kept his hands off. That could just as easily have been wow, he did not want a bite of this crazy."

"Then he would be the king of fools," Adler said flatly. "You would know the difference. Do you think he wanted no part of you? Or was he taking care of you properly, as you should be when you can't look after yourself?"

Adler had seen her in such a state—several times. She could let herself go when he was there, and he always took care of her. Sometimes she needed it, other times—well other times she'd wanted it.

With careful fingers, he massaged the back of her neck, and like the gentle strokes of his nails on her scalp, this loosened more tension.

"Which was it, Rabbit?"

"He was looking after me," she said, licking her lips. "He knew—I think he noticed it when I was kissing him, but he definitely noticed after. No questions, no demands, nothing —he just looked after me."

"Then you have a real chance at something there, Charlie," Adler said, and the fact he used her name instead of Rabbit almost made her eyes well up. "No, you will always be my rabbit, but you have to decide—do you want this chance with him, or are you going to keep running?"

"We are presuming he wants that chance."

"Yes," Adler said with a slow nod. "Perhaps. If he doesn't or he hurts you, there many ways to break his legs —again."

She scowled and narrowed her eyes. "You will do no such thing."

At his grin though, she relaxed and then sighed.

"Crap."

Chuckling, Adler snuggled her close, then nuzzled another kiss to her cheek, and he went back to soothing her. "When you decide, you tell me, and whatever it is, I'm going to support you."

"Even if it's I want to run away and hide in a hole forever? My mother will have kittens."

"I can handle your mother, and if Danes is half the wolf I've heard he is, so can he. As for you, if you want to go, you say the word. I'll protect you."

Surprise arched through her.

"And I won't be remotely insulted that the notion is a shock to you. I love you very much, Rabbit."

Her heart squeezed.

"I've loved you for a long time, but I was not allowed attachments, and you were content with our random assignations. It let me take care of you, and you had your freedom."

Charlie bit her lip.

"None of that," he chastised her, and smoothed his finger

over her lip to free it from her teeth. "We were never in a place where I could take you. I would have had to come to Hudson River, and... I'm afraid that pack life truly isn't for me anymore. Even what we're doing now, the differences are enormous. We spend more time apart than together. It works for us—it would work for you, too."

She sighed. "I never thought..."

"Nor did I, and now you have met Danes and you are curious, and you should let yourself see where it goes. Because of the permanence I could not offer before he can, and he's still here."

"You sound really certain," she told him, searching his face. Adler had always been direct with her. Enforcers, like the Lone Wolves they looked after, had been forbidden attachments. The occasional lover was fine, so that was what she had been. But with all the pack shifts, it never even occurred to her that obstacle was no longer an obstacle.

"I am. Just as I am certain that for all your need for solitude, it's more a craving to be free of judgment. You need your pack, even if it's only to be there for them while living on the fringes."

"I wish I believed it as firmly as you do." Luc was—different. And truthfully, they'd only spent what amounted to a handful of hours over several days together. She could be imagining a lot of this.

Then again...

His reaction to catching her changing? A shiver raced over her skin. She'd been stripping down to get out of her business suit, to get into more comfortable clothes when he came home. He'd called out a greeting, but she'd been reticent to answer before she finished changing. Then the awareness of his nearness swept over her, and she'd glanced back to see him staring through the brief crack where she hadn't closed the door all the way.

Shock in his eyes and the flare of his nostrils, not to mention the swiftness of his apology and retreat. Ogling each other just wasn't done. They were wolves, nudity was natural, but treating anyone that way without their express permission was just plain rude. Yet...

It hadn't bothered her. Was it because she'd already been submerging, or because of his very intimate awareness and overt display of his faux pas? She really didn't know the answer.

Still...

"And around and around my little rabbit races," Adler murmured. "But enough of that."

A knock at the door had him lifting her and setting her down on the sofa.

"Tonight, we are going to drink the wine, eat the Thai food, and enjoy our evening as companions once again." He made it sound so easy. "And if he fails to live up to your expectations," Adler called, "then you know where I stand."

Charlie laughed.

"You think I'm kidding, if I don't like the look of him, I may steal you anyway," he continued as he pulled the door open.

The intense silence pulled her head up, and Luc's scent hit her at the same time.

"Well, you're not here with our Thai food," Adler said, the idleness in his voice a total smokescreen. "In fact, if my nose is right, that's barbecue."

Her stomach twisted. He'd made the most amazing ribs the other night.

"What are you doing here, Enforcer?" Luc's voice held every ounce of warning. "Where the fuck is Charlie?"

"Luc," she said, rising and walking into the hall. "Adler is my guest."

The pack Second looked past Adler, who hadn't shifted

his stance from the door. If Luc wanted inside, he would have to push his way in. Luc's eyes narrowed on her, and she could imagine what he was seeing—disheveled hair, rumpled suit, bare feet, and a glass of wine.

"Adler this is Luc Danes, Luc—this is Adler."

"I presumed," Adler said, offering his hand. "And we've met once or twice. But it's good to meet you again."

The glare in Luc's eyes suggested he wasn't interested in shaking his hand. "I'd say the same if I knew you were involved." He finally took Adler's hand briefly. "What are you doing here?"

"Like Charlie said, we're friends." Adler still hadn't moved out of the way, and Charlie sighed.

At the exhale, the Enforcer cocked his head. "You going to behave in here, Danes? I'm very fond of Charlie, and I'm not going to tolerate you taking your current mood out on her."

Surprise rippled through her…

Challenge flared in Luc's eyes. "Unless you've forgotten, you're in Hudson River territory, and what's more, you're an interloper unless you've got permission to be here…"

"Oh I have permission," Adler said with a slow smile. "I have hers. Brett has us clear it with Charlie when we're only going to be in the city. Sorry to rain on your pissy parade."

For the love of… "Adler, knock it off and get out of the way."

Another laugh as he stepped to the side and glanced from Luc to her. His eyes twinkled with mirth as if to say *see, you do care.*

She was going to punch him.

Luc's scowl said he wasn't far off of it, but he stalked inside and crowded right toward her. His gaze was searching, even as he shifted to keep Adler in his periphery. "I wouldn't have bothered you if I'd realized…"

If he'd realized…?

After closing the front door, Adler closed the mudroom door and leaned against it, arms folded.

"Here," Luc thrust the bagged food. "I grilled up more ribs for you. You seemed to enjoy them last night."

Her fingers brushed his as she took the bag, and a little charge skittered up her arm. "Thank—"

"Just wanted to make sure you were doing all right, and to see you before your day to yourself," Luc continued, then shot a look at Adler, who seemed utterly unmoved by the glare. "But I didn't mean to intrude, so I'll leave you alone. We can—discuss everything over the phone the way you wanted to originally."

Then he pivoted on his heel, and Adler snorted before he stepped to the side and opened the door.

"Luc…" Charlie said, but he didn't slow down as he slammed out of the brownstone.

Oh.

Shit.

"Stay here," Adler told her. "Have another glass of wine and save me some of those ribs."

"What are you going to do?"

"Save him from regretting this, even if I'd rather he just turned tail and went the other way." Adler blew her a kiss, and then he was gone, and she stared at the bag in her hand and then the glass of wine.

Internally, her wolf scrabbled, and she wasn't sure if it was panic or pissed.

Luc just—left.

Closing her eyes, she groaned.

Adler was right… she did like him.

This could be bad on so many levels.

CHAPTER 13

*a*nger and disappointment waged a war inside of him as he stalked down the steps and headed for his truck. He'd left early, taking into account traffic on a Friday night, to drop by and surprise Charlie. After the night before, he'd meant it when he said he wanted to check on her, and he wanted to see the simple pleasure she'd taken in the ribs he'd fixed.

The last thing he expected when he knocked was for an Enforcer to answer her door. Worse, an Enforcer she was clearly close to, and based on her mussed appearance and the other wolf's blocking him from entering until she told him to back off, left Luc with a crap-ton of anger and nowhere to direct it.

He'd had no idea she was already seeing someone, he'd *assumed*. Then again, she'd kissed him the night before. Maybe he had the right to assume. There'd been no trace of the other wolf in her place, and her brothers hadn't brought him up.

That thought brought him up short. Did her brothers even know?

Standing at his truck, his wolf raked his claws at him. The last thing he wanted to do was to get in the truck and drive away. He'd been looking forward to seeing her all day and confirming she was fine.

Then if he were lucky, he might coax her into the spending the evening with him. The more he got to know her, the more he liked her, and she was *taken?*

Something knocking around in the back of his head tumbled forward.

"Colby doesn't smell like you."

Charlie was sweet amber under crushed autumn leaves, while Adler's scent had far more woody notes than she did.

She didn't smell like him, but the Enforcer's scent swirled toward him in the same instant as he turned to find the other wolf staring at him. "Well, it looks like you decided not to bolt after all."

Narrowing his eyes, Luc glared at him. "Are you trying to start a fight?" Because in his current mood, he'd happily toss the Enforcer out of Hudson River on his ass—course, he'd have to explain it to Brett, but it might just be worth it. The Enforcers spent a lot of time nitpicking him while he'd been Lone Wolf, sometimes it was just to fuck with him. But not always.

"I haven't decided," Adler stated as he folded his arms. "At the moment, I'm trying to determine if you're worth it where Charlie is concerned."

"You know what, go to Hell, I don't need to prove shit to you."

"Maybe not, but I care about that woman, and if you intend to play games with her, I'm definitely getting involved."

"She is none of your business. She is not a Lone Wolf, and she *is* my packmate." And he'd like her to be a whole lot more.

"On the contrary, she's my friend, and she's a sweetheart cursed with an ungovernable nature. For all that she has developed control and technique, she will always be a Shadow."

Grinding his teeth, Luc forced himself to keep his fists from launching. At the moment, he just wanted to punch the smug smirk right off his face. "I think I'm more than aware of her nature."

"So she said," Adler continued, surprising him. "She also said you took care of her and didn't take advantage."

"Only a real son of a bitch would manipulate her when she was vulnerable."

The Enforcer laughed without an ounce of humor. "The world is populated by sons of bitches."

A car pulled up, and he tracked his gaze from the Enforcer to the guy stepping out with a bag of—Thai. Very spicy Thai. Luc paced away a few steps while Adler accepted the food and sent the driver on his way. Then he faced him again.

Plastic sack in hand, the other wolf studied him. "If you walk away tonight, you're going to regret it."

"You know that?" Luc challenged him. Didn't matter if the asshole was right, he didn't need some other wolf telling him what he already knew. If he hadn't been so stupid, he wouldn't have handed her the food and then just walked out.

"Yeah, I do. You might want to ask me how I know." The suggestion landed with a wet slap.

"I'm listening." When the other wolf didn't continue, Luc took a deep breath and fisted his temper in both hands. Fine, if Adler had something to say, and it had to do with Charlie, then he needed to hear it, whether he liked it or not. Protecting her was far more important than his wounded pride or ego. "How do you know I'll regret it?"

"Because Enforcers are no longer forbidden long-term

attachments or mating. It's the only thing that has ever kept me from trying to claim her. You walk away, I'll consider the field clear."

The revelation slugged him, and he glared. "Why the hell aren't you going after her anyway?"

"Because for some damnable reason, she likes you, and you faced a real test last night, and you did right by her. I beat the last wolf who didn't."

That stopped him cold. "What?"

"There you go," Adler said slowly. "Now you're thinking."

The night before, she'd gone so sweet and docile. It had been everything he'd ever imagined wanting in a mate, and as much as he adored her, the idea of taking advantage of her when only one part of her nature was surrendering was anathema. But he'd scented her desire then, and her willingness, but he hadn't missed the flash of gratitude in her eyes when he kept his hands to himself.

"A wolf hurt her?"

"He didn't see it as hurting, didn't understand who and what she was. Just met her—she went sweet and pliant, and the next day she hated herself. Didn't mean I wasn't pissed, and didn't mean I didn't deal with it. She is what she is, Luc. You either handle it now, or you walk away. She doesn't deserve more pain, she's done nothing wrong."

His gut knotted. Did Brett know it had happened? Suddenly Brett's warning about not hurting her took on a whole other layer.

"How many Shadows have you known?" The fact they were having the conversation in the middle of the sidewalk on her block wasn't lost on him. They were both speaking in quiet tones, and no one ventured near them, but now that Luc had asked, he needed to know the answers.

"Two," Adler told him. "Part of the attraction in the first

place came when I recognized her nature and understood how desperately she needed a friend."

"And the other you know? Are they mated? Have they settled?"

The Enforcer sighed. "They never settle, they can mate, but their nature will always be variable. It's a fool's errand to think she can just choose to be one or the other. She has control, but only through adapted learning that she has engaged in over time and sheer force of will. But just because they don't settle doesn't mean they can't be happy."

"And how she lives..." She kept her distance from the pack and away from wolves who could pressure her. Her work gave her a modicum of control and allowed her to dictate her schedule. Once a week, she took a day totally to herself.

Even her friends were ones who came infrequently, allowing her the pleasure of companionship without the onus of commitment. She created an environment where she could succeed, and the only wrench in the works was him.

He eyed the food in Adler's hand, then Adler. "You got enough for three."

"With your barbecue? Sure. We can always order more."

Blowing out a breath, Luc motioned toward the brownstone. "Hopefully she didn't just lock us both out for standing out here like a pair of jackasses talking about her."

Adler smirked. "She'll let us in."

Yeah, he didn't need to rub Luc's face in their closeness.

"I wasn't kidding, by the way," Adler told him as they headed back to the brownstone. "You get your shot because she likes you, and you're not a complete idiot. You blow it, and I'll be there so fast, your head will spin."

"Why wait?" Luc had no idea why he was tempting fate. The other wolf already had a leg up on him, there had been an intimacy and warmth between them that Luc hungered for—but she still doesn't have his scent.

That was significant. Enforcers were Lone Wolves, they couldn't mate—before. Now as their own pack, they could and did. In reality, they had. Luc hadn't missed an ounce of the dynamic between Julian and Dallas. The fact Dallas had a kid, and it turned out Julian was the father, said the Enforcers had been verging on breaking the rules for decades.

"Because she likes you, idiot. Try not to prove me wrong in the first five minutes." Then Adler opened the door as if he owned the place and swept an arm to invite Luc in.

Rolling his eyes, he swallowed a snappy comeback and returned the favor by opening the mudroom door for the Enforcer.

"Did you find him?" Charlie asked, the element of worry in her voice raked over him and his wolf, who'd been chomping at him, pricked his ears forward as he settled.

She appeared a moment later, she'd changed out of the pencil skirt she'd worn earlier. Instead, she wore an off the shoulder cream tunic that floated around her and a pair of loose, dark green leggings. She was adorable right down to her bare feet and mussed red hair. Her eyes brightened when she caught sight of him.

"Yes," Luc admitted. "He found me. Beat the stupid out of me, and then invited me to dinner. Do you mind?"

"He what?" Her eyes narrowed, and she glanced from him to Adler with a fierce scowl.

"Nice," Adler murmured, shoulder checking him as he passed him. "Fortunately, the beating was only verbal, Rabbit. He's in one piece for now." He dropped a kiss on her forehead. "Let's feed you, shall we?"

Asshole.

Shaking his head, he followed them as Adler wrapped an

arm around her and guided her back toward the kitchen. The wine bottle he'd glimpsed earlier had been added to the table, and there were two glasses, but Charlie diverted to get a third for him.

It hadn't escaped his notice that she'd immediately leapt to his defense. In fact, despite Adler's affectionate handling—he was very casual and easy with his touches, and she glowed under the attention.

Fuck. Touch starved.

Of course she was, she kept her distance from everyone. It was why her brothers had been all over her at the sawmill.

Okay, Luc, we have to do better. His wolf tensed. They'd been pursuing her with care, but not enough care.

That changed.

Tonight.

"Did you want a beer?" she asked, yanking his attention to the present, and his gaze settled on hers. There was a shyness there that hadn't been visible before.

"Whatever you're having is fine," he told her. "Though—beer is better with the barbecue."

"Wine is fine with the Thai—do you like it spicy?"

Adler was off unloading the bag and setting the containers on the table.

"Let's find out," Luc said. "I like all sorts of things."

The Enforcer snorted softly, but his face was all innocence when Charlie glanced at him. Luc smirked. As irritating as the other wolf might be pretending to be, there was no artifice in the protective look he gave Charlie or the way he invited Luc in for dinner.

He could make the most of it—for her.

AFTER DINNER, ADLER EXCUSED HIMSELF AND GAVE CHARLIE A

kiss on the head before he said he was going up. When she went to rise, he chuckled. "I know where the guest room is." The less than subtle dig reminded Luc that Adler had been a guest—infrequent or not—often enough to be comfortable in her home.

"It was good to meet you Luc," he said, turning to Luc, and Luc rose to take his hand. It was a brief handshake. Neither wolf was all that thrilled with the other, but they were both watchful and minding their manners.

"Adler. Let me know the next time you're in town. I'll buy a beer."

The Enforcer chuckled. "I just might do that. See you in the morning, Rabbit."

"Goodnight," she called, then the wolf was gone, leaving Luc and Charlie alone. He sighed. He should probably offer to leave so she could get some sleep. "Would you like to go up to the roof with me?"

He blinked. "Sure…"

With a smile, she rose. "I'll just get another bottle of wine, unless you want that beer now."

It wasn't like they could get drunk. "Whatever you want," he told her. "The wine's actually not half-bad."

"I like it." She glanced at the bottle. "It's from a vineyard near Niagara Falls. I got it on a trip last spring. They make a better chardonnay than they do a merlot, but the merlot was nice."

He picked up his glass and Adler's. They'd cleaned up in the kitchen before moving to the living room to talk. Over the course of the meal and the after dinner chat, he'd learned a lot about their relationship—including the fact Adler had introduced her to wines by bringing her bottles from all over the country.

Courting her without courting. Yet, the other wolf was folding without a fight.

Well, not without a fight, exactly. One slip, he'd warned. One, and he'd make his play, but he wasn't going to do it right now.

"Because she likes you."

Luc held on to that kernel of knowledge with both fists. She opened her wine fridge then studied the contents. "Oh—this one." The bottle she withdrew was a Crème de Cassis. "It's from…"

"The Andrews winery?"

"Toumont, yes. They had a loan from the company for several years, but they'd finished paying it off and I sent them back the interest they'd paid, because they never should have been paying the pack interest when they donate so much to the gatherings. They sent me several bottles of this. It's *amazing*. And you should feel special," she warned.

"Oh?"

"I don't share it with just anyone." Then she gave him an almost sly smile. "Not even Adler."

The fact it puffed his chest up ridiculously wasn't lost on him. She didn't share this wine with Adler. This was something just for them. He'd take it. "Then I will definitely bask in my special status."

"Good."

Bottle and corkscrew in hand, she motioned to two different glasses that he collected obediently, then she led him up a back set of stairs and then another. The last set took them to the roof. There were four bolts on the door, more than one downstairs, and she grinned.

"Most people don't secure their roof doors, I, however, know I can scale this brownstone, and so could you. I'd like a little warning if someone tried to get in." To break those five deadbolts, she'd get a lot of warning.

It reminded him that she lived all alone in the center of all this humanity, and she'd done very well for herself. Even as one part of him wanted to insist on increasing her security or bringing a Hunter in closer—better still, putting himself closer—the rest of him resisted it. Charlie didn't need him dictating her environment.

Outside, the cool air carried the scent of the river and what was probably someone grilling outdoors. From this vantage, he could see the skyline of the city, and the bridge was in stark relief. It was—remarkably beautiful, considering it made up several canyons of cement and steel populated by an ocean of humanity.

After she'd opened the bottle and filled their glasses, she motioned to a pair of chairs and a small table she had set up. It was cozy and open. In a way, he felt exposed and yet, they seemed to be the only ones out this evening, as the other surrounding building tops were bare.

"It's too chilly for them," she said. "Part of why I picked it. After a certain point in the year, they tend to go in earlier and earlier." It was a little after nine now. "So we'll have some privacy, and I thought you might like to talk without wondering if Adler could hear us. The brownstone is sound-proofed from its neighbors, but not inside, though the walls are thick."

"Thank you?" He frowned. "You don't have to make special considerations for me, though. He's obviously a close friend."

Amusement seemed to flicker in her eyes as she glanced at him. "Yes, he is and has been for a few years."

That gave him pause. "How many is a few?"

"About ten."

Ten years as lovers, and he never chose her over his life as an Enforcer. Luc shook his head. At least he wasn't the only idiot in this equation.

"Okay," Luc said slowly. "You were lovers."

"Yes. We haven't seen each other in a few months, our schedules just didn't allow for it."

He let out a breath. Granted, he and Charlie had known each other a week. It felt like a lot longer. He took a sip of the drink and rolled it over his tongue. It was—strong, but there was a sweetness there. The honey surprised him, but he hadn't really spent a lot of time learning about wine.

Maybe he should add that to the list of things worth knowing, if it was something Charlie enjoyed.

"Thank you for last night," she said quietly, bringing them full circle to why he'd come in the first place.

Meeting her gaze, he said, "You're welcome."

The slightest of frowns gathered her brows together. "You're not going to ask."

"Nope," he told her. "I will absolutely listen if you want to tell me, but...you have a right to privacy, Charlie. You are you. I would never want you to be anyone else. I might be a little behind the curve on learning to court you, but I'm more than willing to learn."

"Court." It was an antiquated term, but it fit.

"I know, sounds old-fashioned."

"I think it sounds charming." The revelation loosened something in his chest, and the edge his wolf had been guarding all evening softened. "And I like you..."

Hearing it from Adler had been one thing. To hear it from Charlie was something else altogether.

"I like you a lot," she admitted. "But I don't know if I'm a good match for you."

The immediate denial was on the tip of his tongue, but his wolf fought him against saying anything. What she was telling him was important. He needed to listen.

She took a long drink and then let out a sigh. "Your job is to be with the pack, to cover what Brett needs you to do, to be involved"

"My job is to help Brett and protect the pack," Luc told her. "But I'm listening."

"I don't do well around all the other wolves. There's always an expectation. The shifting natures—it makes them uncomfortable."

"In what way?" Because he really wanted to understand.

"Did you like it when I challenged you?"

He shrugged. "I could say I don't particularly care for it when anyone challenges me, sweetheart. That's not on you."

"And after last night, if I were to assert my authority…"

"I'd listen," he said, considering the question. "You're talking about expectations."

"Pack hierarchy demands a certain amount of—everyone has a place, and they don't wax and…" She kept starting and stopping, then finally, she shook her head. "The point is, I'm different."

"Okay."

"I mean very different."

"I got what you meant." Maybe it was her nerves that did it, but everything in him settled. "I like who you are."

"You've only had a small taste of it."

"I liked that taste," he admitted, and shifted in the chair so he could meet her gaze. "What do you think is going to happen if you let me pursue you? If you let me court you the way I want to."

The fact he was putting it out there directly seemed to ease some of the tension in her shoulders. "I don't know. But mates are supposed to be together. You live in Hudson River proper—I live here."

"That's a challenge, maybe even an obstacle to be over-come—but it's not a reason to avoid the opportunity." He wasn't dismissing the concern. He couldn't.

"You saw how I was last night," she said, ducking her head and then lifting her chin as she straightened. This time when she met his gaze, she fixed on it, but it wasn't a challenge. Or at least, neither he nor his wolf perceived one.

"You were beautiful."

"I was a mess."

"No," he said, holding out his hand and to his delight, she slid her palm over his. "You were beautiful, and you trusted me. That was a beauty all its own. My only worry was sending you back to the city on your own, but I thought once you got some distance from me…"

She winced. "You figured that part out."

"It wasn't that tough, Charlie. Except I need you to help me understand if I am putting the pressure on, if we're triggering you."

"It's not that simple, and I guess it's not as complicated. Adler said it's because I like you, and he's not wrong."

He held onto his patience by his fingernails, but he kept it there, and he kept his manner relaxed. "Liking me affects your wolf?"

"Does liking me affect yours?" The quiet curiosity beckoned him to answer, and she squeezed his hand gently.

"Without a doubt," he murmured. The urge to kiss her was right there, but he didn't want to make a move. Not until he understood.

"Then you know sometimes it's hard to not react when your wolf wants something."

"Fair point," he conceded, then lifted her hand to his lips. "How is your wolf feeling right now?"

Charlie chuckled. "She's content."

"Good. How are *you* feeling?"

"Honestly?" She raised her brows.

"Please," he said, pressing a kiss to her knuckles. Her pupils flared, and the barest hint of gold began to ring her irises, so he lowered her hand.

"Nervous. Worried. Really glad you came back."

He smiled. "Me, too. I'm sorry I walked out how I did—it was—it was childish."

"You're allowed to have feelings, Luc. I didn't know Adler would be here tonight—I didn't know you would be."

"It was supposed to be a surprise," he admitted. "I want to ask you a question, but it borders on being invasive."

"Okay," she said, lowering the wine glass. "Ask. I don't promise I'll answer."

He could live with that. "If I hadn't come tonight—would you be in bed with Adler right now?" He thought he knew the answer, but he wanted to be sure of it. No assumptions for either of them.

"No," she said quietly. "We were talking before you got here, I'd told him about my slip and about you. He said it best —we always knew this was going to fizzle out. I love him dearly, he's—he's important to me. But no, he would be in the guest room, and I'd be in my bed."

Exhaling, Luc nodded, then he smiled. "Thank you."

She laughed. "You're welcome?"

"Yes, I feel more welcome now." The comment sobered her smile. "Will you let me court you? Will you let me get to know you better? To know your wolf? I want every part of you Charlie—every facet. But I want to earn it from all of you."

"She's half-decided," Charlie told him, but she set the wine glass aside and then rose and moved to slide into his lap. He wrapped an arm around her to balance her and studied her every move intently. "She trusts you and now, so do I."

That was a big step.

She lifted her hand toward his hair and hesitated, but he bumped his head to her fingers, and she stroked across his scalp. Tingles radiated out from the contact, soothing and enticing in the same breath. "Yes, you can court me…"

Curtailing his fist pump was easy because to do it would mean letting her go.

"Do you want to spend tomorrow with me?"

Shock flickered through him. "Isn't that your day to yourself?"

A slow nod. "You want to get to know me—I have to learn to let you in, too."

Fuck. What the hell did he have on his schedule? "The answer is yes, absolutely, I want to spend it with you. But I may need to run back to Hudson River tonight to take care of a couple of things." And to toss at least one ball back at Brett to juggle for the day. Pierce could handle the clearing for the gathering. But there were other tasks on his list, and he wanted to clear them all off.

"Adler will probably leave after breakfast," she said. "So it will just be the two of us."

He really didn't want to leave her, but... "If I make some calls tonight, do you mind if I stay over?"

"And not go back?" She tilted her head. "Can you do that?"

"Yes, I can. I can sleep on your sofa..."

"There's plenty of rooms," she told him, still stroking his scalp. "You can absolutely stay."

He grinned and slid his hand up to her nape. "Wolf still feeling good?"

The barest incline of her head suggested the answer was yes, and then she whispered, "She feels real good."

The barest brush of her lips against his strained his control, but he kept it leashed as he licked the seam of her lips gently, and she opened her mouth. The sweep of her tongue stroking his lit him up, and he groaned as her scent shifted, deepening to something far more decadent. The sweetest amber in autumn, the feeling of home, and the need to lose himself all vied for his attention, but he focused solely on kissing her until her breath came in little gasps, and only then did he ease back.

Her lips glistened, and her eyes shone, but that slender golden ring hadn't deepened, even if her pupils had flared. All he scented was Charlie, and his wolf let out a grunt of satisfaction.

Leaning forward, he rescued her wine glass and pressed it into her hands before picking up his own.

"To getting to know each other..." It had been what he'd wanted from the beginning.

She touched her glass to his. "To you for wanting to chase me."

Laughter swelled in his chest. "You run for as long as you need. I think I'm really going to enjoy this."

No. He knew he would.

But he couldn't afford to screw it up, and for that, he'd keep everything leashed.

Everything.

CHAPTER 14

*I*t proved far more challenging to go to sleep while aware of Luc sleeping down the hall. In fact, she tossed and turned, and then finally sat up. Adler being there was familiar, but Luc being there was a temptation. A scratch at the door had her frowning, and she shoved the blankets back and slid out of the bed to pad over to the door. Her nose told her it was Luc, but...

She opened the door to find Luc standing there on four feet, his dark gray coat with darker points a stark contrast to his dark blond hair. He sat, tongue lolling as he stared up at her, and she chuckled. "Can't sleep either?"

A shake of his head followed by a sneeze.

This was awkward, and at the same time...

Pulling the door wider, she jerked her head toward the bed. He padded into the room, moving lighter than his bulk would suggest. He was huge. His head came up past her waist, and his lanky body elongated as he stretched. Closing the door behind him, she walked back over to the bed—glad she'd chosen to sleep in shorts and a tank top rather than nude, which was her usual.

He waited for her to get settled, and then she patted the bed next to her. Leaping up, he sniffed the covers before moving to lie down next to her, and then he settled his head against her chest, and she chuckled. At her laughter, he pricked his ears forward.

"Subtle."

His mouth opened in a near perfect canine grin. Though it was dark, her eyes had shifted, and she could make him out easily. Raising her hand to his head, she hesitated a beat for permission. Accepting the idea he wanted to pursue her and her own interest was one thing, but this was a little more intimate.

When he bumped his head against her palm, she stroked her fingers through his thick fur and smiled. His eyes closed as she scratched between his ears, and he tucked his head back to her chest. Sinking her fingers into his ruff, she sighed and even exhausted, sleep kept eluding her.

She stretched under him, and he lifted his head again, then she smiled. "Sorry, just… tired, but I'm restless too."

He nosed at her and then moved until he pressed all along her side and settled his head on her shoulder. The soft wuff of his breathing teased her neck, but the weight of him was also a comfort.

Eventually, he drifted off as she stroked his fur, and she settled, but she hovered right at the edge of sleep for so long, it surprised her when she woke up to a light knock on her bedroom door. Luc was still curled up against her, but he snapped his head up and growled.

Yawning, she put her hand over his muzzle, and he stopped snarling abruptly. "Yes, Adler?"

The other wolf didn't open the door. "Sorry to wake you both, Rabbit, but I have to leave soon, and I fixed breakfast."

"Thank you," she said. "We'll be right down."

Luc made a grumbling noise as Adler's footsteps echoed

his passage away from her door. Giving Luc scratches under his chin, she kissed his nose. "I'm sure he made coffee, too. Go get shifted, and I'll meet you downstairs."

Before she could get to the door though, Luc blocked it and then stared at her steadily.

"Problem?"

The baleful look in his eyes spoke volumes. She glanced down at herself and then at Luc. Gazes locked, she folded her arms and waited. The tank top and sleep shorts covered plenty, and she had no reason to cover up. The brownstone was warm, and she was still hot from sleeping under him.

Another grumble escaped him, and then he made a plaintive noise. She rolled her eyes.

"Fine, I'll come steal your shirt and wear it over this. Would that satisfy your possessive nature?"

He sneezed, but he got out of her way, and she opened the door, then followed after him as he led the way to the guest room she'd put him in—just one door over from her bedroom. His clothes lay neatly folded on the chest at the foot of the bed. Claiming the t-shirt he'd worn the night before, she pulled it over her head. His scent surrounded her, but the shirt hung like a dress and even covered her sleep shorts, so it looked like the only thing she wore.

"You're going to want a shirt. Bishop and Duke have stuff in there." She motioned to the closet. "It's all cleaned, but I keep spare stuff in the other guest rooms too, if I have to entertain for the pack."

Then kneeling down, she wrapped her arms around him and buried her face against his fur. The hug of his head over her shoulder pulled her in, and she sighed. "Thank you for coming to sleep with me last night."

As she let him go, he danced sideways and bobbed his head.

The trepidation from the day before seemed absent.

There was something to not dancing around the fact they were both interested. More, there was something to the idea he understood her eccentricities and seemed to be willing to make accommodations for them.

"I'll see you downstairs?" Even though he needed to change, it was hard not to linger. However, when he just started to shift, her eyes widened, and she laughed before hurrying out and closing the door. "Bad, Luc," she called through the door. It had been far too tempting to stay.

That, and the show of trust in letting himself be vulnerable in front of her. Shifting was when they were at their most exposed. There were a few seconds where, trapped in between forms, they were helpless. It was a minute amount of time, but it only took once.

She followed her nose to the seared ham, bagels, hashed browns—he'd actually grated potatoes, how long had Adler been up?—and huge omelets. "You went to the store," she chastised him, and he just grinned at her.

"You were out of breakfast food, and I wanted to make sure you ate before I relinquished your care and keeping to the brute you picked."

Rolling her eyes, she bumped his hip and headed for the coffeemaker. "My care and keeping. Really?"

"It sounds good, doesn't it?" he teased her.

"Not particularly," Luc rumbled as he strolled into the kitchen wearing just his jeans and nothing else. Oh, that wasn't fair, because he was beautiful. Golden tanned skin, ripped muscles, and easily countable abdominals.

"Oh, it's clothing optional Saturday," Adler said. "Good to know." He followed that up by ripping his own shirt up and off.

Charlie groaned and leaned against the counter, even as Luc smirked. "Nice."

"I thought so." Adler laughed, then they both glanced at her, and she shook her head.

"I'm getting coffee and food, you two can posture all you like. I'm reserving my opinions for another day."

"Diplomatic," Adler complimented her, but he just tucked his shirt over the back of a chair while he served out the food. She poured two huge mugs, one for her and one for Luc. Adler usually drank his coffee first thing and had no more in his day. This pot had just been made, so she'd bet he had a whole pot to himself before he woke them up.

Despite the bristliness of their morning greeting, Luc and Adler seemed to get along well enough over food. Enough, she didn't even object to both of them being there on her day. Adler had joined her once or twice in the past, but even he tended to give her space because she needed it.

Still, Luc's presence wasn't a burden at all, and she had to turn that idea over in her head while they discussed inter pack politics, all useful, but she only half-listened. The idea of courting wasn't anathema. Of course it wasn't, yet at the same time, she'd never truly entertained it. Now, not only was she entertaining it, she almost wanted to rush along. The hardest part had already been faced, right?

The sudden silence had her blinking upward to find them both studying her. "I have to go, Rabbit," Adler told her quietly as he rose and pulled on his shirt.

She made a face. "You need to make time for a longer visit."

"I will see what I can do," he said with a grin. "But I have a feeling you're going to be busy."

They both glanced at Luc, who had leaned back in his chair, but didn't say a word. Though, he did smile.

Pushing back her chair, she stood, and Adler caught her as she hugged him. He smoothed a hand over her back and murmured, "You make him take very good care of you, or I'll make good on breaking his legs."

With a pinch, she leaned away and glared at him. "If anyone breaks his legs, it will be me. You don't get to hurt him."

Luc cleared his throat. "To be perfectly clear, I'd prefer no one break my legs."

"Then don't screw up," Adler told him. "Take care of her."

"I have every intention of doing so." Then Luc stood as she eased away from Adler. Running a hand up her arm, Luc squeezed her shoulder gently. "I'm going to walk him out, okay?"

"All right. Be safe, Adler."

"You too, Rabbit." He winked. Then he was gone, his overnight bag was probably already by the door. Their infrequent visits usually began and ended the exact same. The wistfulness at his departure was also less than it had been in the past.

So many changes...

She took the time while they were outside discussing her, or maybe just discussing more politics, to clean up from breakfast. Everyone had eaten, and she got herself another cup of coffee before heading upstairs. She needed to change, and while she enjoyed wearing his shirt, he would definitely need it back for the hike.

The sound of Luc on the steps pulled her out of her closet a beat before he knocked on the door.

"It's open," she called, and he pushed it inward.

"Damn," he said with a grin. "I was hoping I'd make it before you changed."

"You and Adler apparently had a lot to gossip about." She was already in comfortable, but loose jeans, her own t-shirt with a sweatshirt pulled over it, and had her sneakers in hand. "Your shirt is here."

Not that she minded in the slightest the view he presented as he crossed to where she perched on her bed. The muscles along his chest rippled with each movement. Upon closer inspection, there was a trace of golden hair across his pecks and down his abdomen, a happy trail that vanished beneath the jeans.

Tucking a finger under her jaw, he closed her mouth even as he nudged her gaze upward. "Hi."

"Hello," he murmured. "Enjoying the view?"

"Yes, but then you knew that, and it's why you came to breakfast that way."

"Is it? Hmm..." But a smile hovered in his eyes. "It's possible that I wanted to entertain you with the possibilities."

Laughing, she snagged his shirt and handed it to him. "Well it's time to put that back on, because we're going to go get my car and then head up to the Water Gap."

"Why do we have to get your car?" he asked as he pulled on the shirt. "My truck's here."

"Well, that's much more convenient. Do you mind driving us up to the Water Gap? I want to take you to one of my favorite trails, and it's closed right now, so no people to find us—although Bishop hunted me down there last week. Luckily, since I was there last week, he won't likely look twice in a row."

"If he does, I can send him on his way. Since you invited me today, I intend to be a little selfish with your time."

A little thrill skated through her. He waited as she finished tying her shoe. When she stood, he wrapped his arms around her, and his mouth slanted over hers. It was the most natural thing in the world. But unlike the kiss at his place, this one didn't devour her senses or drown her.

No, the massage of his lips on hers teased her mouth open. He slid his hand up into her hair, cupping the back of her head as he tilted her just so. Fingers digging into his shirt, she clung to him as the first sweep of his tongue teased at hers. There and away again. Shivers eddied over her skin as he repeated the move, and then he broke the kiss to nip her lower lip gently before he nuzzled his nose to hers.

The thump of her heart sounded loud to her own ears, and at the same time, she couldn't stop staring at his lips where they glistened with moisture from the kiss.

"That's a much better—" he began before she cut him off to kiss him again. Arms looped around his neck, she arched up onto her tiptoes until he lifted her. It was her turn to kiss, then nip, tease at his lips with her tongue, then suck on his tongue gently as he swept it against hers.

Her wolf shivered as they were torn between demanding more and begging for it, but this time, she broke the kiss by dragging out his lower lip then releasing it with a little pop.

They were both breathing a little harder, and his eyes had gone pure gold. She had a feeling hers had, too, as their wolves stared at each other. "You were saying?" It almost sounded like she purred the words out, but she wasn't a cat. Didn't change the feeling, though.

"That's a much better good morning," he murmured, his voice hoarse. His desire scented the air around her, and the length of his erection pressed against her stomach.

"I liked it," she told him. "Water Gap?"

He chuckled. "You're a cruel woman."

Giving him a little shrug, she said, "You let me see your wolf. I want to show you mine."

For a moment, he tightened his grip, and his fingers were firm against her hips before he set her down. "I would love to meet your wolf."

"In all her aspects?" She couldn't help teasing him.

"Absolutely."

Nerves fluttered in her belly, but she wasn't sure if it was from excitement or worry. Excitement, she thought. Her wolf writhed around inside of her, eager to get out. They both wanted to run and to play, and they were taking a play-mate with them.

"Let me get my duffle and my GPS tracker…"

He was a half step behind her. "Your what now?"

"My GPS tracker. When I run—I usually do it on my own. It's easier than the gatherings. The large crowds of wolves… it's just harder for me. But Brett worries, so I wear a GPS tracker when I run, so he can find me if he has to."

"You won't need it today," Luc told her, and she hesitated at the door to the hall and glanced at him.

No. She guessed she wouldn't. She grinned. "Then I better text Brett, because he knows this is my day to go, and if it doesn't come online, he'll be vexed with me. It's really hard for Brett to yell at me."

"Well, we'll just have him yell at me. Trust me, he has no problems there." The delight underscoring the words made her laugh. His eyes brightened, and the blue began to bleed back into them. "Anything else we need to take with us? Food? Wine?"

She snorted. "I eat off the hoof or paw, as the case may be. The wine will be here when we get back."

"Well," he said slowly. "Look at you."

"My wolf needs her time, even if I prefer the city and the solitude, I don't begrudge the time to run and race the wind. I just prefer to do it alone—and now with you." She bit her lower lip. "Hopefully, it's something you'll enjoy."

Linking their fingers together, he tugged her back to him then cupped her face. "I want to be very clear on two fronts here. I'm not just interested in you because you're beautiful, smart, and beguiling. I'm not just interested in you because I expect you to do the things I do. I'm interested in all of you—what you enjoy, what you don't, where you like to go, what you like to avoid."

She exhaled a shaky breath. "Okay, and the second thing?"

"This only goes a step further when all sides of you are in agreement." Then he narrowed the distance, and his gaze held her captive. "You decide. But my wolf and I are already in agreement on what we want, and that's to wait for you. If you want to go on this run alone...I don't expect you to change for me, even if I very much want to go with you."

"I wouldn't have asked..." She lifted her chin, holding his gaze. "I wouldn't have asked if I didn't want you to go with me."

He grinned. "Well then, by all means, let's go for a run."

Ten minutes later, they were in his truck and on their way to the Water Gap. She let Brett know she wouldn't be wearing the GPS today and why. Brett's only comment had been: *Have fun!* Halfway there, her phone buzzed again, and it was Duke.

He wanted to know where she was heading because Brett wouldn't tell him.

"Want me to deal with him?"

"No," she answered with a chuckle. "As tempting as foisting my family off on anyone else would be, I actually like my brothers. But shh, keep that part a secret."

She texted him back with a simple message. *Not today. I have plans. No, I won't tell you. It's none of your business. Consider me dutifully guilted and recalcitrant. I'll be in Hudson River on Friday getting ready for the gathering. Staying with Luc. Get the boys, and I'll take you four out to eat.*

Before she hit send, Luc said, "Invite them over. I'll grill and help run interference. Then you don't have to worry about them interrogating you about me."

With a snort, she glanced sideways at him. "You do recall the last time we were all in one place."

"I do, and I don't mind, Charlie. They're your brothers.

You still have to meet my family. I think it's only fair that I help you with yours."

Unease seesawed inside of her. "Oh, I hadn't thought about that."

"Don't worry," he cautioned, settling a warm hand on her thigh. "I mean it. My mother already likes you."

"She doesn't know me."

"You have my interest, and you might eventually give her grandchildren. Trust me, she adores you."

Panic scrabbled through her, and she and her wolf both stared at him in shock. Kids were not on any list she'd been considering, and at the same time...

His bark of laughter had her slapping him. "You're an ass."

"Your face was great though, and now you really want to sic your brothers on me."

She snorted, but he wasn't wrong. Amending the message to invite all of them to Luc's for dinner, she added: *behave. I like him.*

That one line would send them into a tizzy, and they'd aggravate Luc all week. His grunt said he recognized, and she smiled sweetly.

"You do not fight fair."

"I wasn't fighting," she murmured. "I was winning."

The laughter filling the cab warmed her all the way to her toes. Being with him was a lot easier than she expected, and it delighted her. While Adler had been convinced, and she'd enjoyed those kisses—attraction wasn't the question. Luc was a gorgeous wolf, strong, capable, and he had a sweet and protective streak. No way he could be Brett's Second without all of those qualities. His patience and kindness though had been unexpected qualities, particularly after their rather tempestuous meeting.

Once they reached the Gap, she slung her backpack over one shoulder and led the way toward the trail they would hike. They took a roundabout route; the colorful fall colors had pulled more than a few people out to venture into the park. But they were heading toward higher territory, and she knew a lot of the trails here, she knew which ones doubled close to the closed trail, and when she broke into the woods proper, Luc was right behind her.

The fact he was content to let her lead warmed her, and she found herself hard-pressed not to smile. In fact, each time she glanced back, she discovered he wore a similar grin, and it buoyed her. As they finally reached a good spot to shift, she dropped the backpack and pivoted to face him.

"I don't know how she'll react—not totally. If there's a repeat of Thursday…"

"Then we'll look after her," Luc said. "No expectations, Charlie. Just be yourself and relax, please?"

"Easier said than done," she admitted, because all the relaxation from the ride fled as she reached for her sweatshirt and tugged it off over her head.

His expression gentled. "No expectations," he reaffirmed, and this time, there was just the hint of command in his voice. Tilting her head, she studied him. The wolf in his eyes gazed right back at her, as unblinking as the man. "We're going to run, play—eat off the hoof, as you call it. Any special requests?"

"I like venison," she admitted. "Though it's a challenge to find them. Sometimes there are too many people."

"Hmm," he said, eyes narrowed thoughtfully as she slid off her shoes, then reached for the buttons on her jeans. "I'm not a half-bad tracker, I'll see what I can do."

It was her turn to snort. "My understanding is you have a very keen nose, you scented a latent and managed to land in her hospital to cleverly ambush her into taking you back to the pack."

The exaggerated roll of his eyes made her laugh, and she

said nothing about his lack of touching his clothes while she stripped. With care, she rolled up and packed her things into the backpack, then glanced up at him from where she crouched. His gaze was on the surroundings, his nostrils flared, and his eyes damn near glowing.

He was protecting her, making sure no one came too close. Some of the nerves evaporated under the warmth burning in her chest.

"Thank you, Luc," she whispered, then closed her eyes and let go. Her wolf surged upward. The burst of pleasure and pain rolled over her as her body shifted, muscles realigning as her bones restructured, and then she was on four feet and gave herself a good shake before she bounded forward and rolled in the crunchy leaves.

Luc's laughter washed over her as she rolled, then writhed, twisting her back to get a good scratching going before tumbling back to her feet and facing him.

Instead of looming over her, he crouched and smiled softly. "Hello there..."

Charlie opened her mouth, she and wolf grinning as they paced up to him, side-stepping. Just when he would have touched her, they streaked away.

"Ahh, I see," he called as she peeked at him from behind a tree. "When you said I could chase you, you meant it literally." Sweet amusement licked every word, and she let her tongue loll out. No, not really, but it was a lovely idea. More, now that he was here with her, she wanted to explore all their opportunities.

Pacing out from behind the tree, she tilted her head as he studied her. Luc remained crouched, then he smiled.

"Watch my back?"

Ears forward, she bounded in a circle and then moved closer toward the woods leading out to the trail. This was a good spot, not immediately visible. The presence of evergreens gave them cover, but a lot of the trees had begun to shed their leaves, and the colors, while startlingly beautiful, also allowed for sight lines not otherwise present.

The rustle of his clothes teased her, and she glanced back to find him already stripped down to his jeans, and they were swiftly removed. Like her, he crouched and folded his clothes and fit them into her bag. Then he secured it. As much as she'd like to get a good eyeful, she returned her attention to the woods. Birds called in the distance. A few squirrels chittered among the treetops. At least one rabbit sat quivering a half-dozen yards away. The racing cadence of its heart attracted her, but she wanted to look for bigger game.

The swiftness of Luc's change tickled her, and then the big brute bumped into her side, rubbing along her fur one way before sliding up the other. She rocked from side to side at the pressure, but let her mouth open and her tongue loll out at his deep woof before he caught one of her ears. It was the barest of tugs, a playful one with no harm, and she wagged her tail as she watched him.

Her lack of reaction seemed to puzzle him. After bounding away a couple of steps, he lunged at her again, and she snapped at him. That got her a start of surprise, and his ears perked forward. Undeterred, he repeated the maneuver, and she snapped at him again. This time, confusion layered his scent, and she grinned before racing around in circles, kicking up the leaves.

It was ridiculous and fun. She did several swift circuits, then altered course abruptly to charge him. With a deeper bark, he leapt clear. She threw a look at him over her shoulder before she raced away, trusting him to follow.

The next few hours passed in bliss as they took turns chasing each other, twice he caught her, and once he pinned her before slurping her face. Tickled, she returned the favor and pounced him by emerging from a pile of leaves. It had taken everything in her to hold still while he stalked her scent. But she'd been rubbing against everything as they passed it to deliberately confuse him.

Just as he neared her hiding spot, she sprang out and hit him full force. He was bigger than she was, but catching him unawares allowed her to bowl him over. She got her teeth against his throat, but he shook her off and tumbled her before pouncing. The wrestling tore them all through the trees as they vied for dominance, but the more they struggled, the greater her thrill, until he finally had her down and laid on her while holding her by the scruff.

She wiggled against the ground, but couldn't dislodge him. Happily satisfied, she settled, and then he began nuzzling her ear before rising and licking her muzzle. When she returned the affection, he rubbed against her side before settling next to her, and they panted together.

They'd spent hours romping—so much for a hunt—then his head snapped up, and his ears pricked forward. Like a gust of wind blew him away, he vanished. She hurried after him, racing to keep up with him as he flew through the woods. It didn't take her long to catch the scent trail he followed, and it took everything she had to resist the howl.

Ten minutes later, they struck—the buck was mature, his shoulders and chest one mass, and his rack impressive. He also was full of enough piss and vinegar, he charged them rather than bolt away. It was a glorious hunt, but they didn't linger over the take down. His death was as swift and merciful as they could make it.

Luc positively glowed as he looked over the downed buck at her, and then he lifted his nose, as if to say *go ahead*. He was giving her the first taste. Only after they'd had their fill, did they drag it deeper into the woods for the other scavengers to enjoy, and then she made her way toward a stream. Luc caught up with her easily, and she drank several droughts before settling on a rock in the sun. When he curled up around her, she rested her head against his ruff and dozed.

It really was the best day. She wasn't sure how long she slept when Luc nudged her to get up, and then she followed him as they returned to the clearing where they'd left their gear.

When he went to shift, she studied the area and guarded him. But the moment he was on his feet and stretching, she gave into the urge and shed her fur for her skin. Surprise flickered in his eyes when she rolled to her feet, and he barely had time to brace when she threw her arms around him. His skin was glorious against hers, sending electricity skittering across her oversensitive flesh.

Then Luc claimed her mouth, and she clung to him, drunk on the day and utterly intoxicated by him. Her nipples strained against the contact of his skin, and his erection smeared a streak of dampness against her belly, but he held her tight and deepened the kiss, until they both had to let go to suck in air.

Eyes bright, he grinned. "Good day?"

"The best," she whispered, giddy as hell. "The absolute best."

CHAPTER 15

*M*iracles happened. He'd proven it by not giving in to the flammable need consuming him when she threw herself in his arms. Skin still prickling and hypersensitive, he'd gone hard at the first glide of her smooth skin against his. The soft weight of her breasts—swallowing a groan, Luc kept his grip on the steering wheel and stole a sideways look at the woman next to him, only to find her watching him with a smile.

"What are you laughing about?" Because hearing her voice would at least satisfy part of his need for her.

"Not really laughing, so much as enjoying," she admitted. "I really liked today."

"Yeah, I got that," he teased. "I had a great time." It had been a while since he'd just been able to roam, to hunt and pounce and play. He hadn't really thought about it. "Weirdly, a lot of my free time when I would just go for a good run has been spent training Colby, and that takes a lot more focus."

"Because she's still learning, and you're a good teacher," Charlie's compliment was a caress he wanted to roll under.

"How do you know if I'm a good teacher?"

"If you weren't, Brett wouldn't have you doing it." Always reasonable, even as she zeroed in on her point. "Colby's different—she's a healer that tends to make others want to coddle her more, and you don't coddle her."

"That woman is velvet wrapped around barbed wire, coddling her is a mistake," he stated firmly. "She's a lot tougher than some people think. She's had to be."

"She's perfect for Brett," Charlie said with a smile, satisfaction eddying off of her.

"Yeah," Luc agreed without an ounce of hesitation. "She really is... It was that stubbornness that made me ask her to bring me back to Hudson River. She wanted to head down to Florida, restart her life—find a place in the world, and I coaxed her into giving the poor, wounded guy a ride home."

He was especially proud that being pathetic as he was at the time worked out in their favor, even if he could have lived without the hospital stay, or the fact that he'd been in a lot of pain. Thankfully, Gillian and Brett had both been able to help him get it together.

Settling back into the pack had been an awkward combination of familiar and alien. He had his best friend back, and between himself and Colby, they'd helped drain the wounds left by betrayal in the pack and galvanize Brett back to his old self. Well, as close as they were ever going to get. One thing Luc and Brett couldn't do was go back to being stupid, idealistic kids. Too much had happened, but it made his best friend an even better Alpha than the promise he'd already shown.

All the way back to the city, he basked in Charlie's company. She told him about going to law school, and what it had been like in college. The fact she'd spent so much time on her education didn't surprise him, so much as impress him. It wasn't just a couple of years, she'd spent just under a decade on developing the critical skills to thrive in business, and Brett tasking her to the company had been nothing short of brilliant. She was more than capable of handling all of it and took a kind of enthusiastic interest in things Luc couldn't imagine being engaging, much less as infused with the excitement she seemed to possess.

Arriving to find Adler in her brownstone the night before had been a slam at his pride and his ego, more because he hadn't thought she would have had relationships. Talk about being a blind idiot. It was the height of arrogance to presume Charlie lived so isolated she never had a lover. It also flew in the face of his own opinions—just because she was a Shadow didn't mean she wasn't a fully functioning and sensuous wolf with her own needs and desires.

The slap had been vital, if he were to be completely honest. While he might never admit it aloud, the more time he'd spent around the pair, the more grateful he found himself for Adler. The Enforcer had given Charlie access to real intimacy that she might have otherwise denied herself, and they were wolves. They were meant to be tactile and connected. Her isolation, self-imposed as it might be, was also fundamental to her own mental comfort with her status.

He had to respect all sides of her nature. Fortunately, the more he learned and the more layers he peeled away, the more intoxicated he grew. Charlie fit him in so many ways and challenged him on so many levels. He wanted more.

He wanted everything.

Patience, he reminded his wolf, but he needn't have bothered. His wolf was more aware of hers than even Luc was. They'd already pressed too far too fast without even meaning to, and the result hadn't dissuaded him so much as amped up his need to protect her—even from himself.

"You're thinking very hard over there," she murmured. The soft rasp of her voice teased over his senses. Like her wolf, Charlie was a mass of luscious contradictions, and all of them enticed him. Delicate in her submissive side, but sharp in her dominance—she was at her core one of the *kindest* wolves he'd ever met. It was a mistake to believe she needed his protection, she obviously thrived without it, and at the same time, he *wanted* to protect her. From her family. From the pack. From everything. But he couldn't just stand in front of her.

"I have a lot to think about," he teased.

"Oh?"

"Hmm," he said, sliding a look at her. "What do you do in the evenings after your day to yourself?"

"A little dinner. A little wine. Maybe a long, hot bath—I was going to do that last night, but I ended up having company instead."

He chuckled. "What do you fancy for your dinner, pretty lady?"

"You pick," she told him. "We did what I wanted to do."

What he'd like was *her* for dinner, but they were supposed to be pacing themselves. It hadn't been quite twenty-four hours since she agreed to his pursuit. He'd promised her patience, and he would damn well give it to her. "When we get back, let's pour you wine, and you can go take your bath while I hunt down dinner."

If he were there while she was taking a bath, that might be just a bit too much torture.

"That doesn't seem fair to you," she murmured.

"Oh, it's plenty fair. I like making sure you get what you want." Heat licked through him. He definitely planned to drown her in pleasure so she got everything she wanted, when the time was right. "Any foods that are definite no no's?"

"I'm pretty easy," she admitted, and he bit his tongue to keep the smartass comment at bay. Nothing about her was easy. She was complicated, enticing, delightful, and intriguing. Never easy. "One of the best parts of living in the city is the access to so many different kinds of food. I have a stack of order in menus in the kitchen, I only keep the ones from the places I like."

"Very helpful."

She grinned. "I try."

The bubble of warmth carried them almost to the city when his phone rang—well vibrated in his pocket. Grumbling, he glanced at the screen on the dash that showed who was calling.

Brett.

Not someone they could just blow off.

Tapping the button on the steering wheel, he said, "Hey Brett—Charlie's with me, and we're in the truck." Better to just let him know right up front the conversation wouldn't be private.

"So I heard, I hope you two had a good run."

"It was wonderful," Charlie hummed, and he swore she almost purred. She was definitely all wolf, a fact he'd vastly enjoyed during their mock battle. More, she was damn tough and clever. He couldn't wait for a rematch.

"Good." Brett's voice warmed a notch as he spoke. "He's being good to you, I presume?"

"He's sitting right here," Luc reminded his best friend.

"And if I wanted your opinion, I'd ask you. I'm asking Charlie."

For her part, she just laughed. "He's being amazing, Brett. I might just keep him."

Electricity scaled his spine at the comment. It might have been delivered in a light tone as a jest, but her eyes heated when their gazes collided.

"Well, he is *my* wolf, if you'll remember," Brett teased, and Luc glared at the man, even if he wasn't there.

Making static noises, Luc said, "Sorry, you—cut—ou—"

But Charlie's laughter only deepened. "He doesn't smell like you, Brett, or like Colby." Then she leaned over and rubbed her cheek to Luc's shoulder. "He's starting to smell like me." Then to Luc's shock and entertainment, she stretched to nuzzle his cheek, then licked his ear. "There, I licked him. Now he's mine."

Brett's bark of laughter flooded the cab, and Luc's face ached from grinning. "Oh well, I'm taken," he said happily. "You and Colby will just have to muddle on without me."

"I heard that," Colby called from the background. "I assure you, I can put Brett through his paces."

"Hush," Brett growled playfully. "I have to work before I can play."

Luc shared a grin with Charlie before he said, "Now I know you didn't call to check in on us, because that would be rude, especially if we'd been in the midst of play ourselves."

Charlie slid her hand onto his thigh, and he covered her fingers with his own.

"Well, unfortunately, I do have to interrupt. Trask is on his way to the city."

Some of his good mood evaporated. "Excuse me?"

"Trask, Second to Cassius…"

"We know who he is," Charlie said, her tone soothing and conciliatory, where Luc just wanted to growl. Her way might be better for the moment, so he let it go. "We just spoke to him a couple of nights ago. He didn't mention coming here."

"Cassius called an hour ago, he wanted to negotiate safe passage for Trask, and it was their opinion that the first meeting between you three should be in our territory rather than theirs. Not sure if it's a power play or…"

"No," Charlie said slowly, her somewhat blissful expression retreating as a thoughtful mask took its place. "This is a sign of respect and a show of strength. He respects the importance enough to meet us in our territory, and he is not intimidated by giving up any advantage he might have in Sutter Butte. This could be good."

"When is he coming?"

"He's driving, doesn't care for flying. I expect him in the next ten days or so. Charlie, he'll be staying with you for the immediate arrival."

Everything in Luc objected.

"How many are coming with him?"

"Just him."

Luc blinked. "Seriously?" That was unusual.

"Ballsy," Charlie commented. "He doesn't need backup. He can handle all of us on his own."

With a grimace, Luc sighed. "And you want him to stay with Charlie?"

"It's not my first hosting job," she said, squeezing his thigh. "So after the gathering then?"

"Yes, which I insisted on. I need you two focused here. Then after the gathering, you can take your work on the road, if necessary."

Nearing her brownstone, Luc said, "Then we have time to plan for his arrival. Thanks for the heads up."

"What are you two up to now?"

"Hanging up on you," Luc said with a grin.

"I see how it is," Brett said, but the smile in his voice rang through each syllable. "Behave yourselves."

"Absolutely not," Charlie answered him, and Luc didn't think he could love her more than he did in that moment.

Laughter echoed over the phone line, and then Brett was gone. He found a spot just a couple of brownstones down from hers and pulled in. She waited for him on the sidewalk, and he caught her hand as they walked. Once they were inside, it took all his will not pick her up and slam her against the wall and just have her right there.

"Go run your bath, I'll bring up your wine, then figure out dinner."

But there was no missing her shiver. "You're taking care of me."

"Yes, I am," he told her, and kept his tone firm. "Now get going." She nuzzled a kiss to his jaw, and he afforded himself one gentle squeeze before sending her up the stairs. When she was halfway up, he said, "Charlie?"

"Hmm?"

"We're absolutely not behaving ourselves tonight?"

Her slow grin promised him he hadn't misheard or misread that statement. "I really hope not."

Fuck.

The growl rumbling through him as he exhaled had her pupils flaring, and the scent of her desire teased through the air. "Bath." He pointed upward. "Go on. Pamper first."

Then pleasure.

She blew him a kiss, and for the first time in his life, he caught himself miming catching it, then pressing it to his lips. The thrill shooting through him at her grin was nothing short of ridiculous, and he really didn't give a good goddamn what anyone else thought.

Perfection. She was perfect for him.

Fisting his control, he went for the wine and the takeout menus. Still, he whistled as he went to work.

Course, when he carried the cold wine and glass up to her, she damn near destroyed him by already being in the bath when he got up there. One bare leg up on the side, immersed in hot, fragrant bubbles, and her glorious red hair all pinned on top of her head.

"Cruel woman," he whispered as he poured her glass.

Glancing at him from beneath her lashes, she smiled. "You pursue me your way, I'll run mine."

"Noted." Kneeling close, he leaned in and brushed a kiss

to her mouth that she arched up to meet, but he kept the contact light before setting the glass in her hand. Brushing his knuckles down her cheek, he whispered, "Enjoy your bath and take your time."

His cock was as hard as stone, but the smile in her eyes tickled him. Then her stomach growled, punctuating the tenderness, and she giggled. Tearing himself away, he went downstairs and got himself a beer. Time and patience.

Time and patience.

But the scent of her was in his nose, and the taste of her on his lips, and fuck if he didn't want to pound her scent into him.

An hour later, he set dinner on the counter and called up the stairs to let her know the food was ready. He'd taken the time to set up candles that he'd light when she came down and picked out a few songs for some *spontaneous* dancing. When she didn't answer or come down, he headed up. The door to her room was wide open, and he slid to a halt at the sight of her, arms folded, utterly nude with her back to him.

"Charlie?" He kept one hand braced against the doorframe. "Dinner's here."

Glancing over her shoulder, she smiled. "Will it keep?"

Eyebrows raised, he nodded slowly. "Something wrong?"

"Nope," she said. "I told you—I don't plan on behaving tonight."

His whole body leapt at the invitation, but he remained where he stood. "I said I could wait…"

"You said you wanted me to choose—all of me." Turning, she faced him, arms open and the look of her devastated his senses. All sleek curves and soft skin gleaming under the low light burning next to the bed. Her scent teased and beckoned to him. "We played today."

"We did."

"I had so much fun." There was a note of wonder in her

voice. "I've never played like that with anyone—there's always an edge. A fine line I had to dance."

He could understand that.

"I want to keep having fun with you." She licked her lips. "We can keep waiting if you want, but I like you. A lot."

The last band of control keeping him anchored to the doorway snapped, and he was across the room and wrapped his arms around her. With a gentle twist, he settled her back against his chest and buried his face in her hair. One arm around her middle and the other across her breasts, he just held her close.

She stroked his arm, melting against him.

"Charlie," he whispered against her ear. "I don't want to move too fast."

"No?" The rich humor in her husky voice teased over him like its own caress. She was even softer up close than he imagined, and he rubbed his cheek against her hair. "Luc, I'm not delicate, nor are my feelings that fragile."

"Maybe not," he conceded. "But you are precious, and I don't want to screw this up…"

"If I were any other wolf, what would you do?"

He nipped her ear for the impertinence in that question. "If you were any other wolf, you wouldn't be you, and I wouldn't be here." Lips against her throat, he kissed a path to her jaw, and she tiled her head back, resting all of her weight on him. She was so light, it disguised the strength and the tremendous courage she housed.

"Mine," he whispered, almost too quietly. "I want you to be mine. That's why this is so important." If he overstepped, pushed too hard, or drove her away—he wouldn't forgive himself.

"Shh," she murmured, gliding her palm over his arm. "I'm right here, Luc. I'm right where I want to be." She twisted against him just enough to angle her head to look up at him. Her eyes were pure gold, not even a trace of the green.

"Who is 'I', Charlie?" He had to know as he loosened his arms and allowed her to turn. The glide of her body against his the most sensual torture. "Which Charlie?"

"All of me," she said. "Sometimes it's a struggle, and other times it's so easy—this is one of those times it's so easy."

Sliding a hand into her hair, he held her head still so he could brush his lips across hers. He'd meant it to be a light touch, but he fell into the kiss, sealing his mouth over hers. Stealing away her breath, he sucked deeply against her tongue until she relented and thrust it against his.

The tangle of her fingers in his hair sent pleasure sparking through him. She fisted his hair, holding onto him as desperately as he clung to her. It was like kissing her for the first time—he'd finally found her, the wolf he wanted. Found the green eyes and red hair he craved to see everyday. Found the taste of her, the sweetness on his tongue and the bite of her teeth against his lips

She rapidly embedded herself within him where she belonged. Never had he imagined pitching so wholly into another person. He loved women, all women, and he enjoyed them—or he had. Now he didn't want any other woman. Just this one. Just her.

He hungered for her sweet submissiveness and the sharp claws of her more dominant side, but most of all, he enjoyed the woman in all her contradictions. One arm around her waist, he lifted her clean off the ground, and then her thighs locked on his hips as she balanced herself. The position lifted her higher, and it was her mouth coming down on his, her hands pulling his head back—it left him curiously vulnerable and open to her.

Neither he nor his wolf objected as she devoured his

mouth. The bite of her nails against his scalp and along his nape just left him hungry for more.

He swung her around, took a single stride to the bed, and settled her with exquisite care, not once letting go of her mouth. She fisted his shirt collar, and though he half-expected it, the shred of fabric as she tore it open made him growl, and she answered his with her own, then bit his lower lip. Jerking his head up, he ran his tongue over the welt, and then she matched him, licking at the hurt even as she reached for his jeans. He got his shoes off.

Together, they pushed them down his hips, and then she ran her hands up his back as he shoved them off, and the whole time, they fought to hold onto the kiss interspersing tiny nips with longer, deeper and far wetter kisses. The copper taste of his blood faded under her gentle care.

He could kiss her for hours, suck on her lower lip, tease her tongue, and drink in her taste and her scent. She smelled like the vanilla from her bath, but beneath it she was all subtle amber, crushed leaves, and woman. All the stunning color of autumn and promise of warm fires. He glided a hand down her side, even as he braced himself on one arm. He wanted to explore everything about her, every curve, every tilt of her chin, and every simmering look coming alive in her green and gold eyes.

Beautiful. Brilliant. Intoxicating.

When she fisted his hair and tugged once, he lifted his head, breaking the kiss and hungry to return. She gazed up at him, those unfathomable eyes so full of questions and heat.

"Luc," she whispered it like it was a revelation, and then, "Please." Both syllables sent electric shocks through his system. Pleasant ones. Igniting his desire, and shredding the leash he'd kept on his control.

He wanted her.

All of her.

"Charlotte." He teased the word with a trace of his finger along the curve of her breast. Her skin was like the finest silk, soft and warm and perfect. The pucker of her nipple tightening into a hard bud drew his attention, and he circled it gently, not quite giving her the pressure she wanted. "My Charlie."

Mine.

The word stamped somewhere deep, so far below the surface, it could never be erased. The gold in her eyes faded, leaving her unguarded and open. Wolf and woman very much present together.

"Charlie." He repeated it like fucking prayer, reverent and loaded with every conviction. She tugged once, and it was all he needed. He dropped his weight down and their lips fused together again. Nothing else mattered but this...

A laugh bubbled out of her, and he paused to marvel at the sound of it. Lifting his head to study her flushed cheeks, bright eyes, and swollen, pink lips, he groaned. She glided her tongue over the lower one, and it glistened. He tracked the motion with a hunger he couldn't comprehend, it consumed all of him and longed to consume her and yet, he wanted to give her everything in the same breath.

"What?" he asked after searching for the word he needed.

"I think I just came," she told him, her eyes widening as she ran her hands over his shoulders and then down his back. "You're beautiful." A slow smile spread across her face. "So gorgeous, I think I came just from kissing you."

"Not yet," he promised, a sly grin of his own coming into play. The wolf settled within him, they were both so hungry for her, they'd been ready to gnaw through the leash and just like that, she set him free. They were where they belonged. He dipped his head toward her neck. "But you will," he promised her.

Against her exposed nipple, he breathed and grinned

when her thighs clenched him tighter and she shifted her balance. Dropping a hand to her hip, he pinned her to the bed.

She wasn't flipping them over. Not now. Not when he hadn't had a chance to play. Cupping her breast with his right hand, he rolled the nipple and focused on her face. With every teasing stroke of his thumb, every light squeeze, he studied her to see which elicited the most pleasure, what could make her gasp, or what sent her pupils dilating. Light pressure, firm pinches, teasing rolls—they all did something different. When he locked his lips around her neglected nipple, her whole back arched as a pleased moan escaped her.

He could do this all day.

But he had other plans, too. After time spent in wonder, teasing each of her breasts, he kissed a path down her abdomen and froze briefly against the flat plane of her tummy.

She shifted restlessly beneath his hands, her fingers in his hair and pulling at him, but he caught her wrist, before kissing her abdomen just above her core, teasing his nose against the red curls waiting for him.

He dragged his kiss lower, and eased between her already spread thighs. Kissing her sex, teasing at her labia, and then sucking on her clit could keep him satisfied for days. Easing a finger into her slick channel, he smiled at her fist thumping the bed, even as she arched her hips in an effort to make him add more pressure—but he wanted every little sound he could wring out of her, explore how many fingers could he slip into her, and when he curled his fingers, she came with a sharp cry.

Savoring every reaction, he resumed his teasing. He wanted to build her to another orgasm while licking, nipping, tasting every sweet drop of her release. After dragging his index finger through the slick, he eased it beneath her and teased the puckered ring of muscle at her anus. Above, she stiffened, and he relaxed the touch and then looked up across the sweet plane of her body to meet her gaze.

"May I?" he asked, teasing his breath against her clit. The pulsing, swollen button of flesh beckoned his lips but he wanted—more.

He wanted everything. Every single facet...

A catch in her breath, then a slight nod, and he pressed his finger back to the tight ring, and eased past it, even as he locked his lips on her clit and sucked fiercely. Her body bucked under his, her thighs locking on his shoulders, and he groaned at the reaction and worked his finger deeper into her ass.

Drunk on her taste, he delved deeper. And she rippled above him, hips rolling as her sex fluttered, and he curved his fingers inside of her again. Hot spikes drove through him, images of beds, of closets, and even cars—stolen moments where they couldn't even take off their clothes, and long, indulgent days when they never bothered to put them on. He was hungry for every experience.

He ramped up the intensity, wanting—no needing—her to come again. When she shuddered and spasmed through a second orgasm, he lifted his head to gaze up at her. His mouth was wet with the taste of her, and his fingers damp.

"Luc..."

Easing his hands from her, he wiped them on the comforter. Then he gripped her hips, and flipped her over. The curve of her ass teased him, and he eased his palm along her spine. "Is this all right?" Manhandling her if she let him was fine, but he wasn't taking a damn thing she didn't give him.

"Yes," she exhaled, and then glanced over her shoulder at him as she tilted her hips and then wiggled her ass. "Like something you see?" The teasing remark dragged him forward with a laugh, and he leaned over her to kiss that smart mouth.

"I adore everything I see." Then he tangled his tongue with hers as he fisted himself once, then twice. Hard enough to send a spark of pain up his spine. He wasn't going to come as soon as he slammed into her. He wanted to make this last —for her, for him—for them.

He took his time teasing his length against her sex, slicking himself up before easing inside of her, and he took his time, inching in as he trailed kisses over her shoulders and slid his hands down to settle on her hips. His whole body laser focused on where he joined hers, and he looked down, tracing the way she took him inside her like it was where he belonged.

"Fuck yes," she whispered, and he grinned. It was a stupid, silly smile, and it stretched his whole face. A nudge forward, then another, and the hot, wet heat enveloped him, and he had to lean his head back and look away from the elegant lines of her back, or all his efforts would have been wasted. Slowing, he tried to catch his breath and gather his self-control, and then she pushed back, taking him to the hilt, and in a single movement, she shattered nearly all of his restraint.

Satisfaction and pure need collided. His grip on her was too tight, he was going to leave bruises, but she pulled away a fraction and then drove back. The movement jerked him out of his stupor. "Yes?" He demanded—he had to know. Had to know it wouldn't hurt her—that it was what she wanted.

"Yes, dammit...Luc." She pounded a hand against the bed, frustrated with his need to know. Loving her meant loving all of her, and he would always need to know. She would always have her say. "Move, please..."

It was all he needed to hear, and then he fucked into her hard and fast. His skin slapped against hers, and the sound played out the beat of his heart as he thrust. Every part of his body focused on hers, on joining her again and again, and his control shredded, even as white-hot heat unfolded down his spine. His balls dragged up tight, and he stretched beneath her, dragging his fingers over where they joined and then found her clit by some miracle.

One stroke. Two...and then she spasmed around him, even as he danced along the line of pleasure and pain before it all melted away, and he came. The shock of it held him rigid, and he wasn't sure which of them let out the shout, or maybe it was both. When she collapsed beneath him, he eased down along her back, careful to keep from crushing her, and then he rolled them onto their sides and kept her close, he hadn't slipped free yet and he wanted to stay there forever.

Wrecked.

Destroyed.

Together.

They lay there for hours, he stirred only long enough to use the restroom and then returned with a damp cloth to ease over her. She might have slept, but he didn't. Refusing to look away, not even once. The idea she might disappear kept him awake, stroking her flank, then along her sides. When she stirred and he began to stiffen, she turned to meet his kiss, and he began to move with her again. The desire to bite her and claim her once and for all was a living, visceral thing inside of him, but he settled on loving her for now.

CHAPTER 16

*T*he week had been an exercise in decadence—and exhaustion. Luc stayed through Monday morning, but he had to get back to the pack, and she had to work. Monday evening, as soon as she finished her last meeting, she got in the car and drove up to his place. It was worth every minute of fighting through traffic to see the delight on his face when she pulled in next to his truck. He got up with her before dawn to see her off, and she was tired when she got to the office.

Tuesday, she had meetings run long, but Luc met her at the brownstone with dinner and a hot bath—only he joined her in this one. He couldn't stay the whole night, but she woke briefly when he kissed her goodbye.

Wednesday frustrated both of them because he was tied up with the gathering, and she had two unexpected conference calls that pushed her schedule. He left her a message, and she sent him a text, but the busy carried them right through Thursday and into Friday morning. The only good thing about Thursday was a call from Harris Ryder and his parents. She'd spent an hour on the phone with them making arrangements for Harris to intern with her.

But the success of that moment didn't allay her agitation for long. Antsy didn't begin to cover her mood through her daily routine. She'd gone months between visits with Adler, but two days seemed almost unbearable. At lunch time, Debbie walked into her office with the take out order and closed the door before crossing to put it on the desk in front of her.

"You know I love and respect you, right?" Debbie asked, and it left Charlie gaping at her briefly. The question was so far out of left field, she didn't know how to respond immediately. "You do, I know you do. Because you're amazing. You think of everything, and you're always a half-dozen steps ahead, which means I need to be a step or two ahead of you, and I'm telling you right now—eat your lunch, I'm canceling the rest of your day, and I'm wiping out your Monday schedule. Eat, have coffee, and then get out of here and go find that gorgeous man who sent you the gorgeous flowers and get laid."

Eyes narrowing, Charlie stared at her.

"Yeah, that's not going to work on me." Dramatically unimpressed didn't begin to describe Debbie's manner. "You haven't *quite* been moping since Wednesday afternoon, but you are more like a sore and grumpy animal just waiting to take a bite out of someone." She nudged the food. "Your favorite roast beef sandwich with triple meat, some cheddar cheese, and that spicy horseradish you enjoy." Then she tapped the other container. "Spicy fries from the shop down the street." The last thing she set there was a cup of coffee. "Dark roast, extra bitter—like your soul is going to be if you don't take care of this issue."

No amount of scowling would neuter that last statement

of its humor, and Charlie pressed two fingers to her lips to suppress a smile. "I've been that bad?"

"Honestly, they're out there drawing straws on who has to go to this afternoon's meetings. You took a strip off marketing for that mistake…"

"It was a hundred thousand dollar mistake that I have to now own to Brett," Charlie pointed out.

"And you will spin it around and repurpose those materials for something else in order to clean it up from being a complete loss." Debbie wasn't wrong, the problem was more Charlie hadn't thought of *what* to do yet. "So, in the meanwhile, eat, drink the coffee, and I'll go take care of everything, and then on Tuesday, you can treat me to my favorite lunch and tell me how wonderful I am."

Chuckling, Charlie said, "I'll probably do that."

"I know you will, because you will be in a much better mood."

Had she been chewing on everyone? "That bad?"

"Worse, but we love you, and we can all tell you're distracted. So—do as your told." From anyone else, Charlie might have snapped at the last, her wolf's restlessness thrashing inside of her as though she'd been caged. Even her skin itched with the need to shift. She wasn't as dictated by those needs as others in the pack, she could usually contain her to one good shift per week.

"Clear the calendar, and if I'm leaving early, so are you." Charlie tapped the desk. "Got it?"

"I'll need a couple of hours to rearrange things, and then I'll go get happy hour started." Debbie winked as she headed for the door. "Also, details—is the yummy guy really yummy?"

"He's better," she murmured, but waved her off before she could demand more details. Now that the decision had been made, she just wanted to go, but eating before the drive was a good plan. She'd skipped breakfast that morning because she'd been irritated at the fact they hadn't been able to work out Thursday evening. One night had been fine, but the second had been overkill.

That evening, she had to share him with her brothers.

I like him. As she devoured the food, she turned that thought over in her head. She'd all but declared her feelings to Adler and to her brothers. In fact... She reached into the drawer and took out her cell phone. There were easily a half-dozen messages from her brothers, including a couple of really colorful comments from Noah and Sullivan. They were stuck on an outer loop circuit and would make it back in time for the gathering—barely. So they may or may not make it for dinner.

If Luc *liked* her back, he'd let them come back early. Amused, she forwarded the messages to Luc. Fifteen minutes later, Noah sent her a middle finger emoji because Luc thanked them for volunteering to ride herd on the youths, since they wanted to come back early.

She'd grinned. Luc could definitely handle her brothers. There was a message from him too, or a more recent one than the others he'd sent.

Luc: *I vote we just ditch the gathering and run away together. You in?*

Laughing softly, she typed in. *Sure, about to ditch the office and just head up now. I miss you.*

The message was read a second after she sent it, and then the three dots popped up that showed he was writing.

Luc: *Have you left yet?*

Sandwich consumed and fries almost gone, she'd begun to feel a little better just from two sentences with Luc and the food.

Leaving in ten.

Luc: *Text me when you're in the car.*

The order amused her. Even more when he added on a separate *please* a moment later. Food finished, she cleaned up the trash, packed up the desk, then slid her laptop and tablet into her backpack. She'd brought her overnight bag with her, since she planned to leave directly from the office. Backpack over her shoulder and overnight bag in one hand, she rescued her coffee and phone, and headed to the door.

Debbie glanced up and then pushed away from her desk to head to the executive elevator. "You already look like you feel better."

"I do," Charlie assured her, guilt stabbing her for her earlier mood. As she stepped into the elevator, she faced her to add, "And you were right, I do love you. Have a great weekend." Then she winked as the doors closed. Debbie's laughter rang out as the elevator descended.

It took her fifteen minutes to get down to the subway, ride it a couple of stops, and then go to the garage where she parked her car. Another five minutes to get it down, and then she was behind the wheel. She'd finished the coffee on the subway. Setting the phone in the holder on the dash, she let it queue up to Bluetooth before sending an *on the way* to Luc.

The phone rang seconds later. His name popped up on the screen, and she grinned as she hit answer. Before she could say anything though, he said, "Are you here yet?"

Laughter swelled out of her. "I'm not even out of the city yet."

"Then drive faster," he teased. "I wasn't kidding about ditching the gathering and running away."

"Brett would kill us," she reminded him.

"Nah," Luc said. "He's a lot of bark and no real bite." A distinct thump echoed over the phone, and she raised her brows. "Then again, he does have a mean right hook."

Fresh laughter buoyed her, and she grinned. "Do me a

favor, try to stay in one piece until I get there. I'd rather not have another evening interrupted…"

"Your brothers are coming for dinner."

"Yeah, don't remind me. Whose terrible idea was it to invite them to your house?"

"It's going to be fine, Charlie," he soothed. "I've already got the steaks marinating and the perfect sauce to grill them with. I stocked the fridge and bribed my mother into making more apple dumpcake."

"Hmm, I think you might just like me there, Mr. Danes."

"No thinking required, it's just a fact. Now pay attention to the road and drive safe. I want you here in one piece, too."

"See you soon…and Brett?"

Their Alpha chuckled. "Yes, Charlie?"

"Would you like to have my brothers for dinner, so Luc and I can be alone?"

"No can do," Brett said, his mock sympathy amusing. "I have a date, and she doesn't have any brothers to cockblock me."

"Ass," Luc said, and Charlie grinned.

"Damn, I had to try."

"It was an admirable attempt, drive safe."

"See you soon," Luc told her. Then they were gone, and the silly grin she'd begun wearing when he called just grew.

Two days had been two days too long.

She'd become absolutely ridiculous. Turning up the music, she focused on the drive. Hopefully, she could get out of the city ahead of the rush hour traffic.

THE DRIVE TOOK JUST OVER NINETY MINUTES, BUT SHE managed to hang onto her good mood right up until she pulled into Luc's drive and found her mother leaning against the side of her car—and it was the only car in the drive. Luc's truck was not there. Exhaling, she debated sending a message to Luc or just handling her mother herself. Constantly avoiding her hadn't worked as a plan so far, even if it did buy her weeks, sometimes months, of quiet.

Gazing at Adele Miller was like looking in a mirror sometimes—a mirror of who she could have been if she'd just *sucked it up* as Adele had often encouraged her to do as a child. She reached for her wolf and found her alternating between almost plaintive and aggravated. Getting her bearings around Adele could be a challenge.

But she had to handle this today, or the gathering would be absolutely unbearable. Pushing the car door open, she tugged off her shoes before stepping out barefoot. It didn't matter she was still dressed in a black skirt and jacket over a deep green blouse.

Eyes narrowing, Adele straightened as Charlie approached. The grass was cool beneath her toes, and damp. There was the faintest hint of rain on the air. She could have just missed a storm.

"Charlotte," Adele said slowly. Tanner than Charlie from years of working outside and with darker hair, though it was shot through with only hints of the red Charlie had, Adele had the same green eyes Charlie saw in the mirror. They were near enough in height that her mother couldn't use that as part of her dominance, and hadn't in years. Another source of frustration, though height didn't stop her from dealing with the boys, and they towered over both her and their mother.

"Mom," she said. "It's good to see you."

"No, it's not," Adele retorted, then invaded her space and pulled her in for a hug. Charlie's back stiffened, and she ground her teeth. It was an aggressive demand, and her wolf's hackles went up. Fisting her response to it, she endured the hug for a moment, then pulled back. Wolves were tactile, and maternals more than most. As it was, Charlie was damn tactile, particularly when she was in submissive mode or needing the comfort of leaning into it.

But with Adele, even hugs were a form of combat. A demand for affection, whether she wanted to give it or not. A requirement to respect and obey, whether earned or not—shaking her head, Charlie pushed aside her need to reject the contact, but still created space between them.

"Your brothers told me you were planning on staying here for the weekend." It wasn't a question.

Folding her arms, she inclined her head. "That is the plan."

"I don't think so," her mother stated. "In fact, I believe that would be another poor decision on your part."

Charlie raised her eyebrows. "I don't think I asked your opinion."

"Of course you didn't, the only thing you know how to do when you fail is run away." It landed with all the delicacy of one of her mother's typical rants. They made her so tired, keeping her wolf in check to not lash out or worse—crumble and fold in on herself. Aggression was how Adele showed affection. She pushed and pushed, demanded perfection from her children, though the woman herself would never achieve it, and despite her many superior qualities, her empathy and compassion always seemed in short supply where Charlie was concerned.

"Is that all you came here to say, Mother?" Relying on the title that would yank her mother's chain, she increased the emotional distance between them, and her wolf paced restlessly inside of her. They were already agitated after the separation—albeit temporary—from Luc. Now they had to deal with her mother standing between them and the goal they desired—which was to go inside and text Luc so he would show up.

Her brothers would be here shortly enough.

"Charlie, I didn't raise you to run from what you could be."

"No, Mother, you most certainly did not. Amazingly enough, I haven't run from a single thing I can be, quite the contrary. I embrace it. The problem here is *not* with me." Her wolf stretched, and Charlie lifted her chin. They had been the butt of one too many micro aggressions from the woman who was supposed to love and protect her. "You know what —I don't care anymore."

The truth in those words shocked her, but nowhere near as much as they did Adele. Her eyes widened even as her scent changed. The anger threading through her transformed to something milder, but no less choking.

Hurt.

"I don't care what you think about me or my choices. I'm a Shadow. I'll always be a Shadow. There's nothing *wrong* with being a Shadow. I live a wonderful life that you refuse to be a part of, and I refuse to keep subjecting myself to your judgment. It's petty and serves no purpose."

When her mother glared at her, Charlie just raised her brows and didn't blink or look away.

"You don't outrank me, Adele. I report to Brett and no one else. I run a multi-billion dollar company and arrange trade with multiple packs and corporations around the world. I speak five languages. I host Enforcers and foreign visitors all the time, and I do it *well*. Just because I'm not a Hunter, doesn't mean I don't serve the pack."

Nostrils flared, Adele studied her. "Then why do you avoid me so much? Why are you always running away? You have the capability of being strong, why do you fold?"

Charlie rolled her eyes. "I am who I am—all I am. There is

no shame in being a submissive. They care for the pack as much as a dominant. I am both, and if you can't accept that, you are *never* going to accept me, and I don't need to subject myself to that."

"Oh." A woman's voice intruded, and Charlie jerked, even as Adele did the same. They'd been so focused on each other, they'd failed to notice the new arrival. "I *like* you." Babette Danes stared at her with a wide smile. "I like you just fine." Then she glanced at Adele. "Do take the stick out of your ass, sweetie. You have a wonderful daughter."

Haughty fit her mother when she was in a mood, as it was, Adele merely glared at Babette. "Mind your own business. You deal with your daughter how you wish, and I will deal with mine as I see fit."

"My daughter is not ashamed of me as a parent."

Wait...

"Charlie isn't ashamed of me," Adele argued, her glare intensifying. "What are you doing here, Babette? We were having a private conversation."

"This is my son's home," Babette informed her, and Charlie had to bite back a smile. Luc's mother said it with almost the same easy-going charm her son employed when he was going to get his way and was willing to be nice about it. "And I'm expected. What's your excuse?"

Frustration etched into every line of Adele's face.

"Mother," Charlie pulled her attention back to her. "You have to stop now. I'm *fine*."

"She is fine," Babette wrapped an arm around Charlie's shoulders and pulled her close, almost hugging her from the side. It was both warm and discomfiting all in the same breath. "She's a wonderful girl. My son..."

"...is ten feet away and can speak for himself."

Charlie's wolf bounded happily inside of her, and she twisted to see Luc arriving between the trees. His own grin grew as their gazes locked, and she let out a slow sigh. There he was, and he was fine. Better now.

Peeling away from Babette, she met Luc halfway, and he scooped her up when she threw her arms around him. It didn't matter which of them initiated the kiss, she fused her mouth to his and clung to him as she reveled to his touch. It was ridiculous how much she'd missed him.

"You're kidding?" Adele stated, shock rippling through her voice.

"Adele, darling, I do remember when you and Jesse met… if I recall, you couldn't keep your hands to yourselves, and you were forever finding the most inappropriate—"

"Babette!"

"Weren't you even at Hatcher's once? Having a bad sprain looked at? He stepped out—"

"They don't need to hear that."

"Then there was that time you two seemed determined to christen…"

"For the love of the pack, woman, is there no gossip you don't listen to?"

"Nope," Babette said. "It's how I keep my finger on the pulse of things. Now, come along. I promised Luc I'd get supper started for your sons. They're coming to dinner, and I'm sure if you behave, we'll be invited, too."

Lost in the kiss, Charlie barely noticed when the conversation faded away, until he lifted his head and let out a sigh. "Much better…"

"Hmm, I missed you."

"Fuck," Luc exhaled. "You have no idea."

"I growled at people in the office," she informed him. "I have some idea. Debbie kicked me out at lunchtime and told me to go find the yummy guy who sent the flowers and get laid."

Luc threw his head back and laughed. "I'm sure that can be arranged."

"Hmm...I wish it was just the two of us."

"Soon," he promised. "Dinner, some conversation, and then I'm kicking all of them out. We have to be at Brett's at nine tomorrow to kick off the gathering, and I plan to have you all night long."

A shiver raced up her spine, and she stroked her nails through his hair. It was a little sweaty and sticky. In fact, all of him was a little sweaty and sticky. Rubbing her head against his chin, she tucked her face against his throat and inhaled his scent.

"You need a shower."

"All right," he murmured, balancing her as he walked toward the house.

"My bag is still in the car."

"I'll come back out for it."

Inside, Adele and Babette were still arguing in the kitchen —though they both went quiet as she and Luc came inside.

"My mom is here," she whispered.

"Mine too," Luc said, and he didn't whisper. "They're adults, they'll be just fine." He carried her straight through the house to his room—not the guest room. "And if they need anything," he called. "They'll wait until we come out." Then he kicked the door closed and his mouth was on hers again.

She liked this plan.

He barely set her down before trying to peel her out of the jacket. In the bathroom, they were all hot, hurried hands, and then he had the shower on. His jeans seemed to take forever, and she almost ripped them in her haste, but then her back was to the tile wall and Luc was buried inside her to the hilt, and she could breathe again.

The feel of him, all hot and heavy as he stretched her,

made her keen, and her wolf all but rolled over and gave her throat. He stroked his hands over her, whispering nonsensical things that were so soft, even as he drove her pleasure higher and higher. Something white hot and desperate flashed up and filled her whole body. She dug her nails into his back and kept her thighs locked to his hips as he rocked into her, and every word he spoke was interspersed with a kiss.

When she trembled on the edge of orgasm, he lifted his head, and his deep golden eyes met hers and she grinned, clinging to him. Tense, she strained with him toward orgasm, and his hand skimmed along her body, even as he kept thrusting.

Oh, she was so close, it was right... *oh right there...* Her mind blanked as she let out a long cry, and he claimed her mouth, swallowing the sound, and then he was pulsing inside of her and his mouth was on her throat. The scrape of his teeth set off another spark of pleasure through her system, but he didn't bite.

Not yet.

And as much as she wanted it, she and her wolf both rolled around in the sense of his affection. He could have claimed her, and he continued to hold back because he wanted her to choose—all of it.

Panting, they clung to each other as the floated back down to earth, vaguely aware of the shower splashing against her.

"Much better," she sighed, and he chuckled.

"All fixed, you can go back to the city now?"

Lifting her gaze, she smiled. "I don't know... it's been two days."

"In that case, we have some time to make up."

And oh boy, did he.

CHAPTER 17

*D*awn edged the window when Luc opened his eyes. The warm press of Charlie's body against his registered a heartbeat faster, and he stroked his hand over her shoulder. The steady cadence of her heart, the soft feather of her breathing, and the weight of her thigh resting on his was a delight. He'd run most of the way back to his place rather than grabbing his truck. Needing to be there when she arrived, and even happier to find her already present when he got there.

Everything was ready for the gathering. Hunters had their circuits and would keep any wandering hikers out—though so far none had been encountered, they had to plan for the accidental few. He'd worked nearly forty-eight hours straight, coordinating with the various groups from the families hosting the feasting and providing buffet style meals for the hundreds who would be in attendance at each location.

It wasn't that he resented the work, but he'd loathed the enforced separation no matter how "short" it had been. Charlie's work was as important as his own. Still, the awareness she was on her way made him speed through the final checks while delegating specific follow-ups to Pierce and the others. The gathering would be a success and in... he snagged his phone off the nightstand and checked the time.

Two hours.

Plenty of time to savor her before the madness of the weekend truly began. Stealing a glance down, he smiled at her scrunched nose. His movement had disturbed her, but a few soothing strokes of his hand over her shoulder, and she settled right in.

Adele Miller was every bit the battle-axe he'd been expecting. By the time he and Charlie had emerged from their shower, and after he retrieved her bag from the car, dressed in clean clothes, their mothers were still in the midst of a fierce debate. Though instead of discussing them—or Charlie more specifically—they'd been arguing about two wolves Luc had never heard of before.

Frankly, he didn't care.

One by one, her brothers had arrived, and their shock at finding their mother there had been almost amusing. For the most part, Charlie relaxed as her brothers teased her. But Luc hadn't missed the assessing gazes they'd each given her and then him. It took about an hour for everyone to settle, but the disapproval in the air began to dissipate, and by the end of the night, Bishop had clapped him on the shoulder.

"Good luck—and take care of her," her brother advised.

"Agreed," Duke added, and he'd glanced to where Charlie stood listening to Noah and Sullivan, her eyebrows raised. The amusement in her eyes kept Luc from wanting to thump either of the brats. They kept invading her space and pushing her to see if she'd push back. "She seems happy. I like it."

"Mom seems happy, I want to write the day down in stone. What did you do to her?" Duke wasn't wrong. Adele hadn't said a single, critical comment, and even Charlie had begun to relax.

Adele and Luc's mother had ignored all of them as they settled outside with a bottle of mead that Babette had brought with her, and were currently debating yet another pairing Luc had never heard of.

"Mom's gossiping," Bishop said with a note of wonder. "I never thought I'd see the day."

"My mother has that effect on people," Luc told him. "Now go away. I want your sister to myself."

"TMI, Luc," Noah declared. "TMI."

Charlie punched his arm, and Noah clutched at himself. "You wound me."

"Not as much as I will," Luc said idly when Noah picked her up and spun her around.

Sullivan had laughed. "We can still pick on our sister. She was ours first."

"Hmmm," Luc had been undeterred. Still, her smile lit him up, and she'd threaded her arms around one brother after the other. Each got a firm hug, and there was a sense of relief around them that couldn't be missed. One by one, her brothers shook his hand and then made themselves scarce, leaving Luc and Charlie with their mothers.

"Don't worry," Babette said. "You two can go play, we're just going to sit here and drink a while. We haven't caught up in ages, and Adele's actually not quite the bore she likes to pretend to be."

Charlie's mother snorted. "Just because I don't spend every hour of every day discussing the lives of everyone around me, doesn't mean I don't notice things."

"I noticed," Babette said with a grin. "You have some wonderfully juicy details I've been missing..."

Luc rolled his eyes, but Charlie let out an almost wistful sigh, and the sound caught his and Adele's attention.

"Don't be so dramatic," Adele informed her, then set aside her glass to rise and approach them. With a firm look at Luc, she held out her hands to Charlie. Tension threaded through her, but she took her mother's offered grip. "I *am* proud of you. I know you don't believe that. I *wanted* different things for you, that doesn't mean I don't admire what you've accomplished."

"Thank you." Surprise glittered in those words, and Luc had to resist the urge to tug her back. Family relationships were thorny enough to navigate in the best of relationships, much less troubled ones. "I'm sorry I couldn't be who you wanted me to be."

When Adele snorted, Luc tensed, but his mother shook her head and mouthed *wait*.

"My sweet darling, I pushed you because that's what mothers do, and I was always worried someone would take advantage of you. You bring out every protective instinct I have—far more than your brothers do..." Then she gave a look to Luc. "But you're right, you have built a life for yourself where you thrive. I've just hated that the life has been far away from us. Maybe now you'll be around a little more often?"

"We're not always going to agree."

"Good," Adele told her. "Because a good fight helps clarify the argument. Your father and I have been fighting for over fifty years, and we're doing just fine."

When Charlie laughed, Luc settled and left her to talk to her mother as he went to speak to his own. Crouching next to her chair, he said, "Thank you." He didn't have to explain why.

"My pleasure," she murmured, then stroked a hand over his hair. "She's the one, isn't she?"

He grinned. "Do you believe me about Colby now?"

When she tugged his hair once in reproach, it didn't

diminish his grin one bit. "I like her."

"Me, too," Luc said, and before she could say a word, he said, "One year."

"What?"

"One year. Let us get our feet under us for one year before you start nagging for grandkids."

"I do not nag, Lucas. I resent that inference."

"It wasn't an inference, it was a flat statement. One year. Promise me." Besides, after the announcement at the gathering, she would have plenty to keep her busy.

With a long-suffering sigh, she met his gaze, then leaned forward and pressed a kiss to his forehead. "I start counting today, so one year from today, I'm going to ask."

He chuckled. "Thank you, Mama."

"I really do like her, Luc." His mother glanced to where Charlie and Adele had walked, nearly to the edge of the woods. The conversation between them was intense, but not combative. "Are you ready for this?"

"Yep, now, if you and Adele would kindly find somewhere else to gossip, I want time with Charlie."

The brush of fingers against his cheek brought him to the present, and she smiled up at him sleepily. "You're a thousand miles away."

"Not even," he said. "Not when I have you right here."

Yawning, she stretched and then rolled to lay on top of him, and he settled his hands on her hips. Propping her chin on her folded hands, she said, "Have I mentioned how much I like being chased yet?"

"Hmm," he said, rubbing his hands over her ass. "I thought you preferred being caught."

Playfulness lit her eyes. "Haven't been caught yet, have I?"

"You need to run," he reminded her. "Running *to* me, doesn't count."

"True." She let out a little sigh, and her whole demeanor

softened as she snuggled up to him, and he wrapped her up tight. "Do we have time to nap?"

He chuckled, then pressed a kiss to the top of her head. "We have time." The soft warm weight of her was a delight. "We have all the time in the world," he whispered.

Two hours later, he walked with her toward Brett and Colby's. The gathering would be kicking off from their place, and then turn into the woods and out toward the national park. Nearly half the pack was already in wolf form. At the sight of so many, Charlie gripped his hand a little tighter.

More than one rushed up to say hello, and the ripple of double takes they were getting was *almost* insulting.

Charlie leaned up to press a nipping kiss to his jaw. "I think I'm both breaking hearts and offending people."

He laughed, but kept them moving. Brett strolled out at their arrival, and Charlie walked right into his hug. With a smirk, he gave Luc a once over. "What did I tell you? You survived."

"What can I say? My mood is good enough to not slug you today."

Chuckling, Charlie pulled away from Brett and to Luc's pleasure, just leaned back against him, and he wrapped his arms around her. "You shouldn't slug Brett anyway, Colby likes his face this way."

"Yes, she does," Colby answered, peeking out from behind Brett. Her scent was as sweet as always, but it had just the same amount of bite as the woman herself. Brett's eyes flashed, and the same fierce tension that had kept him rooted near her all week while Luc ran his ass off appeared.

There was a beat before Charlie stiffened, and Luc leaned closer and pressed a kiss behind her ear.

"Shh," he whispered in her ear, and she grinned.

Pride shimmered in Brett's eyes, and then Colby slid around him, and Charlie pushed away and she gave her a hug. Luc kept himself braced between the Alpha pair and the pack. Very shortly, the announcement would be made—the reason behind the gathering, and there were still wolves arriving.

The next few months were going to be insanely busy for both of them. But he was ready for it. They would find a way to make it work. Brett would be with Colby, which meant Luc and Charlie would have to pick up all the slack, in addition to tackling the treaty negotiations.

They could do it.

When Charlie's gaze collided with his, he read the understanding there. It was another reason why he told his mother to leave them alone for at least a year. Besides, he had to seal the deal, and while they were close, he didn't want to push her—Brett whistled.

Luc shifted, turning to face the pack as the whistle pierced the air and pulled their attention. Charlie slid into place next to him and linked their fingers together.

"Good morning," Brett called as the volume in the crowd dropped. His presence was a beacon at the center of the pack. Charlie leaned her head against his arm and sighed. She wasn't the only one. The ripple effect of their Alpha addressing them pulled everyone's attention.

It didn't seem all that long since he'd come back to find Brett chewing on his own wounds and isolating himself. Now he had Colby, and the pack thrived, and there was a kind of satisfaction in the air, particularly after the troubles of the last few years.

Threats defeated. Mad wolves dead. Invaders gone.

"I know not everyone could make the gathering—so for those of you here, we celebrate you, and we need to remember those whose work or duties prevented them from joining in on the party. Those Hunters of ours who continue to run our borders. Those maternals with pups too young to race, and the children—who I see we have a lot of—who need special tending." Brett's voice was strong and carried easily. "This is only our third gathering in as many years, and we will be doing this more often, we're returning to the seasonal cycle, to allow everyone who can a chance to come together."

He called out specific wolves who contributed—particularly those providing the food, and there were many cheers. Luc swept his gaze over the gathered. Trent appeared out of the crowd and trotted up to lean against Colby's legs. The young healer had already shifted, and Colby crouched to scratch under his chin. The two worked well together, and they'd make a dynamic team when Trent grew up and developed his skills.

It also meant Hudson River would have two healers. Gillian and Owen were amongst those gathered. Soon, they'd be returning to Willow Bend, though. Years of helping out could not be overlooked, they may never be Hudson River's to claim fully, but Hudson River wanted them nonetheless.

Charlie rubbed her cheek against his arm, and he glanced down to find her grinning at him. When she winked, his own grin grew, and he tuned back into Brett as he said, "I'm not going to bore you all with speeches. This weekend, we run, we hunt, we play, and we renew pack bonds. But we will also be celebrating one last gift, and it's a personal one that I am more than delighted to announce."

Turning slightly, Brett held out a hand, and Colby gave Trent one last pet before she rose and caught his fingers and let him pull her forward.

"In six months—just around the time of the spring thaw, we'll be welcome our first child..."

Whatever else he had to say was utterly lost in the roars and the cheering. It was a good sign, a positive one on the health of the pack. A whole mated Alpha, his chosen mate, a healer, and the strain put on pack bonds by betrayal and grief had healed.

While controlled chaos was the only description for it, Luc drew Charlie back as the pack surged forward to congratulate the happy pairing. This was all part of the gathering, renewing those pack bonds and forging new connections, even as they strengthened the old ones. When an Alpha pair reproduced though, it was the sign of a healthy pack, and Hudson River was more than ready to demonstrate how healthy she was.

"Where are we going?" Charlie murmured as he guided her around the house toward the back. The sound diminished some, but the volume was too loud to fall away completely.

"To begin enjoying our last few days of freedom," he told her. "I talked to Brett yesterday, he's going to be very focused on Colby, and being away from her will be hard, so a lot more is going to fall on our shoulders."

"I figured," she said as he set off for the woods. "But they deserve it."

"Yes," Luc said. "They absolutely do. In the meanwhile..." He cut a glance down at her. "You and I deserve some time, too. You have the next week off, if you want it. He was going to tell you, but..." He motioned behind them to the crowd.

"A whole week?"

"A whole week. He's going to handle things, and he had Debbie reschedule your time. After that, Trask will be here, and more work begins. Fortunately, he stopped for a visit on the way and bought us more time. We're going to have to juggle. I thought—if you didn't mind, I would try to get into the city twice during the week, but you could come here on the weekends. Then we'll have to try and make do on the other nights if we have to be apart."

She made a face. "I'm not sure I'm onboard with that plan."

His heart sank. "No?"

"No, because that means sleeping apart almost as often as being together."

He frowned. "It doesn't have to be, and it won't be forever, just until after Colby has the baby, and the first couple of months after Brett stops walking around in a daze."

Laughter eddied out of her. "Oh, is that all?"

"Charlie," he paused. They were deeper in the woods, and he faced her. Everything from the tilt of her head to the shimmer in her eyes threatened to beguile him. She'd enchanted him in Brett's office even as she challenged him. "This—this works." He licked his lips. "You and I... you're perfect for me. You're everything I ever wanted and more. I adore your mind. I adore your body. I adore your sense of humor—I love your wolf almost as much as I love you."

She blinked, and her eyes went from green to gold. "Almost?"

With a slow grin, he cupped her chin and tilted her head up. "Yes, almost. Your variable, unpredictable wolf. Whether she's snarling at me and showing her teeth, or demanding affection and beckoning me to look after her—or when she's standing right there defending me. I love every part of her. But you, Charlie? You I love. I love your fierceness and your strength. I love that you *know* your value, and you own your mistakes *and* your triumphs. I love that you go after what you want, and you put others in their place when they try to interfere. Most of all—I love that your heart is still so big that you love even the people who frustrate you."

It never occurred to him that it would take everything he had to bare his soul like this, and as difficult a task as it was—it was also the easiest thing in the world.

"I promised you time, and I'm giving it to you... but this works. I want you. I want us."

Charlie didn't respond right away, her expression pensive and thoughtful as she studied him. Scraping her teeth over her lower lip, she murmured, "I can work from here two days a week."

"What?" That was not what he expected her to say.

"I'd have to build an office and wire it—but there are days when it's just video conferences, and I don't have to be in the office for them. If I did them here...then I could work here two days a week, and then we would have the weekends. As for the other three days, you could come to the city with me. I know it's not perfect but—"

A list of what he'd need to build an office tumbled through his head. "Yes," he said. "Yes. We'll do that. Just tell me what you need, and we'll set it up."

The corner of her mouth tilted. "There will still be times when I can't stay, but they would be the exception and not the rule."

"Agreed, and times when I'll have to stay here, but always an exception. Never the rule."

"Adler is my friend, and he'll still be my friend."

"I can live with that," he said, and he meant it. "Just as long as I can still pick on him."

"Since he'll pick on you, I wouldn't have it any other way." Then she grew thoughtful again. "You do realize the more I'm around, the more you have to put up with my brothers."

"I still have siblings you haven't met, and you get my mother, too."

She threw head back and laughed. "I like your mom."

"I like yours too, mostly. That's better now, yes?" He hoped so. They seemed to be getting along better.

"I think so, and even if we're not, I told her I didn't care anymore. I wasn't going to try and impress her. She had to respect me for me, and that was that."

Oh, he could kiss her for that, and he did. "Good," he murmured against her lips. "Anything else?"

"We still have the treaties to negotiate."

"But that we do together. Here. There—wherever there is —and then here again. We do that as a team."

She chuckled. "Very diplomatically said."

"I have an excellent teacher. She's persuaded me to the art of negotiation. "

"Has she now?"

"Yep," he said, then winked. "She's also proven to me that there are a lot of ways to negotiate and get what I want. Sometimes slow and steady wins the race."

"Even when you want to go full tilt at it and charge?"

"Even when."

"There is something to be said for directness, though," she countered. "For presents, unexpected visits, and listening."

"Agreed," he said. "There's a lot to be said for those."

"So we can still do both?"

"Court you? Tease you and spoil you with gifts? Enjoy when you indulge me and look after me?" He laughed. "God I hope so. I promise you, I want everything."

Her grin was like a burst of sunshine from behind the clouds, and pleasure eddied in her scent.

"Then we have a plan?"

She leaned up to press a kiss to his lips, teasing her tongue along the seam of his lips and taking her time to suck against his tongue when he opened to her. Then with a hum, she leaned away. "I think so—well, save for one small matter."

"Name it." He'd take care of it.

"Do you have to work this week?"

"Nope," he said with a grin. "From now until next Sunday at midnight, I'm all yours." He and Brett had hashed that out while he'd been stuck here for the last couple of days. He *needed* that time with Charlie, and as much as Brett teased him, he'd given it to him willingly.

"Good," she affirmed. "Very good."

"That was it?"

"No, I just wanted to know how much time we had…" She slipped from his arms, and he frowned as she backed away, and he followed her a couple of paces. "Ah-ah… stay there. You said you like surprises."

"I do."

"Close your eyes?"

He raised his brows. They were deep enough in the woods that they had no audience, but it wouldn't be long before the pack joined them if they weren't already on their way.

"Why?"

Hands on her hips, she said, "Does it matter? I just want you to close your eyes for a moment."

With a long-suffering sigh, he folded his arms and closed his eyes. "Better?"

"Yes." The crunch of leaves alerted him to her movement, and her voice came from farther away when she called, "No more leashes, Luc!"

"Hey," he opened his eyes to find her on the move. It took him a moment, but then she threw a glance over her shoulder and laughed as she picked up speed.

"I love you, too!" She yelled.

She was running.

Running so he could chase…

His brain and heart kicked into the same gear, and his wolf let out a howl. Not wasting any time, he raced after her. They had a week. Oh, he was going to make the most of that.

◇

By nightfall, he sat with her curled up against him back at his place. His mark bright against her throat, and hers firm over his heart. Claiming her filled him up inside, filled him to bursting. She'd led him a merry chase, and he'd let her keep her lead—for a while, but when missing her grew too strong, he'd tackled her carefully and tumbled them both to the ground and taken the brunt of the fall. She'd been laughing as she wrapped around him, and her bite had struck so hard and swift, he damn near came in his pants.

Claimed.

Wanted.

Loved.

He saved his bite for when he had her naked, some things were just worth savoring. But her dominant side claimed him, and her submissive side held him captive and surrendered so sweetly, it took his breath away.

He loved her. Every variable inch.

He and his mate.

A whole week.

Then a lifetime to work together after that.

No more leashes.

For either of them.

Negotiations will continue in *Wolf Spirit*, in the meanwhile please join my reader group to stay on top of all updates!
https://www.facebook.com/groups/HeathersPack/
I look forward to hearing from you!!

ABOUT THE AUTHOR

USA Today bestselling author, Heather Long, likes long walks in the park, science fiction, superheroes, Marines, and men who aren't douche bags. Her books are filled with heroes and heroines tangled in romance as hot as Texas summertime. From paranormal historical westerns to contemporary military romance, Heather might switch genres, but one thing is true in all of her stories—her characters drive the books. When she's not wrangling her menagerie of animals, she devotes her time to family and friends she considers family. She believes if you like your heroes so real you could lick the grit off their chest, and your heroines so likable, you're sure you've been friends with women just like them, you'll enjoy her worlds as much as she does.

Keep up with Heather
www.heatherlong.net
heather@heatherlong.net

ALSO BY HEATHER LONG

Always a Marine Series

Once Her Man, Always Her Man

Retreat Hell! She Just Got Here

Tell It to the Marine

Proud to Serve Her

Her Marine

No Regrets, No Surrender

The Marine Cowboy

The Two and the Proud

A Marine and a Gentleman

Combat Barbie

Whiskey Tango Foxtrot

What Part of Marine Don't You Understand?

A Marine Affair

Marine Ever After

Marine in the Wind

Marine with Benefits

A Marine of Plenty

A Candle for a Marine

Marine under the Mistletoe

Have Yourself a Marine Christmas

Lest Old Marines Be Forgot

Her Marine Bodyguard

Smoke & Marines

A Man Called Wyatt

Going Royal

Some Like It Royal

Some Like It Scandalous

Some Like It Deadly

Some Like it Secret

Some Like it Easy

Her Marine Prince

Blocked

Heart of the Nebula

Queenmaker

Deal Breaker

Throne Taker (coming soon)

Lone Star Leathernecks

Semper Fi Cowboy

As You Were, Cowboy

Madison, The Witch Hunter

Every Witch Way But Floosey's

Magic & Mayhem

The Witch Singer

Bridget's Witch's Diary

The Witched Away Bride

Mongrels

Mongrels, Mischief & Mayhem

Wolf Unleashed

Wolf Spirit (Coming Soon)